MARK S. VARNUM

THE Hawk's CROSS

THE Hawk's CROSS

MARK S. VARNUM, O.D.

COLD BROOK PUBLISHING

Cold Brook Books, New England

Cold Brook Publishing
8 Waterville Common, suite 125
Waterville, ME 04901
www.coldbroookpublishing.com

Although inspired by real events, this book is fictional. Characters within this work are the invention of the author and are not meant to portray any actual person, living or dead.

Cover design Kico Passalacqua

ISBN 978-0-615-24191-3

If this book was sold without its cover, the publisher and the author were not paid for their work. If this is the case, the novel was likely reported as "not sold and destroyed", this is known as a "stripped book."

20 19 18 17 16 15 14 13

Acknowledgements

A completed novel begins much like a compost heap. Bits of inspiration accumulate over long periods of time, piled high and loose. Eventually, time and energy compact these scraps into something capable of growing fragrant flowers and succulent fruit. Here is the place to thank those unwitting contributors to the pile.

First, my family, both those related by blood and then those not: You know who you are and the things you did to aid this endeavor – thank you. Second, my line editor and agent Sammie Justesen. Without her assistance, this book would have remained lines and circles in the memory of my computer. Third, my writing buddies John C. Karrer, Claire Hersom, and Jesse Estevao, who took turns holding the carrot in front of me.

Chapter One

Late.

Very late.

Ken flicked his wrist to see his watch: thirteen hundred hours. He pressed harder on the Jeep's accelerator. The gang would already be at the quarry and he hadn't even checked in at his new post. Perhaps he could skip checking in. His orders didn't call for him to be there until zero six hundred. No, that wouldn't work. If he didn't swing by the post, he'd have nowhere to sleep, and he certainly wasn't going to stay with his parents his first night back in town.

He drummed his fingers on the steering wheel. Imagine what his mother would say if he stayed with his friends all afternoon, then dragged in after midnight. Better she didn't know he'd arrived. What was he thinking? Of course, she'd know. This was Machias, Maine, for Christ sake. She'd know before his Jeep had a chance to cool off.

The post was just up ahead. He could breeze in, drop his gear, and be back on the road in two shakes of a dog's tail... or was that a lamb's tail? Ken shook his head. It didn't matter; fast anyway. After all, he was going to be senior officer on this post. He snorted. Twenty-three-year-old, Lieutenant Junior Grade as senior officer. Did that make him – the junior senior, or the senior junior? The sign for the post was little more than a plank with the words, "Machias Coastal Watch" scrawled on it in gray paint and tacked to a white pine. It would have shown up better in black, or at least if they'd bothered to trim up the branch that hung over the top. He decided right then, that would be the first thing he would change.

The Jeep lost traction in the hard right turn. Ken spun the wheel hand over hand, off the asphalt surface of Route One, and onto the gravel access road leading to the post. His foot didn't leave the accelerator as he blew by the guard shack, waving a salute to the young sailor who had his feet up on the windowsill. Ken watched him in the rearview mirror. The man sprang to his feet, rushed to the doorway, half-removed his side arm from his holster, then apparently thought better of it. He tossed a salute to the ass end of the speeding vehicle. That's right, shoot me for running the gate. Put me out of my misery.

Two makeshift buildings sat beyond the gate; the farthest one Ken guessed to be the mess with stacks of empty crates and trash barrels acting as bookends to the side door. He concluded the other had to be the office. The Jeep skidded ten feet before it finally came to rest near the front door of that building. Ken grabbed the manila envelope containing his orders, which now lay on the floorboards, climbed over the passenger seat, and burst through the screen door, letting it slam in his wake.

Four walls, two desks, and a file cabinet. All gray.

A skinny little Petty Officer vaulted out of a chair, sliding it back across the painted wooden floor.

He snapped to attention and saluted. "Officer on deck!"

Ken hurried in, unbuttoning his uniform as he went. He slapped the envelope on the table and finished stripping off the tunic. "File these orders, get this shirt laundered, and where the hell am I sleeping?"

The Petty officer remained at attention and nodded toward the back. "Sir, your billet is in the rear."

Ken glanced at the human question mark; even at attention, his back was crooked.

"Petty Officer Durning at your service, Sir."

God couldn't be accused of lacking a sense of humor, he thought. Here Ken was stuck back in Hicksville, USA, with a reject from 'The Justice League' at his side. This just kept getting better. So much for join the Navy, see the world, and fight the bad guys. Ken tucked his white T-shirt into the Navy issue shorts, his pasty legs extending to his dark socks and dress shoes. His legs were almost as pale as his shirt. He turned and headed back toward the front door.

"I'll be back by zero six hundred. Don't lock me out."

The sailor manning the gate was still on his feet when Ken flew past him in the opposite direction. The man saluted again, still looking befuddled. Ken would have to have a word with him when he got back.

Fifteen minutes; he'd be there in fifteen little minutes. His pals from school, the girls, Barbara... Maggie. Especially Maggie! Why the hell did he ever break up with her? Oh yeah, that's right, his bright idea. Break up with Mags, tour the world, have an adventure.

He looked up into the sky, tried to see beyond the clouds, and shook his head. End result: get sent back home to protect hayfields and blueberries from the Germans.

The Jeep struck a pothole and kicked toward the shoulder. Warren Sims was working down the far side of his field with his Percheron geldings, Tom and Barney. How old was Tom now? Fifteen - sixteen? It had to be fifteen; Warren got him right after the crash in '29. The team made a wide arch at the far end of the field and started a new swath through the hay with the side-cut sickle bar mower. Although too distant, he could conjure the familiar clack of the blades clashing past the stationary teeth; dust and chaff billowing up in the path.

Ken wiped the sweat from his brow.

The quarry lay a half-mile up in the woods just beyond the orchard on the left. A break in the cedar fence line would be just beyond the round stone; it marked the end of a rum wall that lined the path.

The sun was still high overhead, scorching the battered steering wheel of the Navy's Jeep. The wheel was smooth from years of use and his hands slipped on it as he stomped on the brake. The old vehicle ground to a stop at the end of the dirt road, a second ahead of a dust cloud that kept going, and settled on the parked cars on either side of the lane: Josh's '36 Packard rag top, and Luke's black Hudson. The top was down on Josh's two-seater, an empty beer bottle resting on the hood. The gang had started without him.

A row of low, bushy alders shielded the parking spot

from the top of the quarry that lay fifty yards beyond. A worn foot-path led from the front of his Jeep into the brush. A faded "No Swimming" sign dangled from one of the trees – the same sign they had childishly tapped for luck each time they skipped school and snuck up here. Ken stripped off his footwear, grabbed a thin military issue towel from the back seat of the Navy's Jeep, then headed barefoot down the path, making sure to tap the sign as he passed. The trail rose up through a split granite boulder. He turned sideways to slide through, his back rubbing against one side of the rough stone. The pads of his feet were sensitive after wearing boots and shoes all winter. He flinched as he stepped on the occasional pebble or stick, secretly wishing for the barefooted days of his youth.

When Ken reached the far side, he paused and leaned against the boulder, feeling the warm stone rub against his back. His chest felt tight and he had difficulty filling his lungs. His friends would be just over the rise; he should stop dawdling, and get up there. The walk up the trail hadn't been that strenuous. Why was he so out of breath? His hands tingled, he was hyperventilating. He forced the air to stay in his lungs longer. A year and a half wasn't that long, was it?

But his legs didn't move.

Ordinarily, he knew he'd rush through the split in the boulder, race his friends to the opening high over the quarry, pause only long enough to drop his towel and hurdle off the edge to the cool water below. Today, however, the bees hovering near the Nannyberries and the squirrel chattering in the nearby cedar fought for his attention. Maggie's high-pitched tenor sounded above the rustle of the leaves. Her sweet voice sank into him and his mind failed to focus. He hoped she'd kept her hair long, Luke had tried to talk her into cutting it, but he liked it long. He liked her in every way, exactly like she was.

Luke's lower thicker voice penetrated the trees. Ken leaned forward trying to make out the words, but they stalled in the greenery. Maggie deserved better than Luke. Ken knew he was thinking like a father screening potential suitors. But it was true. Luke was three and a half years older than them, he never would've dated her in high school. She should be with him instead. Months before, in a moment of intoxicated ranting, Luke had admitted to Ken that he was in love with her. Although it'd taken enough beer to fill a small milk tub to get him to confess, he'd sounded sincere.

That conversation had gnawed at Ken's thoughts and dreams over the last six months. If he hadn't known Luke almost as long as he had Maggie, he'd do his best to take her away. He bit the inside of his lip. Who was he kidding? She wasn't seeing Luke last year and he could have gotten back with her if he'd asked her to the spring dance. If he'd done that, she never would have started seeing Luke. It wasn't Luke; it was him. His dad was right – he didn't know what he wanted.

A sparrow landed on a branch ahead. Ken watched the bird dig its beak under a wing, preening a feather or perhaps scratching an itch. Blue sky framed the bird on its perch, sunlight gilding its feathers. It had just come from the clearing and knew who lay beyond.

Ken knew what lay on the far side of the brush: the old granite quarry sprawled over several acres. Dark-green water filled the north side, starting halfway across the pit and extending to the high, cleaved walls that rose up from the pool. Local kids had been coming here for years to swim, build campfires, and revel in their summers. Joyful, high-pitched laughter from the plateau above the water crept around the edge of the boulder.

Ken crept closer.

Barbara's squeaky voice rose above the others. "Josh, you're so bad. There's no way I can drink that straight. Don't you have a Coke in your bag?"

Bottles clinked. "I thought you were a daring girl, Babs. It's just grain alcohol, for Pete's sake. I even diluted it for you."

"Okay, but just a taste." There was a pause, then, a choke, a cough. "You liar! That's not diluted, it burns my throat!"

Standing on his toes, Ken leaned into the brush and peered through the branches.

Luke and Maggie lay face down on a plaid blanket next to Barbara. Maggie's long slender legs glistened with a light coat of perspiration. He remembered the feel of those legs, soft under his fingertips, twice as soft on the inside of her thighs.

A red squirrel chattered and scurried past him. He flinched, put his hand to his chest, then looked back through the bushes.

Ken refocused on Barbara's shapely curves completely filling a black one-piece suit. Josh sat across from them, holding a clear bottle.

He held it up. "You next, Mags?"

Maggie adjusted her sunglasses, rolled her shoulders back, and tucked her blonde locks behind her ear. "No chance. I'm not that corruptible."

Ken was pleased she'd left her hair long, she'd talked about cutting it.

Josh took a nip from the bottle. "Oh, I think you are. You just haven't spent enough time with me."

She rolled over and used a towel to wipe the moisture from her legs. "That's just the problem. I already spend too much time with you." She picked up a silver watch that lay on the blanket beside her. "Where's Ken? He should be here by now."

Luke rose up on his elbows. "Ken's slow. That's why we made him play third base in high school."

Josh swirled the alcohol around in the bottle. "Slow?" He snorted. "Now that's kind. I've seen moss move faster."

Ken frowned; they all knew it was because he'd frozen his feet skating on Cathance lake. Why did they always have to bring it up? It wasn't bad enough to keep him out of the Navy. Besides, if his feet didn't get too cold, they worked pretty darn well. His eyes softened at the sight of Maggie's calves; he hadn't forgotten those. He sighed, stooped over and picked up a small stone, then tossed the pebble so it struck Luke square on the back of his head.

"Ouch! What the… ?" Luke rubbed his head and spun around.

Ken pushed though the shrubbery and dropped his towel on the blanket. "Even if I was slow, my talent made up for it."

"Kenny!" Maggie's face brightened for a moment, then she looked away.

Barbara rose and smothered him with hugs. He took her in one arm and twisted her back and forth a few times. Luke reached out a hand and Ken took it, his arm still wrapped around Barbara.

"What about you, Maggie? Don't I get a hug?"

She ran a hand down one of her legs, keeping her eyes away. "Do you think you deserve it?"

Ken watched her hand travel the length of her leg. "Probably not, but a fellow can hope."

Josh offered him the quart-sized, wide-mouthed milk bottle. "How about a starter?"

Ken accepted the bottle as Barbara flopped on the blanket next to Maggie. He took a sip and swallowed hard. "Where did you get this stuff? It tastes like drain cleaner."

Josh grinned. "I have my sources. It just so happens they use this to make the chocolates at the Ganong factory in St. Stephen."

Ken reached into the picnic basket for a Narragansett. "Did you smuggle it or did you let some other sap take the risk?"

Josh shrugged, "Let's say I repatriated it for the betterment of the country's youth."

Ken took a slug of the cool beverage. The bitter twang, coupled with the cold liquid, intertwined with Maggie's words, and washed down into his gullet. Things hadn't changed much, he decided. The water glistened twenty feet below, the green surface rippling with tiny wavelets. The water was clear to the bottom. An old truck lay submerged near one side, and a conveyor of some type leaned against the wall on the far side. The hint of a breeze lifted off the water, rose up the sheer rock face, and caressed Ken's damp body. He shivered.

Maggie was watching. "What's the matter – too cold for you? You're just spoiled by that hot weather in Pensacola."

Ken put the cool bottle against his cheek. "It's just the sight of you, Maggie. You give me chills."

"Apparently not," she scoffed.

Luke lay back on the blanket, put an arm over Maggie's waist, and cocked his head toward Ken. "If it was anyone but you making nice with my gal... I just don't know what I'd do."

Josh swirled the clear liquid in the bottle. "Hell, Ken's a naval officer. I'll bet he has a different girl for every night of the week. Isn't that so, buddy?"

Ken took another sip of his beer, still looking at Maggie, then broke away and stared outward. "If you say so, it has to be true."

Maggie's soft, sweet voice toyed with his ears as she spoke with Luke. He tightened his grip on the bottle. Why hadn't he asked her to the spring dance? She would have gone with him. He'd blown it. He had to force himself to be more decisive.

Ken opened and closed his hand, the bottle rotating in his grasp. He looked down at his plain white shirt and then at Josh's brilliant – red clamdiggers covered with a square-tailed, bright plaid shirt.

Maggie pouted. "I don't want to go driving with you

tonight. I want to do something. We could go to the movies."

Ken drained the last of his beer, tossed it toward the basket, then put an arm around Barbara's sensuous waist, his fingers sinking into her soft side. "Have you been in yet?"

She braced her feet and squirmed, letting her dark loose hair swat him in the face. "No. And you're not going to throw me in."

"You think not?" He pulled her toward the edge, his fingers penetrating further into her flesh. Her waist was plush, lacking substantial muscle tone underneath. "Don't fight it. You know you're going."

She wriggled in his arms until they reached the edge, then planted both her feet into the dirt. "Don't you dare, Kenneth Mitchell! I just had my hair done."

"Sorry, my dear, it's my duty as a naval officer to teach you women how to survive in the water."

Barbara's body relaxed, she leaned into him and put her mouth close to his ear. "Oh really, is that all you're going to teach me?"

Her warm breath tickled the hairs on his neck, and he glanced at Maggie. Her eyes were hard and she glared at Barbara.

Ken spin Barbara around and gave her a nudge over the ledge.

She resigned herself to the twenty-foot plunge and jumped as he pushed her, letting out a high-pitched scream as she flew through the air. She landed feet-first in the cool, bright-green water. Ken jumped after her; he couldn't listen to Luke and Maggie chatter any longer, and the look she had given Barbara, well that was another matter. He landed a half second later, shooting a plume into the air. Piercing the warm surface layer, he plunged into the colder water below the thermocline. A green blur enveloped him and he paused for a few seconds. The silence and tranquility around him were a comfort. Maybe he could just stay down there awhile. Fish are lucky, he thought. No worries. No job. No responsibilities. He looked up at the surface, Barbara's feet kicked rhythmically above him, and felt his chest spasm. No air, either! He shot to the surface, gulped a huge breath, and wiped the water from his eyes.

The others were only a few moments behind, running and leaping as far out as they could, then dropping into the water, decelerating as their bodies plunged into the depths. Their splashes washed over his head. He closed his eyes and turned away to avoid the waves.

The chop churned up the green water, lightening the color. Ken swam over to the ledge and grasped the coarse rock face in his hands. He rotated his body, holding onto the granite with his arms splayed out behind him. The others were treading water in front of him in a loose circle.

Josh dove under, his red shorts streaking toward Maggie. Reaching her, he pulled on her legs, attempting to sink her. She swatted at him beneath the surface as she sank down to her chin, her blonde hair floating around her shoulders, like the tentacles of a jellyfish.

"Cut it out!" She kicked at him. "You know I don't swim as well as you."

Luke splashed Barbara, taunting her, as he treaded water nearby. "You as tough as you think?"

She didn't splash back. "If I'm going to start a water battle, it's going to be with the lunatic who threw me in."

"Lunatic, is it? Just tell me this water doesn't feel good." Ken said.

Barbara paddled over toward Ken and grasped onto the rock, she floated up next to him. Even in the water he could feel the heat from her body. "That wasn't very nice. Are you going to be nice to me now?"

A drop of water clung to the tip of her nose, Ken had the urge to wipe it away, to leave his hand on her check then push back her sopping black hair and pull her hot body closer. He averted his eyes and looked past her. "What do you think Maggie should I be nice to her?"

Barbara tilted her head and turned away.

"Be nice to who ever you want. What do I care."

Luke spun around to face Ken. "Come on – I'll race you to the far side. The loser has to climb back up and get us a beer."

Ken lifted his feet toward the surface, supporting his weight on his arms. Luke always turned everything into a competition. "No, thanks. I'm fine right here."

Luke moved over toward the wall. "Chicken?"

He'd been running every morning through Officer Candidate School, and a part of him felt he could beat Luke. "Yeah, that's me. Lily-livered through and through."

"You're just smart enough to know you wouldn't stand a chance against me." Luke swam to the ledge and pulled himself out of the water. "Well, I'm going to get myself a beer. Maybe I'll be nice and bring a few more."

Ken sighed. Maybe he should have raced Luke. Maggie would at least have to watch them swim, and if he won… but that was stupid. He shook his head and laid it back in the water, half up to his ears. The sounds around him dulled and the voices thickened when his ears submerged, then lightened when his head cleared the water.

Maggie swam to the side of a ledge fifteen feet away, hung onto the rocks, and floated face-to-face with Josh. She dipped her chin below the surface and blew, her lips forming a perfect circle.

Josh touched the tip of her nose with his finger and winked at her. "Why don't you dump Luke and hook up with me? I'd be a lot more exciting."

She looked upward where Luke had disappeared over the top, and then to Barbara treading water nearby. "You're wicked. Don't let Luke hear you say that. Even if it's just in fun."

Josh also lowered his face into the water up to his chin and locked eyes with her. "Who's saying anything just for fun?"

Barbara swam over and pushed between them. "What's going on over here? A little tryst?"

Maggie moved away and floated on her back. "Don't be silly. Josh is just being Josh. He'd flirt with a porcupine if it would lower its quills for him."

But Barbara wouldn't let up. "Well, I figured since Luke and Josh own the Sea Swirl together, maybe that isn't all they share."

Maggie kicked water in Barbara's face. "You have no shame. Besides, what am I, some old fishing boat?"

Barbara lay on her back with both arms outstretched. "Shame is for those who don't know how to have fun."

Ken moved in and grabbed Barbara's ankles and gave her a push, slowly spinning her around in the water. "Biscuit Gilman's band is going to be at the Novella tonight. What do you say?"

She lifted her head a bit. "Are you asking me or the whole group?"

Ken shot a glance at Maggie. "Whoever wants to come, I guess."

Barbara laid her head back, sweeping her arms to the sides. "That's what I thought."

Movement caught Ken's eye. "Luke, you're back." Ken wondered how much he'd heard. "That was quick."

"Yeah, I'm back. Don't act so disappointed." Luke set the beers on the ground in front of Josh, stared at Ken for an instant, then dove into the water, and paddled over to Maggie. He corralled her against the ledge, placed an arm on either side of her, supporting their weight on the rocks with his hands. They began kissing.

Barbara called out to Ken. "Are you sure the navy will part with you for the night?"

Ken ran a hand over his short-cropped navy cut. "Sure. I don't have to be back until zero six hundred."

"Zero what?" Josh said. "This ain't the Navy, pal. Drop the pretense."

Barbara continued. "You are going to wear your uniform aren't you?" she looked toward Maggie. "He'll look great in that huh, Mags?"

Maggie continued to kiss Luke, but splashed her fingers in the water flicking droplets toward Barbara.

"So are we going, or what?" Barbara said.

Luke didn't remove his lips from Maggie's, but mumbled his assent. "Mmm, hmm."

Josh splashed them. "God. Would you two knock it off? It's embarrassing."

Luke pulled back an inch from her lips, his eyes turning toward Ken. "If my lips are here, nobody else's will have a chance to be."

Chapter Two

Thursday, June 29, 1944:
North Atlantic Ocean

Gray.

Steel gray ocean and sky.

The U-boat furrowed through light, rounded swells, churning the cold seawater of the Atlantic off its sides like a single bottom plow through a field. The rain fell straight down, pelting the deck and conning-tower with large, heavy drops. A single dark silhouette under a storm hat and slicker huddled against the fore bulkhead, facing into the mist. Binoculars hung loose around his neck.

The hatch behind him swung open and the Kapitan climbed the ladder.

The figure looked down from under the floppy hat. "Good morning, Kapitanleutnant."

"Good morning to you, Werner," the Kapitan said.

Werner looked out into the mist, barely able to see three hundred meters beyond the forward lookout. He enjoyed his time alone on the bridge and partly resented the intrusion. There were so few places on a crowded boat where one could find solitude. The fresh salt air was soothing, yet the fog made the lining of his stomach quiver.

"With this poor visibility and calm water, we could be anywhere." Werner said.

"Deceiving, isn't it? We could run right by the enemy without seeing him."

Werner passed him the binoculars. "The rain seems to be easing a bit. I can see twice as far as I could an hour ago."

"This should be a safe place to charge our batteries. We're well south of the main shipping lanes." The Kapitan wiped the moisture from his eyebrows then put the glass to his eyes. "This fog is a stroke of luck. We can run on the surface most of the time, and should make the New England coast in four days."

Werner removed his black watch cap from his back pocket, tossed the storm hat through the hatch, and stretched the wool cap over his skull, snugging it tightly over his ears. The Kapitan watched him neatly fold the front of the cap on his forehead.

"You should get a new cap. That one's too small for you."

Werner looked into the mist. "It was my brother's. It'll do."

"You were close?"

Werner wondered if the Kapitan was truly interested in his relationship with his brother or was just making conversation. In the six months the Kapitan had been seeing Werner's mother, Werner still wasn't sure if the man liked him or not. "No, not really. But it's all I have left."

The Kapitan let the binoculars hang from the leather strap around his neck. "Your mother doesn't speak of him."

"I think it's her way of dealing with his death." Werner tried to see into the gray veil in front of the boat. The Kapitan shouldn't be talking like this with him. "Is Mother under the impression you can keep me from meeting a similar fate? Is that why she asked you to get me aboard your boat?"

The Kapitan looked away. "What makes you think she asked me to put you aboard? Maybe I just wanted to get to know you better."

Werner rested his hands on the damp steel plates that surrounded the top of the conning tower, and leaned forward. "I know my mother. She asked you."

The Kapitan raised the glass back to his eyes and remained silent for a brief instant. "I promised her I'd do my best. And speaking of doing one's best, how are you making out with that girl you're seeing? Gert, is it?"

Werner tucked his bare hands under his armpits. "We're all right, I guess."

He lowered the optics and turned to Werner. "All right? At your age, that means trouble."

If there's trouble, it's my trouble, Werner thought. And I'll take care of it. He scuffed a foot on the metal deck plate. And what does he mean at my age? Most officers had their own command by twenty-eight. "No, nothing really."

The Kapitan didn't take his eyes off Werner.

"Seriously, it's all right."

The rain picked up, and as it fell, the curtain of mist receded another hundred meters. The Kapitan turned slowly, scanning the limited horizon, then froze. He thrust the binoculars at Werner and shouted down the hatch. "Alarm! Alarm! Dive the boat!"

Werner's throat hitched, as he grasped the binoculars. He hadn't seen anything and it was certainly was an awkward time for a drill.

The Kapitan lurched toward the hatch, Werner following close behind. As he slid into the escape trunk, Werner slammed the hatch shut behind him with a hollow thud, and they scrambled down the ladder. The Kapitan pushed past a sailor in the trunk, landing hard on the deck plates of the control room. Two men were already at the dive station opening valves and flooding the ballast tanks, the backs of their heads bobbing feverishly as both their hands cranked on the wheels.

"Emergency dive! All outer doors closed. Continue to flood the tanks!"

Werner stumbled on the grates, falling against the hard steel ladder; pain shot up his elbow. He grabbed a pipe on the bulkhead for support, then staggered toward his post behind the diving mate, rubbing the soreness from his arm. "All compartments have white lights. Tanks flooded." He released his elbow and grasped the speaking tube above his head. "Secure the diesels. Switch to the electric motors."

Werner watched the Kapitan's phlegmatic face, a man with much on his mind. No, this was not a drill, he concluded.

The Kapitan pulled down the handles to the periscope and put his eyes to the optics. "Dive planes to maximum. Make our depth twelve meters."

"Twelve meters, aye," the diving mate replied.

The diesels went silent and the boat tipped downward, creaking, and moaning.

The diving mate called out, "Twelve meters!"

The Kapitan peered into the periscope, swiveling it as he spoke. "Level the bow planes and make your speed dead slow."

"Dead slow, aye," came the reply.

The periscope stopped rising, then slowly rotated back and forth a few degrees. The Kapitan clicked the magnification on the periscope and rotated the focus. "All engines reverse. Left full rudder."

"Hard left rudder, reverse full," Werner replied.

The periscope swung as the boat turned. Werner couldn't feel the boat swing only see the telltale assurance of the compass as it ticked off the degrees, indicated the turn. Werner stared at the compass, mentally reorienting the boat in his mind. He wondered what the Kapitan had seen that the lookout hadn't. He wanted to look through the periscope and see for himself, but remained at his station, and quietly looked on.

The Kapitan leaned into the periscope, rubbed his cap on the optics, and pushed it further up on his head. "Slow the rate of turn. Slower, slower, that's it. Good. Now hold that bearing."

Werner moved closer to the bulkhead keeping an eye on the Kapitan. "What is it?"

"Looks like a convoy of Liberty ships and I don't see

an escort." He clicked the magnification on the scope once again. "Three columns, staggered about a quarter mile apart. Maybe a dozen or so."

Oscar Schuch and Wilhelm Franks had slipped into the control room and stood quietly beside the aft bulkhead. The Kapitan ignored them. Werner edged closer to the diving mate to make room for the two men. He didn't like having passengers aboard, but it wasn't his decision. "Are we going to submerge and wait for them to pass?" Werner asked.

The Kapitan gave him a wolfish grin. "I still don't see any escort. I think it would be safe to send a couple of fish at them before we continue."

Oscar Schuch cleared his throat. "Begging the Kapitan's pardon, but your orders don't include putting this boat at risk. Your primary mission is to get us to the coast of Maine intact, before engaging the enemy."

The Kapitan leaned back from the scope and stared at the two *Abwehr* agents. "Mr. Schuch, I don't see any significant risk here. And the time it'll take to loose a couple of fish at them will be minuscule. You are guests on my boat and I ask you to stand clear of the operations." He looked back at Werner. "Set a course of one, nine zero true. When we're out of sight of the convoy, put us on the surface, and start the diesels. Then change course to one, four five degrees so we can get ahead of them."

"Aye, Kapitan." Werner took his place at the periscope and the Kapitan moved to the small chart table on the starboard bulkhead.

He flipped through the charts, then laid his parallels

on one, and then drew a straight pencil line along one side. "Yes. We'll intercept right here."

He circled the spot on the chart, rested his index finger on the spot, and glared at the agents as though daring them to object.

Chapter Three

Biscuit Gilman's Orchestra was in rare form, whipping the club into what sounded like a tempest. Josh steered his Packard into the nearly full lot; Barbara sat quietly in the passenger seat, arms folded across her chest. The rest of the gang followed in Luke's Hudson. Josh wavered as he got out of the car, stepped to the rear of the car, and stuck the silver key into the lock of his trunk. When the boot clicked open, he shuffled through the contents, pulled a bottle out of a case and refilled his flask, while Barbara got out and stood by her door. Luke parked beside them and then quickly hustled around to open the door for Maggie.

Ken slipped out of the back seat and tried to see into Josh's trunk. "That wouldn't be anything illegal, would it?"

Josh put the stopper on a flask, slipped it into the breast pocket of his oversized jacket, and closed the trunk. "Nothing the Navy would have any interest in." He cocked his head, thinking. "Then again, they might. Do you have any buddies in need of anything?"

Ken shook his head. "Let's just get inside before you set up shop right here in the lot."

The music washed over them as they swung open the doors. Josh paid for the tickets and they stepped further inside. A large banner hung over the stage:

BISCUIT GILMAN'S ORCHESTRA RETURNING
JULY 28TH AND 29TH.

Tables surrounded the dance floor – and red, white, and blue crepe paper streamers dangled from the rafters. The band had just started a jitterbug. Maggie grabbed Luke's hand, and dragged him out on the floor. Ken pointed to the punch bowl. "You get us some seats and I'll take care of the drinks."

Josh escorted Barbara to a round table. The hall was jumping. The people not dancing swayed to the music and those on the floor hopped and twirled. The guys wore baggy, high-waisted, Zoot Suits or sharply pressed military uniforms, the girls in snug-waisted skirts, thin dresses, and tight shoes. Biscuit Gilman blew on his saxophone center stage; his band wailed behind him. Ken returned and placed the cups on the table. Josh took one under the table and reached into his coat pocket. He then handed it to Barbara. She took it while he repeated the process with his own.

"How about you?" Josh bellowed over the music.

Ken held up a hand. "All set. Thanks."

Josh took a big slug of the punch, then rose and took

Barbara's hand, pulling her onto the floor, leaving Ken alone at the table.

Josh and Barbara were aggressive dancers, spinning and stopping in the center of the floor. Quick abrupt movements, then a smooth twirl. Luke and Maggie were far more conservative, hanging to the side, slow and deliberate. Maggie's blonde hair bounced on one shoulder, then the other, as the music pounded.

The song ended and the Biscuit Gilman Orchestra shifted tempo to a foxtrot. Luke and Maggie sashayed onward, but Barbara and Josh broke away, and returned to the table.

Josh plopped down on the wooden folding chair, slung an arm over the back, and wiped the perspiration from his forehead. Barbara gave him an irritated look. Ken began to rise for her, but was too slow and she seated herself. Josh drained the last of his punch, then took Luke's cup under the table, fortified it, and drank half of that as well.

Ken cocked his head. "Hey, remember you and Luke are fishing in the morning. You don't want to be seasick."

Josh laughed. "I've never been seasick in my life."

Ken nodded. "No. Not seasick exactly."

"Mind your own business. Besides, aren't you going to be back on the base in the morning, playing sailor?"

Ken laughed. "Base? More like a shack with a clerk and a couple of enlisted men milling around with nothing to do."

Josh took another drink. "Well, at least you're the big cheese. You can slack off all day and watch them work."

Ken wondered just what his duties would entail, but didn't want Josh to know that. "I wish that were true, but I'm sure I'll find plenty to keep me busy."

"Just what do you do there anyway?" Barbara asked.

Ken leaned forward, raised his voice over the band, and guessed. "It's mostly administrative stuff. Make flyers to tell people about blackout curtains – or rationing, and what to do if there's an air raid. Check the fuel consumption of fishing boats. Stuff like that."

Josh finished the punch and refilled his cup from the flask, without the punch this time. "Ken's a regular Yankee doodle pencil pusher. He'll win the war one flyer at a time." He laughed.

Ken scowled, but remained silent. This posting wasn't his idea; he'd rather be on a destroyer in the middle of the Atlantic. Hell, even an administrative position in Washington would be a step closer to the war.

Barbara leaned over the table, the top of her low-cut dress opening, a bit. "If you have any cute sailors out there, keep me in mind."

Ken grinned. "What about Josh here? Why don't you two start seeing each other?"

Josh leaned toward Barbara. "Sure. What do you say, Babs?" One of the dancers lost his balance and bumped into Josh's chair, pushing him into Barbara.

She gave him a gentle, good natured shove. "I'm game." She winked at him. "But you're such a rogue. I'd end up having to scratch your eyes out the first time you looked at another woman."

Josh glared at the man who'd stumbled into him; then

his eyes softened as they refocused on Barbara. "Maybe if I was with you, I wouldn't need to keep looking."

She rolled her eyes. "Yeah, that would last about one hour."

Josh drained the rest of his cup. "I'm going to get another. Anyone else?"

Luke returned with Maggie in tow. She sat down and fanned her face with her hand while Luke slid in next to her and nodded at his empty cup. "Josh must be at it pretty hard already."

Barbara shook her head. "Oh, leave him alone. He's fine."

Maggie watched Josh walk to the refreshment table. "He's not fine."

Ken rose as Biscuit Gilman signaled a change to a waltz. "Luke, do you mind if I steal Maggie for a dance?"

Luke raised a hand, palm up. "Don't ask me, ask her."

Maggie smiled, accepted Ken's hand, and followed him onto the floor. Ken slipped his right onto her slender waist and took her right in his other hand. Gently releasing and increasing pressure on her back with his hand, he led her around the floor. Her feet skimmed effortlessly over the hardwood. She kept her eyes on him and matched his movements, falling quickly into a familiar pattern.

"Your dancing has improved," she murmured.

Ken stared down at her thin cheeks, then her slender nose, and locked his gaze onto her bottomless eyes. "When I was at Brunswick, I was in charge of the hangers for the night flights. An empty hanger with nothing to do gave me plenty of time to perfect my footwork. A homemade radio left by the maintenance crew provided the ambiance for my solitary evenings."

The pace of the music escalated, and with it, the quickness of their steps. "Who did you dance with?"

Ken tightened his hand on her taut back, his fingers finding their old, familiar place against her spine. "Let's just say I'm on a first name basis with a certain mop at the hanger."

She smiled and looked back at the table; her face stiffened. Ken stepped back, turning her body so he could see the table. Josh and Luke were leaning toward each other, their faces red. Luke's jaw was tight and Josh's head shook at the same pace as the finger he pointed at Luke.

Maggie sighed. "I think our dance is over."

Ken reluctantly released her, letting his hand to linger on her hip as they left the dance floor.

"What I do on my own time has nothing to do with you," Josh shouted as Ken and Maggie approached.

"If it concerns the Sea Swirl, it damn well does," Luke replied.

"What is it? Do you want a piece of the action or something?"

Luke threw up his hands. "You friggin' moron. No, I don't want anything to do with it. But I also don't want my boat being taken by Customs, either."

"Easy, fellas!" Ken put a hand between them. "This is supposed to be a dance, not a boxing match."

Luke looked toward Maggie; Josh's eyes stayed locked on Luke.

Ken removed his hand and pulled out a chair for Maggie, seating her beside Luke, then moved his own between them to push the men further apart. "Josh, why don't you and Barbara take a spin on the floor?"

Josh slumped back in his chair and turned his attention to the dance floor. "I'm not in the mood."

Luke kept glaring at Josh, but didn't speak.

Maggie reached for Luke's hand. "How about you? Do you want to finish the waltz?"

He turned to look at her, his eyes still hard. "Maybe I should ask my partner first."

Josh took the last of his drink in a quick shot. "Screw you!" He rose and moved unsteadily toward the door.

Barbara touched Ken's hand. "Do something!"

Ken watched him leave, then turned to Barbara. "Leave him be." He stared past Barbara to Maggie. "You know Josh – he's always been quick with his temper. I think it has to do with his father. Josh never talks about him."

Barbara leaned forward and folded her arms on the table. "Josh's dad is strange. He only comes to town once a month and when he does, he lurks around like a ghoul. It's creepy."

Chapter Four

Thursday, June 29, 1944:
North Atlantic ocean –
Three hours after first
contact with convoy.

A steady thread of water ran down the side of the periscope, dribbled onto the grates of the deck, continued over the reserve torpedoes, and then disappeared into the bilge. The roar of the twin four-stroke, supercharged Germaniawerft diesels filled the passageway and rumbled up through the control room. Everything in the room was painted light gray, except the bright-red valve wheels, black control gauges, and green levers that stood out amid the intertwined gray pipes, wires, and cylinders.

The diving mate sat beside the steering *matrose*, a hoop-like wheel in front of each of them. Oberleutnant Zur See Werner stood behind the diving station to the left of the steering mate watching the Kapitan at the periscope.

He swivelled the periscope, changing the magnification as it moved. "The convoy is approaching from the west. Turn the boat a hundred and eighty degrees to line up our stern tubes."

Werner bobbed his head. "Turn the boat. Aye, Kapitan."

As the boat swung, the Kapitan kept his face against the periscope and shuffled around with it, the black dial above his head registering the swing of the boat. "The convoy is still staggered in three columns."

Werner knew the most valuable cargo would be in the center column, loosely screened by the outside ships. Behind him, the two *Abwehr* agents slipped back into the control room and took positions as before, against the bulkhead. Oscar, the older agent, kept his face stern and tight. Mr. Franks seemed more interested in the running of the boat than the delay in his mission.

Werner continued to study them, wondering what kind of a man could be a spy. How could anyone live with that level of deceit and treachery every day, betraying the people who trusted him? It was a life he couldn't fathom. Then again, what was the Kapitan doing shooting at a convoy in the middle of a mission? "Sir? Perhaps Mr Schuch had a valid concern earlier. Is it wise to go on the offensive? Isn't our primary goal to get these men ashore in America?"

Kapitanleutnant Steiner pulled back from the periscope and glared at Werner without saying a word. Werner cleared his throat and looked down through the grates. "Sorry, Sir. My apologies."

The sound of the convoy's *screws* in the water echoed

through the hull, the noise growing as the distance between them closed. The Kapitan returned his attention to the optics. "I want a five-degree spread on two fish; then reload the tubes for two more shots."

"Aye, Sir." Werner put his lips to the communication tube. "Load the stern tubes. Five degree spread, and prepare to reload."

"Engines back slow. I want our speed at two knots, just fast enough for our drift to steady the boat," the Kapitan said. "Almost there."

U-233 backed toward their quarry, allowing the ships to steam directly into the path of the stern tubes. Mr. Schuch wiped the sweat from his brow; Mr. Franks drummed his fingers on the bulkhead.

Franks whispered to Schuch, "Why are we backing into them?"

"Because it will make our escape faster." Schuch answered.

Werner stifled a laugh. No, you idiot. It's because we're a mine layer and we don't have any bow tubes. They'd been on the boat for three days. They should have known that. What kind of spies were they?

The Kapitan ignored the exchange, tightening his grip on the handles. "Almost there. Almost there."

Werner wrapped his fingers around the speaking tube. Come on, fire the fish and get us the hell out of here!

"All stop." Kapitan Steiner reached for his stopwatch. "Fire the first tube!"

"Fire one," Werner repeated into the communication tube.

They heard the high-pitched whoosh of pressurized

air being released into a column of water, immediately followed by the release of the torpedo. The Kapitan clicked the stopwatch then looked at it. A few seconds ticked off the stopwatch before he said, "Fire two."

Werner repeated the command and the second tube emptied. Kapitan Steiner looked at Werner, smiled, and then put his eye back to the scope. "Looks like our friends up there are about to have a surprise." He rotated the scope to the west, then snapped the scope back to focus on an image.

He slapped the handles up and lowered the scope. "All ahead full! Emergency dive!"

Werner stepped to the main vents and spun the round handles. "Full down angle on the bow planes! Flooding all ballast tanks!"

Mr. Schuch and Mr. Franks latched onto pipes running along the bulkhead as U-233 tilted forward and slipped into the depths.

Every muscle in the Kapitan's face stiffened. "Cut the diesels and get the electric motors on line! Turn us forty-degrees to port and make our depth sixty meters."

"Sixty, Aye."

The diesels became quiet and the boat slowed under the power of the electric motors. The hull protested the increased water pressure by snapping and creaking as she sank deeper into the frigid water.

Kapitan Steiner moved to the forward watertight door and looked into the communication and sonar room on the port side, across from his cabin. "What do you hear?"

The man at the sonar rotated the oscilloscope dial,

keeping his other hand over his headset. "Engines gaining on us, Sir. Matching our bearing."

"Sixty meters. Leveling the bow planes," the steering mate called.

"Continue your dive. Turn to one, two, zero degrees magnetic and take us to one hundred meters."

Werner relayed the order and then stepped closer to the Kapitan. "What is it, Sir?"

The Kapitan rested his arm on the chart table. "A light cruiser."

Mr. Schuch snapped, "I told you this wasn't proper. Look what you've done."

"Shut up! If you want to live, you'll let me do my job. The last thing I need is some landsman telling me what I should have done."

Schuch scowled, but remained silent.

"Splashes!" the sonar mate shouted.

"Damn it!" The Kapitan slapped the surface of the chart table.

Mr. Franks tightened his grip on the pipe above his head and looked at Werner. "Have you ever been depth charged?"

Werner nodded.

"What's it like?"

Werner stared at the top of the compartment as if he could pierce the steel and water to see the barrels raining down on them. His throat was dry and his mind jumped back to his last tour when they narrowly escaped a British destroyer in the Baltic Sea. "Imagine clutching a case of dynamite while lying under a cast-iron tub. Then imagine someone's tossing hand grenades at you."

Franks put his hand on his stomach, turned, and headed for the exit.

While the boat was submerged, the heads didn't operate. Mr. Franks would have to retch into a bucket placed in the aisle of the engine compartment. Even seasoned sailor's bowels failed during an attack. The smell of adrenaline-laced excrement and vomit would remain in the air for hours, provided the men were fortunate enough to escape the attack.

Franks disappeared down the passage just as the first charge exploded. It rattled the boat, but sounded shallow and distant. The next two were progressively closer. The fourth nearly knocked the men off their feet.

"They're right over us, Kapitan," Werner said.

"Ten degrees to starboard!" the Kapitain ordered.

Werner moved further from the bulkhead, his eyes darting around the compartment. What was it the Kapitan had said? "Fire a couple of fish and be on our way." Was he trying to show off for his sweetheart's son, was he looking for a medal, or did he really just want to sink those ships?

"Mr. Schuch, move toward the center of the compartment." Schuch looked at the Kapitan, but didn't move. "It'll lessen the shock to your body." Schuch took two steps forward and latched onto a pipe above his head with both hands.

Two more charges detonated near the hull, one just below the stern, lifting it and twisting the boat. The second charge, amidship, pushed the boat sideways. Water flowed into the compartment around a valve that carried seawater to the ballast tanks. Schuch glanced at the water and moved forward another step.

"They've still got a fix on us. Full speed and take us deeper! One hundred and fifty meters and turn twenty more degrees to starboard as you go."

Werner leaned over the diving mate and watched the depth meter edge around the gauge. This was a risky maneuver. With the added stress to the hull, a depth charge, that wouldn't kill them higher up, but might do the job here.

Schuch edged closer, squinting at the gauges. "How deep will she go?"

"The hull will crush at two hundred meters," Werner answered.

Another charge shook the boat. Werner slammed against the bulkhead and his head struck the steel plates. The blow made the action around him appear to slow. Blood trickled down his face. He covered the wound with his hand and tried to keep the blood from going into his eye. He blinked hard, trying to focus. The voices around him seemed hollow.

The Kapitan shoved a handkerchief at him. "Use this."

Werner took the cloth and held the cotton square over the wound. A drop of blood oozed into his eye and blurred his vision. The room suddenly became one-dimensional.

The boat slid further into the darkness. The bulkheads groaned and snapped as pressure rose on the hull.

"More splashes!" the sonar operator shouted.

The explosions came after fifteen, maybe twenty

seconds. They wrapped the boat in a water fist and the ship jolted again, like a toy in an angry child's hands. Men fell onto the grates and stumbled into the bulkhead. A second blast; then a third. More leaks came from pipes and valves, spurting seawater onto the bulkheads and grates. No major ruptures, just steady streams and fountains. Enough to completely unnerve Mr. Schuch.

"Kapitan, they must have turned with us," Werner said, holding the cloth to his head.

Schuch grabbed the Kapitan's arm. "Do something!"

Kapitan Steiner looked down at his arm. "Let go of me! Let go of me now!"

Schuch didn't release his grip. "For God's sake, get us out of here!"

"Release my arm now." The Kapitan pushed Schuch away from him, and another charge exploded on the port bow. Schuch lost his grip and fell to the deck. He grasped at the grates and wobbled on all fours. The Kapitan grabbed the periscope with both hands and swung on it lurching his feet forward to catch up with his body.

Werner blotted his head, unsure if it ached from the blow he'd suffered or the concussion of the blasts. The boat was holding together, but it would only take a single well placed charge to change all that. He tightened his free hand on the speaking tube and watched Schuch wobble to his knees.

"Sonar, can you find a thermocline?" the Kapitan asked.

"Checking." A two-second pause. "Two hundred and twenty meters."

"Werner. Make our depth is two hundred twenty meters."

Werner pulled the rag from his face. "Sir?"

"You heard me. Two twenty." The Kapitan righted himself and grabbed the chart table with both hands.

Schuch pulled himself up, holding onto the cable conduit for support. "You're crazy!" He turned to Werner. "You just said the boat will crush at that depth. The damn gauge only goes to one fifty." He moved toward the Kapitan and reached once again for his arm.

Kapitan Steiner blocked with his left and landed a solid fist on Mr. Schuch's jaw with his right. Schuch went down like a ship with her back broken, then lay still on the grates.

Werner was surprised by the speed of the older man's movement and the apparent force of the blow. Mr. Schuch's eyes fluttered, yet he remained otherwise still.

The depth gauge was already pinned at one hundred and fifty meters, its deepest reading, when the diving mate angled the bow planes. Kapitan Steiner clicked his stop watch and began to listen to the sounds of the ship.

Werner fumbled with his watch, finding it with his fingers. He, too, clicked the button and then tried to read the Kapitan's face; it was tight, yet stolid. "I estimate one-sixty, Sir."

The ship creaked and whined as she dove, sounding like metal plates were compressing the hull from all sides. Werner's eyes jumped at every snap and crack, looking for new leaks and popped seams.

"One sixty five."

The sonar operator leaned into the passageway. "The

cruiser's coming at us again, Sir. Her screws are getting louder."

"One seven five," Werner said.

Mr. Schuch put one hand to his jaw and tried to sit up.

"One eight five." Werner's eyes continued to sweep the room, the blood clearing from his eye more each time he blinked. Would the old gal handle the strain?

A pipe burst in the passage behind the control room, spraying water against the bulkhead. A steady stream flowed out of the pipe and washed down onto the grates.

The Kapitan took little notice, continuing to stare at his watch.

Werner shouted into the red-painted speaking tube. "Damage control to aft of the control room!" Then he looked back at his watch. "Coming up on two hundred."

The Kapitan put his hand on the bulkhead and closed his eyes for a few seconds. "Sonar."

"Splashes." Then a pause and, "Thermocline eighteen meters away."

Schuch moved as if to stand. The Kapitan pointed a finger at him. "Stay down." He glanced at his stopwatch. "Continue the dive. Prepare the Kobold."

Werner shouted into the tube. "Prepare to jettison the Kobold!"

Mr Schuch released his jaw. "What's that?"

The Kapitan ignored the question.

"Two ten."

The steering *matrose* stole a nervous glance at the diving mate beside him.

"Two fifteen."

Depth charges exploded above them, again drawing closer, with each blast."

Again, the Kapitan held fast to the chart table. Then a charge went off to starboard side and the ship listed hard to port.

Werner stuck his ear to the tube, then relayed the message: "Engine room reports severed bolts on the packing gland around the starboard shaft seals, Sir. We're taking on water around the shaft on that side!"

The Kapitan looked at his watch, placing his other hand against the pressure hull again. "Continue the dive. Shut down that motor and pack it off as best as they're able."

Bang!

The head of a bolt snapped off a coupling and flew across the control room, passing so near the Kapitan's face that he instinctively reached up and touched the tip of his nose. The bolt head blasted across the control room and struck the steering mate in the shoulder, the force of it ripping into the muscle tissue, nearly severing his right arm. Blood splattered onto the gauges and controls as the mate flew off the seat and hit the deck. The mate ended up sprawled sideways across the passageway. Arterial blood spurted in an arc above the man's body. The Kapitan rushed to his side and covered the wound with his hands.

"Werner, take over the steering!"

Werner hesitated for an instant, the sight of the

wriggling body on the deck freezing him. Then he shook his head and slid into the vacant seat. He removed the bloodstained cloth from his head and wiped the seaman's blood from the wheel.

"Sonar!" The Kapitan looked up, keeping his hands tightly wrapped over the seaman's shoulder.

"Penetrating the thermocline now, Sir."

The steering mate writhed in pain under the Kapitain's grasp. Steiner tipped his head at a seaman in the forward passage. "Get over here and take care of this man!" Turning and releasing his grip as the other man took over, the Kapitan told Werner, "Level the boat and turn ninety degrees to port!" He shouted into the tube, "Release the Kolbod! Total silence on the boat!"

A mechanical clank followed; then a hissing sound that slowly trailed off. The seawater was mixing with calcium and zinc in the released canister, forming hydrogen gas. The canister spun violently in the water and rose toward the surface, imitating sounds similar to the U-boat.

Steiner took a towel from the chart table and wiped the blood from his hands as he listened. He heard the faint sound of screws at the surface and more explosions, but further away and shallow. The cruiser was dropping depth charges on the "deceiving spirit."

Kapitan Steiner whispered, "Twenty more degrees to port and full on the port electric, Mr. Werner.

Chapter Five

The tires of Luke's Hudson spun on loose gravel as he turned onto the Lubec boatyard. The rough-sawn, barn board building sat parallel to the water, yet back from it a hundred feet. An old weathered sign blended into the graying boards of the structure and hung under the eaves, Cox Marine. A pile of lumber was stacked nearby and would someday be the machine shop, but it, too, showed the gray of exposure to the elements. The sandy driveway was pockmarked with water filled holes, some deep enough to bathe a large dog.

Three fishing boats were up on stands for repairs and painting; several others hung on moorings in the bay. Five boats rested against the dock, swaying with the tug-o-war between the outgoing river and the incoming tide. A few men rattled around on the boats getting ready for the day, but the yard held the stillness of morning. Luke waved at Stan McPherson as he stacked traps on the stern of the

Miss Jenny. Stan's hands were occupied, but he smiled and raised his head.

The Sea Swirl lay tied to the dock at their slip with Josh's car parked at an angle in front of the ramp. Luke pulled the Hudson in beside it, whispering under his breath, "Miracles never cease. He made it, and on time, too."

Luke grabbed his foul-weather gear, work gloves, and sack lunch from the trunk, then strolled across to the main seawall, his boots grinding in the loose sand of the drive. The seawall was constructed of old railroad ties that had been soaked in creosote and stacked into the bank. The floating docks ran perpendicular to these and into the harbor. One boat was tethered on each side of the floats. A long boarding ramp ran out onto the float from the seawall and was attached by a heavy galvanized hinge on one end and rollers on the float end. The ramp extended half-way out on the float now at almost high tide. In six hours, the ramp would be at a steep incline, barely reachable. Luke stubbed his boot on one of the wooden cleats attached to the ramp as he walked onto the float and nearly dropped his lunch into the water.

The *Sea Swirl* was motionless on the water, tiny ripples reflecting her green hull like a disheveled twin. Dew clung to all her surfaces and his foot skidded as he stepped aboard. A seagull perched on a pylon watched him set down his lunch. Knowing the habits of the gulls, Luke set the lunch further into the cockpit away from the wretched scavenger.

He tried to open the hatch to the V-berth. It was locked. He felt a bit silly having missed seeing the padlock. Banging on the wooden door, he called out, "Josh? Josh?"

No answer. He noticed the dew was undisturbed on the deck. He banged again. "Josh!"

Luke looked back at the cars. A flurry of movement in the seat of the Packard, then Josh's head rose beside the steering wheel. He looked around in a daze and then staggered out of the car, rumpled and half-asleep. Pushing himself away from the car, he walked a slow, unsteady line to the boat. "Damn! Morning comes early."

He tossed his gear onto the boat, held onto the gunwale with both hands and stepped aboard the wet deck. His dark hair rebelled over his right ear and stood up straight at the cowlick.

Luke unlocked the V-berth and tossed the padlock on the dash behind the compass. "Earlier for some than others. I didn't know if you'd show up after last night."

Josh rubbed at his scruffy face. "Aw, I was just being a jerk. You know me."

"So are we all right then?"

Josh picked his gear off the deck and laid it on the engine hatch. "If you can put up with me, then yeah." He stuck out his hand.

Luke took the hand and gave Josh a slap on the shoulder. "It's not the first time we've gone at it, and I'm sure it won't be the last."

Josh picked up his gear and headed into the cuddy cabin. "You're probably right."

Two tall bait barrels waited on the stern. They'd been delivered by Joel Cox, the marina owner, earlier that morning. They held trimmings of small herring from one of the sardine factories.

"What time did Joel come by this morning?"

Josh leaned his head out the entrance to the berth and frowned.

He inspected Josh's haggard face. "Right. My mistake."

Luke stepped over to the wheel under a short shed-type roof and turned the key to the left to engage the glow plugs. After a minute, he turned it to the right and the diesel cranked over slowly. It groaned, coughed a few times, and finally fired up. A black plume of smoke shot into the air as the old diesel came to life, shattering the morning quiet. The seagulls on the dock didn't fly away at the racket; instead, they hopped closer to the herring bait.

Luke leaned over and shouted into the berth, "I thought you were going to get us a new fuel pump? This one's going to give out on us any day."

"I can get just about anything, but engine parts are a bit tricky. Everything's going overseas."

"Well, just try, huh? I don't fancy being stranded somewhere."

"You're welcome to try yourself. It's not like you'd think. A simple cash payoff at a back entrance might work, but we don't live in Detroit. I don't even know anyone from there, let alone have a connection."

Luke played with the throttle mounted to the right of the wheel; the engine dutifully responded in pitch.

Josh came back on deck wearing an ancient set of orange, waterproof bibs, stained from use, and a pair of cotton-lined leather gloves. He wobbled to the gunwale, stepped onto the dock to release the lines, and jumped back aboard. Luke engaged the throttle and the boat lurched into Johnson Bay, which lit up like an undulating mirror in the morning sunlight.

Josh pried the lid off a barrel of the bait with a screw-driver, picked up a well-worn metal grain scoop, and ladled batches of the slimy mass into the small fishnet bait bags. Much of it missed the bag or dripped through the netting onto his pants and boots. More ran down his arm and soaked through his leather gloves. He'd fill one, pause, tie it, and then slowly fill another. On the third bag, the scoop hung up in the net and as he pulled it out, the fish slime splattered across his face. He tried to wipe it away with the back of his glove, but only succeeded in smearing it around. He coughed and gagged at the foul stench, then resumed working. As he started on the fifth bag, he rushed to the side and threw up into the water.

Luke smiled to himself and looked back over the bow. "You should wait to do that until we get out there. It would make good chum for the lobsters."

Josh wiped his lips with the back of his glove. "Funny. Very funny." He looked back at the sloshing bucket of guts, heads, and slime.

Luke reached for his rubber gloves. "Come on. You drive this morning. I'll fill the bags."

Josh headed for the helm, removing his gloves as he went.

"Head straight out. We'll pull the traps off West Quoddy Head, then swing down into Wallace Cove."

"You got it, boss." Josh tossed his gloves onto the deck beneath the wheel and placed a hand on the throttle.

The morning warmed fast, with the sunlight dancing off the smooth water. Luke shaded his eyes with one hand and stared at the channel between Lubec and Campobello Island, a body of water forming the border between the United States and Canada. The highest tides in the continental US battered the solid granite ledges that lined each side of the bay and islands.

He finished loading the bags, laid out the sorting table on top of the engine compartment, then checked the winch arm and electrical connection. Finally, he joined Josh at the wheel. As they cleared the inlet, the sea breeze picked up and a light chop rocked the water. The bow sliced through it without lifting or bouncing. The light wind swept away the stench of the boat and replaced it with salty sweetness. Luke closed his eyes and faced into the breeze, feeling it sweep across his face and take with it his worries.

"Couldn't ask for a better day," Luke said with his eyes still closed.

Josh swallowed hard. "Still looks a bit hazy to me."

"Well, a few hours of hauling traps will clear your head faster'n anything."

"Cure it or kill it. I'm not sure which."

Luke moved to the locker on the far side of the wheel house, removed a set of stained coveralls that matched Josh's, slid them on, and fastened a belt around it to keep the loose fitting garment from catching on the rigging.

He pointed toward the shore. "There's our first

string. Come around from the east and keep us headed into the wind."

"Sure."

Luke stepped up to the winch and grabbed the boat hook with his left hand, while Josh piloted close to the red buoy marked by a white handle and blue nose. Luke braced himself against the gunwale, reached over the side, and snagged the line with the hook, pulling it to him. He dragged the loop of line onto the boat, wrapped it over the winch with his right hand, then hung up the hook with his left, and hit the power switch. The trap began rising from the bottom toward the Sea Swirl. The winch motor strained under the load and the arm that held the pulley swivelled on its hinge in the direction of the load, squeaking and creaking as it worked. The wooden trap broke the surface, the light swells sloshing over the top, dunking it in and out of the water. Luke grabbed the chipped, wet frame and pulled it out of the bay. The water ran out of the mesh and gushed over the side, revealing the empty bait bag hung from the top of the trap and a number of skittering crustaceans climbing onto the red-brick weight wedged into the corner. He rested the trap on the gunwale, unhooked the line from the winch, and took a bite of the rope below the first trap, threaded it through the pulley, and slung it over the wheel.

Releasing the wooden toggles that held the cover of the trap closed, he flipped open the mesh top, pulled out three good-sized lobsters, and tossed them onto the sorting table. Next, he unloaded two short lobsters and a crab, tossing them overboard after a quick examination. He left the trap on the deck while he double-checked the line to pull the second trap from the same buoy, and hit the switch to the winch. It, too, held three keepers and a couple of shorts.

After re-baiting the two traps, he set them on the rail and shoved the first one over while Josh headed for the next pot. As the line drew tight, Luke pushed over the second trap, then finally the rest of the line and the float.

They repeated this maneuver for several hours, taking breaks to sort the lobsters by size and condition, storing them in wooden crates on the stern. Single-clawed lobsters were separated from the rest. By mid-morning, Luke was sweating hard as they began pulling the pots in Wallace Cove. His damp shirt clung to his shoulders; the thought of a cold beer tortured him. He looked at Josh at the wheel and considered asking him to switch places, but shook off the idea and reached for the boat hook.

That double haul contained a nice surprise – four good-sized lobsters and two smaller ones in the first trap, and six medium-sized lobsters in the second. He held up one of the green-speckled, spiny creatures. Its eyes twitched back and forth on short stalks, apparently looking for escape. Luke smiled and tossed it on the table with the others. Luke grabbed another bait bag and hung it from the top of the trap, then set it up on the rail with the first one. The moment he shoved the first trap over the rail, the lobster snapped its tail and flopped off the sorting table. Luke lunged for it, and as he moved forward, the line in his hand looped over his wrist. The boat kept moving ahead, the line pulled snug, and the second trap went over the side.

The combined weight of the two traps and the boat's

momentum snapped the line tight around Luke's wrist and yanked him to the starboard side. He slammed into the gunwale, clawing at the rope. A knife. He needed a knife. There was one on the sorting table, if he could just get to it.

Before he could react further, the line flipped him over the side exactly like a cull lobster. He plunged head-first into the cold Maine water, managing to gasp a breath of air before the weighted traps dragged him down.

The traps sank quickly, dragging him further and further below the surface. The suddenness of being pulled over didn't allow his body to fully register the cold water, but the pressure to his ears felt as though they'd been stabbed by ice picks. He had to get his hand out of the loop in the line. What could he use? He thought about the contents of his pockets, but they were empty. The water appeared murky-green at this depth, but his vision was fuzzy, with the only distinct object being the line that was hauling him to his death.

He yanked at the rope, but it clung around his wrist like a vise. His ears continued to throb and his heavy clothes acted like an anchor. Kicking in vain as the thick slicker coveralls filled with water, he looked up at the surface. Maybe he could hold his breath long enough for the traps to settle and slacken the line? The sun reflected down through the water, breaking it into distinct planes of light tantalizingly flickering off the air above. You can't get free, he was thinking, so use the time you're sinking. He clawed at the belt and managed to unclasp the hook. The belt drifted into the darker water below. He tried to rip off the coveralls, but they hung up on his wrist, still tethered to the line.

In the world above, Josh swung the bow toward the next pot. "I don't know about you, but I could use a cold drink."

No response.

"Luke?" Josh turned toward the stern and scanned the empty deck. No sign of Luke.

His stomach tightened and he had difficulty catching a full breath.

He slammed the throttles ahead and spun the wheel. The bow rose from the water and swung around, heading for the last buoy. Josh stripped off his rubber boots and coveralls as the Sea Swirl raced toward the pot. When the boat came up to the float, he grabbed the filet knife off the sorting table, pulled the throttle back to neutral, and dove over the side.

He struck the water hard, and at first couldn't see much of anything; then slowly his eyes adjusted, and he spotted the line descending into the deep. He grabbed it with one hand and pulled downward, kicking hard. The water pressure compressed the air in his lungs and his brain demanded a new breath, but he ignored the sensation and kicked harder.

Where was Luke? He had to be down there somewhere. The knife in his right hand made it difficult to claw at the water with his fist, so he kicked harder, feverishly pulling himself deeper.

A shadow at first, then a grotesque form flailing on the line. Luke struggled with his coveralls and the line around his wrist. Josh grabbed the upper part of the line and pulled himself toward his friend. Luke must have felt the pulling on the line and looked upward. Luke's panicked eyes gaped at him. Josh latched onto his wrist. He swept the knife through the water and sawed at the line, parting it below the point where Luke was attached. The rope curled free. Josh dropped the knife and dragged him toward the surface. Luke pulled his wrist away, to strip away his coveralls. Josh stopped his ascent and watched his friend. Only after Luke had freed himself from the garments and began to follow, did Josh resume his climb. The surface seemed a lifetime above them, and as the pain in Josh's ear subsided it was replaced by an ache in his chest. A dark blur at his side and Luke shot by. Josh continued to paw at the water and kick as hard as he could muster and the surface eventually neared.

Luke broke the surface first and took a huge breath. Josh surfaced half a second behind him and immediately attempted to slow his own frantic gulping. They bobbed in the water kicking rhythmically and fanning their arms at their sides, drinking deeply of the sea air.

Luke's eyes were still wide. "Thank God you found me! I was right at the limit."

"What the frig happened?"

"I got my hand caught."

"Duh! I mean, how'd you manage that?"

Luke coughed and gulped more air. "Got distracted, I guess."

"Yeah, I'd say so." Josh looked toward the boat, now drifting with the ebbing tide. "We'd best be swimming to her before she drifts too far away."

Chapter Six

The sun hung low over the bull grass. The last sliver of crimson retired below the horizon with a final burst of orange rays dancing across the water. Seabirds nested in the dark silhouettes of the pines and aspen, their cackles quieting as they settled into the blackening wood. Ken shivered at the sudden chill rising off the water.

Turning from the water's edge, he trudged through the coarse grass and up the gradual slope towards the office. The frogs began to serenade their mates behind him as he walked. If there hadn't been a war, what would he be doing right now? The Navy had seemed like the perfect choice at the time, but now he wasn't sure it suited him. It wasn't the adventure he'd expected. Maybe he could use the time to reconnect with Maggie; then at least his time here wouldn't be wasted.

The single bulb hanging above the door flipped on, and illuminated the steps to the temporary structure. Ken's clerk must have seen him coming. The building was a single-story, wood- framed structure with white clapboard siding and a black asphalt roof – all perched atop concrete blocks. The office consisted of two wooden desks up front and cramped sleeping quarters in the back for Ken. His bunk area also doubled as the post armory.

He swung back the squeaky screen door and let it slam behind him as he stepped inside.

The clerk's chair scraped on the wooden floor and almost toppled over as Petty Officer Third Class William Durning rose and saluted. "Officer on deck."

Ken hesitated then returned the salute. "Bill, do you realize you're the only one here?"

Durning remained at attention. "Protocol, Sir. The Navy lives and dies on repetition and drill."

Ken rubbed his eyebrows. "Fine. As you were."

Durning was relentless. "Sir, the daily reports are waiting on top of your in-box, followed by the fuel consumption data from last week, and lastly the duty roster."

"Duty roster? This post consists of a cook, two Seamen first-class, and us. I know what I'll be doing and I assume the cook won't have any surprises about his job. The two Seamen alternate duty at their post guarding the entrance." He paused. "So that leaves you. And since you make up the roster, I expect you already know what's in it." Ken raised a brow. "So I think we can stop posting the roster."

Durning's eyes shifted around the room.

"Sir, Command requires a duty roster each day. At the end of the day, it should be signed by the commanding officer. One copy is placed on file, and the second forwarded to Portland for review." He tightened his jaw. "I can't be a party to shirking my duty, Sir."

Ken walked past Durning, slumped into his gray metal

chair and stared at his desk and the papers in the box on the corner. "And I'm sure the entire Navy will collapse if they don't receive it. Carry on."

"Thank you, Sir." Durning reseated himself, took a sheet of paper from the neat pile on the corner of his desk, and fed it into the Smith Corona typewriter. Mechanical clicks followed as he plunked the keys with two fingers.

Ken removed the daily reports, scanned them briefly, and signed the bottom of each page. Next, he set the fuel reports aside on his desk and also signed the duty roster, without reading it. Lastly, he placed a pen in his pocket, gathered up the fuel reports, stood and headed for the door. "I'm going over to Mabel's for a bite."

Durning snapped to his feet. "Yes, Sir! I'll send a runner if there's anything to report."

Ken pushed open the screen door. "You do that."

After the door slammed, he heard Durning's voice behind him. "It's lasagna night, Sir. Should I have the cook hold you some?"

Ken shook his head and walked away, rolling his eyes.

———

Mabel's diner was two miles east of the post off U. S. Route One, situated on the north side of Court Street in Machias between the hotel and Alton Bridgham's barbershop. Mr. Bridgham had been Ken's scoutmaster and always kept a supply of stick candy in a jar on the counter. A glow from the glass-fronted diner spilled out onto Court Street and illuminated the parked cars. Bright lights from Emma Mean's theater across the street intertwined with the lights from the diner in the middle of the street.

Ken parked his Jeep beside a dusty Plymouth, set the parking brake, and gathered the fuel reports that had blown around the front seat. He waved at Barbara in the glass booth at the theater and turned toward the diner. A bell above the door announced his entrance, jangling dutifully.

The two men who occupied the first booth looked up at him while a waitress he didn't know leaned over them pouring coffee. The men stared at his uniform instead of his face.

This was not only a welcome change from the dreary mess hall at the base, but the surroundings gave him with a rush of warmth and security. The red vinyl seat covers looked cheerful against the yellow linoleum floor and silver-based stools. The coffee smelled twice as rich as it did back in his office and the pies on the shelf behind the counter would fill any gaps the coffee might have missed.

He nodded to the men as he passed and headed to a booth at the far right side. "Al... Phil."

Albert, the heavier, balding man, nodded. "Geez, Ken, I didn't recognize you. You wear the uniform well."

The other man spun in his seat to look at him.

Ken wondered how many other people he'd known all his life would see the uniform first, perhaps forgetting this was his home and these were his folk. "Thanks. It's not as comfortable as dungarees and a T-shirt."

Ken headed for his usual booth on the far side where he had a view of the whole diner. The waitress behind the counter had dark hair and a sallow complexion – pleasing, but plain. Maggie backed out of the kitchen balancing two plates in her left hand and two glasses of ice-water in her right. The kitchen door swung shut behind her, barely missing her shapely rear. She caught Ken's eye and smiled.

Her figure was captivating; her movements smooth and graceful. She made the simple chore of carrying plates as enchanting as a ballet.

Ken watched her finish serving Al and Phil. Her hair was pulled back, her slender neck rising out of her open-collared dress. The hem was hidden in front by her white apron, yet the back snuck upwards to the back of her knees as she bent at the waist to lay the plates on the table. Taut and smooth, her legs held Ken's attention until her silky voice drew him away.

"You boys need anything else?"

"No thanks, Maggie," Phil picked up his fork and began rearranging the food on his plate.

A few seconds later, she sauntered toward Ken and slid into the seat across from him. "Well, hello stranger."

"I'm no stranger than anyone else you know."

She laughed. "I didn't expect to see you here, what with your own cook at the post."

Ken pushed the stack of reports toward the window. "The company's better here."

"You want dinner or just a pop?"

"A Coke would be great." He could smell the light scent of violets from across the table.

She called to the other waitress: "Juliana, would you get a Coke for him and a coffee for me? Thanks."

"Who's the new girl?"

"Bill Holmes' cousin from Ellsworth." Maggie pushed her hair back behind her ears. "She's real nice. Maybe you two should go out."

Juliana approached with a cup of coffee in one hand, and a bottle of Coke with a glass filled with ice in the other. She kept her eyes on Ken as she slid the coffee in front of Maggie. "Just the way you like it, Maggie, with a spoonful of vanilla ice cream."

Ken knew this about Maggie – always a small dollop of vanilla to sweeten and cool her coffee.

Juliana slid the Coke in front of Ken. "Who's your friend?"

Ken reached for the plastic-covered menu wedged behind the salt and pepper shakers and the window.

"Juliana, this is Kenneth Mitchell. Ken, this is Juliana Munson."

"Nice to meet you." Ken half rose and shook her hand, then reseated himself and opened the menu, studying the daily special.

"A pleasure."

He continued to concentrate on the menu. "So, Maggie, what's good tonight?"

Juliana tossed a napkin in front of him and flounced back to the kitchen.

Maggie grabbed the menu from his hands. "You're a real charmer tonight. I told you she's a nice girl."

"I'm sure she is." Ken leaned toward her and tried to take back the menu. "What makes you think I'm interested?"

Maggie set the menu in her lap and took a sip of her

coffee. "We've got baked beans tonight. I cooked them myself this afternoon."

Ken reached for the menu under the table, grazing her knee as he did so. "How do I know what I want if you won't give me the menu?"

She jiggled the menu in front of her. "So you need a menu to figure out what you want?"

Ken eased one hand across the table. "I'm more decisive than you think."

She laughed. "Oh. The still waters run deep thing, huh?"

"Something like that."

She lifted the menu over her head. As he lunged again, she tossed it into the booth behind her. "You need to learn some manners. Maybe I should have a talk with your father."

"I'm not the one tossing things around the joint." Ken settled back in his seat and poured Coke into his glass, then stirred it with the straw. "Speaking of which, how's your dad? Any chance he'll be back at work after his heart strain?"

"Don't know We'll just have to wait and see." She leaned toward the table, her apron strings restraining her breasts, and raised her chin as she kept her eyes pinned on his. "Are you flirting with me?"

Ken's peripheral vision noticed her absentmindedly rub her finger tips on the Formica surface of the table. Her slender fingers, strong from work. "Just because the new seed hasn't arrived, doesn't mean you shouldn't plow the fields."

Her fingers stopped.

Their eyes remained locked. Ken knew he should look away, but couldn't.

Maggie's gaze broke from his and she set the spoon aside on the table. "Why did you leave college when you could've gotten a deferment and finished?"

Ken stared out the window across the dark, quiet street, where Barbara was admitting an older couple to the theater. "I haven't told anyone this, but I really didn't like it."

Maggie stopped with the cup halfway to her lips. She lowered it back to the table. "No kidding? What didn't you like?"

"It was too rigid. They want you to learn everything their way. If you don't agree with them, you're wrong. Sort of like with my dad."

"Couldn't you have finished, then done something else?"

He shrugged. "Maybe. But with two years of college behind me, I could get into Officer Candidate School. Besides, my family didn't have the money. I barely made tuition. I wasn't going to ask my dad for more money and give him poor grades in return."

Maggie frowned and slapped her hand on the table after rethinking his words. "Oh, who's kidding who? Like the Navy isn't rigid. Besides, you're way too smart for them."

Ken smiled. "Okay, maybe that wasn't all. I guess I couldn't see myself teaching English for the rest of my life. I thought I could see the world. Have an adventure maybe."

"Are you twelve years old and need to run away from

home? Surely you aren't going to come back here and work in the blueberry factory."

"No, definitely not the factory. That was a disaster, if you remember. All three of us guys worked there after high school. It was fine when we were all on the loading docks together, but Fred Ames, the owner, took a liking to me and moved me up to overseer. That sure didn't make it easy to live with Josh and Luke. Especially Luke, being older, he'd already been there over two years when I started, he couldn't stand the thought of me being above him. That's why he quit, remember."

"Yeah, I remember. So, are you going back to school after the war?

"Maybe. I mean, I'd like to." Ken decided to change the subject. "You were always the inquisitive one. You should've been the one to go."

She began to rub her fingers on the table again. "Me? College?"

"Do you think you might?"

She twirled her cup on the table. "Well, maybe if Mother was alive, but that isn't important. It is what it is. No what if's." Her face brightened. "Hey, Luke's going to pick me up at seven and we're seeing the new Olivia de Havilland picture. You want to come?"

This was typical Maggie. She didn't like talking about herself, so she'd adroitly changed the subject.

"Another western?"

Maggie smiled. "Of course. What girl wouldn't like to be rescued?"

Ken touched the back of her hand. "Is that what you need?"

The bell over the door jangled and Maggie withdrew her hand, placing it under the table. Luke paused in the doorway, then headed over to the booth. He pushed in next to Maggie and gave her a peck on the cheek.

"Has my girl been working hard?"

Ken leaned back. "Of course. In fact, she was about to get me a plate of beans. Weren't you, Maggie?"

"Yeah, that's right" She pushed against Luke. "Excuse me."

Luke picked up Maggie's cup, reached for the glass sugar jar, and added a teaspoon of the coarse granules from the little silver trap door on top. "Listen. The town team is short a man. Johnny Beal cut his arm on a sickle mower the other day and can't play. You want in?"

Ken watched him stir the sugar into what remained of Maggie's coffee and put it to his lips. It was her coffee. Why did it bother him so much to see him drinking it?

He looked away. "I was going to drop in and see my folks tomorrow."

Luke frowned. "You can do that anytime. The games more important."

He thought of all the ball games they'd played; hitting balls in the park until well after dark, playing catch in his yard after school. He knew his mother would already be muffed that he hadn't stopped by, what would one more day hurt. "Sure. You want me to play first?"

Luke sipped the lukewarm brew. "Nah. We've got a first baseman. You'll have to play third."

"But I'm a first baseman."

Luke finished the cup and held it up to Maggie as she came back from the kitchen. She nodded and headed for the coffee pot. "This is my team. You'll play where I say. Besides, it's the same thing as first, just the opposite side of the diamond. Anyway, Josh and I do all the real work. If I turn up the heat with my left-handed magic and Josh manages to catch everything I throw at him, you won't have to do much."

Maggie filled Luke's cup while looking at Ken, a blonde lock of hair tumbling over her ear and curling inward. "I'll finish up here in a minute. Then we can wander across to the theater. You sure you don't want to tag along?"

Luke's head snapped toward her. "What?"

Ken looked at the stack of fuel reports. "No, I really should be getting back. I'll take a rain check on the food, too."

"So we're on for tomorrow?"

Ken rose, flipped fifty cents onto the table and gathered up the papers. "Yes, nine. At the field?"

"Yeah."

The soft wind blowing through Ken's hair rustled like wheat in a breeze. When he left the lights of town, the sky blossomed in all its glory. The big dipper was directly off his right shoulder, the moon on his left, and the smell of salty air streamed past. Thoughts of Maggie clouded his vision. He caressed the wheel with his hand just as he'd touched the inside of her thigh as they lay naked on the shore of Cathance Lake two summers ago, moonlight reflecting off her moist skin, the light breeze keeping her nipples erect. He shook his head and slapped the wheel with his hands.

Leaning back in the seat, he pushed hard on the top of the wheel and shouted into the wind. "Aahrr! Think of work. Get your mind busy."

Ken thought of the drudgery of his job; then thought of the fuel reports and whose name would be on top. Outside the guard shack, a lone seaman sat on a wooden folding chair, tilted back against the wall, listening to a radio. He rose and gave a weak salute as Ken drove past. Ken parked in front of the office, where the single light bulb still burned over the steps.

The door was locked and he fished in his pocket for the silver key that let him in. Petty Officer Durning's desk was neat, typewriter square to the corners and covered smartly with a plastic shield. Ken's desk had been straightened as well. Even the file box on the corner had been moved an equal distance from the corner of the desk. He stripped off his tie and unbuttoned his shirt, then fell onto his bunk, facing a rack of carbines and Thompson's on the far wall. He kicked off his shoes, flipped the switch on the reading light over the bed and held up the reports.

Fuel Usage by Commercial Boats
Week of June 18 to June 24, 1944
List compiled in order of greatest to least usage.

Boat	Gallons		Owner
1. The Annabelle	Stinson Canning co.		750
2. Sea swirl	Josh Halley and Luke Morgan		480
3. Miss Jane	Mike McPherson		110

The list went on, but Ken focused on line two.

He rested the pages on his legs and stared at the ceiling, then spoke out loud. "How do you expect me to fix this one, Josh? When Customs sees these reports, they're going to wonder where you've been to burn that much fuel."

Chapter Seven

Oberleutnant Zur See Werner ducked through the water-tight hatch and headed toward the galley. Not a room; but more an alcove off the passage, it held a gas four-burner stove with a small oven underneath. Metal lockers filled every centemeter of free space, allowing barely enough room for the cook to slip between the stove and the forward bulkhead. A table attached to the hull on the far side acted as the officers' wardroom.

Werner lifted the blackened coffeepot from the burner, filled his mug, and reached for the powdered milk. The stench of the U-boat overpowered the coffee beans, but the liquid was hot and took the chill out of the soul.

Low voices came from the berth behind the galley. Werner stepped close, curious.

"Make sure to double-wrap the radio in oilcloth. If it gets wet our whole mission will be in jeopardy." It was Oscar Schuch's voice.

"I've got it. I've got it. Just worry about the money and diamonds. We'll need all of it." Franks responded.

"The harder part will be getting to the railroad station in Bangor. Once we reach New York, we can blend in."

"Der Falke should have arrangements for us. We needn't worry about that."

Werner leaned closer to the curtain. A brief pause, then, "I'm sure we can..."

The curtain whipped back and Werner stood face to face with Mr. Schuch.

"Something we can help you with?" Schuch stared at Werner, his beady eyes unwavering.

Werner cleared his throat and stepped back. "No, sorry. I just needed coffee. My apologies." He gazed at the stacks of US currency on the bunk and small piles of glistening diamonds.

"What did you hear?"

Werner took a step backward, bumping into the corner of the table.

"Nothing. My apologies for disturbing you."

Schuch stepped closer. "That's not good enough. How long were you there?"

Werner leaned back on the table, trying to get more distance between himself and Schuch. "Just a moment, really."

Franks scooped up the diamonds in his fist and dribbled them into a blue cloth sack. "He's on our side and an officer. We can trust him."

Schuch turned toward Franks. "I don't trust anyone with my life. If you weren't so young and inexperienced, you might realize the peril he could put us in."

Franks tied the strings on the top of the bag. "He's on board a U-boat. Who's he going to tell?"

Schuch turned back to Werner and eyed him. "You've already heard too much." He paused, "But, I think Franks may be right. We have no choice but to trust you as an officer. You'll keep this to yourself?"

"Of coarse. It's my duty." Werner nodded.

Schuch considered something for a few seconds. "Since you're here, you may as well help us. Besides, Franks might be right. Who could you tell aboard this boat?" He looked at the bunk, but his jaw remained firm. "We need a good coat of oil on the Lugers. Then load the spare clips."

Werner squatted down and picked up one of the butt-heavy pistols, turned it in his hands, then field-stripped it with efficiency. "Looks like we could be a few days late delivering you to Maine."

"No matter. Our timetable can be re-arranged by radio," Franks said.

"The Kapitan has been tight-lipped about you two. Where will you put ashore?"

Franks shot a look at Schuch, who shrugged. "Somewhere between Calais and Ellsworth."

Werner slid the rod with an oiled patch through the barrel. "If you're headed for New York, do either of you have knowledge of the area?"

Schuch's eyes hardened. "So you were listening for awhile."

Franks tied off the string over the oilcloth. "I went to school there before the war. My sister still lives there." He paused and sighed, nodding toward the stacks of bills.

"She's not well off, but I think we can help her out a bit."

Schuch reached out and slapped Franks shoulder. "Shut the hell up! It's one thing to accidentally let something slip, but you don't have to make it worse."

Frank's head dropped and he stared at the bunk. "I thought you said we could trust him."

"Damn, you're stupid. With what he already heard, not something new." Schuch picked up a stack of bills and slid it into his brief case. "Why did I let them stick me with a boy still wet behind the ears? You're going to get me hung."

The speaker squawked as Werner slid the action back in place. "Surface the boat. Repair teams to the stern. Divers ready your gear."

Werner placed the Luger back on the bunk. "I'm needed on deck. Excuse me." He rose and headed for the control room.

Behind him, Schuch picked up the Luger and snapped back the action with a metallic crack.

The boat hit the surface and the Kapitan was the first up the ladder to the hatch. He swung the crank and water rushed in around the seal, gushing over the men in the tube. The first breath of fresh air was worth the drenching as it flowed downward and swept into the control room. Kapitan Steiner's feet landed on the bridge at the same time his binoculars hit his brow. Scanning the night sky toward the horizon, he barked orders.

"Mr. Werner, supervise inspection of the starboard screw. I want watches fore and aft, and man the two guns on the platforms." He paused, gazing at the horizon. "Make sure to charge the batteries."

The watches were first out, followed by the gun crews, then finally the engineers and mechanics. The gun crews had stripped off the covers and removed the muzzle plugs before Werner even reached the stern. One of the mechanics hooked a line onto the deck and walked down the side of the hull like a climber down a steep hill.

He inspected the shaft and screw as best he could without getting into the water, then climbed back up, and reported to Werner. Werner hurried across the deck and climbed up to the conning tower beside Kapitan Steiner.

"It appears the initial assessment was correct. The shaft seals were damaged. We'll need braided flax, impregnated with wax, several new bolts, and a shaft cover.

"Can the men manufacture it?" Kapitan Steiner asked.

"I'm afraid not, Sir. We'll need to acquire it. But once we have it, we may be able to make the repairs at sea."

Steiner put the binoculars back to his face. "Send a radio message to our weather station in Greenland. Have them relay a message to Admiral Donitz for instructions." He paused and lowered the glasses to his chest, but didn't turn. "Leave out the part about our failed attempt on the Liberty ships, won't you?"

"Of course, Sir." Werner turned, then stopped halfway into the hatch. "The *Abwehr* agents will want to send a message as well. Shall I let them?"

Kapitan Steiner took a deep breath. "Yes. Just monitor what they say and report back."

"Aye, Sir. Count on it." Werner stayed in the opening,

looking at the Kapitan. "You have doubts about our guests?"

"I don't trust anyone who's in the secrets business."

Chapter Eight

Petty Officer Third-Class Durning was already up and thumping on his typewriter in the next room when Ken opened his eyes. The papers had fallen off his legs, but the light still burned above his head. He reached up and flicked it off, then glanced out the window over his bunk. This would be a perfect day to make hay. A cool morning without any dew, the sun full of itself already and working hard to heat up the fields. The clouds had slept in late, promising to arrive only when the workers would need afternoon shade.

Rising, Ken rubbed his face and looked down at his wrinkled uniform. After stripping it off, he took a wash-cloth bath at the sink, dressed in a clean uniform, and headed through the door into the office.

"Officer on deck." Durning snapped out of his chair.

Ken looked at the empty office, saluted his junior, walked to his own desk, and slid the fuel reports into a drawer. "I'm going to the mess for breakfast and then into town. I didn't get a chance to look over the fuel reports. I'll do it tomorrow."

"Begging you pardon, Sir. But they're due today."

Ken paused at the door. "I'm aware of that. If I don't get them in on time, it will reflect on me, not you. As far as I'm concerned, you've done your duty, and I'll reflect that in your fitness report."

He watched During return to his desk and begin typing. Ken stared at the back of his narrow head. Doesn't he know this is Machias, for Christ's sake? No one gives two hoots about these being on time.

Chipped beef on toast. Ken could still taste the cream sauce on his palate as he turned the Jeep onto Broadway, headed north towards Whitneyville, the fair grounds, and the diamond. His father's dark-brown glove, well oiled with Neatsfoot, lay in the seat beside him with a ball stuffed in the palm of the five-fingered mitt. The bottom of his stomach tingled; on a day like this they'd won the county championship on this very field.

He swung the Jeep to the right and onto the grounds, drove past the empty animal shelters, around the grandstand, and parked near the picket fence among a cluster of other cars. The teams were already warming up and spectators milled around the edge of the field or sat on blankets behind home plate. Several rows of people stood along the sidelines, just inside the sulky track that circled the diamond. He sat in the Jeep for a few moments staring at the field, his mind full of memories of youth, friends, and fun.

With the mitt tucked under his arm, Ken jogged toward the home team bench. Luke spied him as he crossed the lot and came to meet him. He tossed Ken a jersey, pants, and socks.

"These are Johnny's things. They should fit. You can change over by the grandstand."

Ken took the clothes and retreated to dress while Luke returned to the team and resumed his warm-up pitches with Josh. Ken waved to Barbara and Maggie, who were sitting along the first base line on a dark-green plaid blanket, a picnic basket at their side.

The practice pitch struck Josh's glove with a crack. Luke grinned. "Hey, Mags. Looks like I'm on today."

She raised her chin, smiled, and then went back to her conversation with Barbara.

Ken dressed quickly, then wandered back to the team. He tugged at the seat of his tight, off-gray pants, and rolled his shoulders in the jersey – *Bulldogs* plastered across the front in orange and black. "Johnny must be shorter than I remember," he mumbled to Josh.

Josh looked up through his catchers' mask. "Maybe you just put on a few pounds, eating all that Navy grub. I hope it doesn't make you slower than you already are."

Ken slapped his fist in his glove. "Don't worry about me. How are your knees holding out?"

"Fine. Now get out there and warm up."

Ken picked up a ball and loped toward third. He could feel the anticipation in his limbs. It was like being back in school. The same fears and performance anxiety; wanting to impress the girls, and the equal desire not to disappoint his teammates. "Caleb, toss me a few."

Caleb Turner knelt by the sideline, tying his shoe, but nodded to Ken, then sprang up from his knees and stuffed his burly hand into his glove. The stocky shortstop was surprisingly agile even with a stump for a neck.

Barbara leaned forward on the blanket. "Nice duds, Ken. Very provocative."

Ken looked down, not sure whether she meant the pants, intentionally long and non-traditional, with elastic stays covering most of his socks and almost reaching his ankles, or the fact that they were wedged half-way up his behind. He'd always felt three inches taller in his base-ball uniform, but after spending the winter in Florida and seeing some of the fancy playing duds they wore, this felt constrictive.

"Yeah, yeah. Loose lips don't just sink ships. They can screw up the game," Ken scolded.

"It may not win games, but it keeps the players on their toes," Maggie added.

"Why don't you distract the other team when they're on the field?"

"Oh, don't worry about it. I've got that covered," Barbara said, stretching her arm out, arching her back, and raising her ample chest skyward.

"Good god," Ken whispered.

The afternoon clouds appeared as promised, casting shadows onto the outfield and releasing the squinted eyes of the infield players. The second half of the ninth inning left the Machias Bulldogs tied with the Calais Blue Socks, four even. The bulldogs had one out and Caleb stood on first, having grounded down the third base line. It was Ken's turn at bat, Josh on deck, and Luke sat on the dugout bench, kibitzing with both of them.

"No pressure, Ken. Just make connection with the ball. Don't try to knock it onto the track. Just get on base."

Josh rested a bat on his shoulder. "Don't you worry. The pitcher's got nothing left in him."

The Calais pitcher scuffed his foot on the mound and leered at Josh.

Ken gave Luke his best "What? Do you think I'm stupid?" look, and stepped up to the plate. Okay, the pressure was on. Just swing through the ball. Make good contact. Don't try and kill it, he told himself. He glanced toward the girls, then stepped into the box.

The first pitch was high and outside. Ken started to swing, but held back. Maybe he'd get a walk. The pitcher really might not have anything left.

The second breezed right over the plate. Ken was hoping for another ball and was a bit slow on the swing. He fouled it over first base. Maggie ducked, even though it cleared her by ten feet. Great. Pay attention. Get on top of the pitch. Make your choice sooner. He took a couple of swipes at the air, then held the bat high.

The third pitch was also right down the middle. He swung, gritting his teeth as his wrists came through. He connected and it popped over the shortstop's head. By the time the ball took a second hop and found the left fielder's glove, Ken was three-quarters of the way to first and Caleb was holding at second.

Ken overran first, turned toward the girls, and walked back to the base. His lungs burned, but his stomach quivered and tingled. He couldn't suppress a smile. He didn't look at Maggie, but could feel her eyes on him.

The fielder threw the ball in by way of the third baseman, bringing Josh to bat.

Josh passed the first two pitches, both balls. The third

he took as a matter of course, hoping for another ball, but it flew right through the strike zone.

"Come on, Josh. 'Do it like the Babe!'" Luke shouted from the bench. "Solid hit coming!"

Ken inched off the base, bent over and shuffled to a good sized lead. Not too much. Be able to dive back to the plate. Yeah, that's it.

Barbara and Maggie rose to their knees and shouted. "You can do it, Josh!"

Josh had never been a big hitter; if not for his great eye and hands for catching, he would have had a hard time making any team, Ken speculated.

"Just advance the runners!" Luke cried. "Watch your lead, Ken."

Ken glanced at the pitcher, who didn't appear interested in anything but his next toss. "Shut up, Luke. I know what I'm doing," he wanted to shout. But he didn't say a word.

The pitch came. A straight fastball. Josh swung low, raising on his toes. The ball cracked off the bat and launched high over the pitcher's head toward center field. Josh remained standing at home plate for an instant, then dropped the bat and sprinted for first. Caleb and Ken held the bases, having to tag up. The ball arched and descended directly into the mitt of the center fielder. Caleb and Ken were running the second it touched the glove. Josh slowed and stopped, never reaching the base.

Caleb reached third just as the ball skipped off the top of the third baseman's glove and hopped onto the grass, rolling toward the sulky track. Caleb rounded third and headed home. The third baseman recovered the ball and rocketed it toward the plate. Caleb dove headfirst and slid into the plate just as the ball reached the catcher's glove.

"Safe!" the umpire yelled.

The catcher slung the ball back to third as Ken sprinted toward the base. The ball reached the third baseman and he tagged Ken out a fraction of a second before his foot touched the base.

The Calais pitcher pointed to the umpire. "That's the third out. The run doesn't count. We're still tied."

Josh flew across the field toward the pitcher and skidded to a stop in front of him. "That's not the damn rule. The run counts. We scored before the out."

The pitcher shoved past him, giving Josh a hard shoulder in his chest. "I'm right. It's still tied. Right?" He pointed at the umpire.

Josh caught his footing, grabbed the man by the shoulder, and took a swing at him. The blow creased his cheek and the pitcher tossed his mitt to the ground with his left hand and swung back with his right. Neither man was a fighter. Their awkward dance in the center of the diamond didn't last more than a few seconds before the other players jumped in and broke it up.

"That's it! The games over! We win by one run," Josh declared, as Ken grabbed one arm and Luke took the other.

"Take it easy, Josh. Calm down," Ken said.

The pitcher looked at the umpire. "Make the call. You know I'm right. The run doesn't count and we're going into extra innings."

The umpire stared between the two men. "The run counts. That's the ball game."

The pitcher lost interest in Josh and turned toward the umpire, following him off the field, ranting the entire way.

"What are you thinking? It doesn't count! Get back out there on the field!"

Luke released Josh and he swung his shoulders and pulled at his shirt to straighten it. "Damn Flatlander! Doesn't even know the rules. Why do they let him on the field if he doesn't even know the rules to the damn game?"

Luke put his arm around Josh's shoulder as they headed toward the girls. "That was a nice sac fly. I thought you were going to let me win the game and become the hero of the day."

"Shoot. You've already got the girl. Do you need everything?"

"Sure, why not?"

They reached the blanket and sank onto the ground beside the girls. Maggie touched Josh's knee. "That was a great play. You really came to the rescue."

"That's me. Alan Ladd, *Gun for Hire*."

Barbara sighed. "Too bad you had to go and ruin a good thing by getting into a brawl."

"Hey, the other guy started it."

She glowered at him. "Don't be childish."

He lowered his chin a fraction and remained quiet, picking at a blade of grass at his side. The sun was still hard at work, but so were the clouds, moderating the temperature.

"I'm sure the Army would still take you if you want

to fight that much," Maggie added. "You could use him, couldn't you, Ken?"

Ken rolled his eyes at Josh. "When are you going to grow up? It's just a game for Christ's sake."

"You know I can't go because of my knees," he said softly. "And it ain't just a game – it's Calais."

Barbara looked back at Ken. "Well, at least we have one patriotic man in the group."

Ken ignored her and lifted the lid to the picnic basket. "And what might you have in here?"

Maggie slapped his hand and pulled the basket towards her.

"Chicken and coleslaw for you boys… if you'll behave long enough."

Barbara didn't let up. "And what about you, Luke? Don't you want to do your part?"

Maggie sensed the uneasy feeling Barbara was causing. "You know very well he has to be here and help with the blueberry crop. That's a legitimate deferment." She opened the basket. "Now come on, let's be civil and eat."

An hour later, Ken lay on his back, Barbara between him and Josh, Maggie and Luke ten feet to his left. Barbara twirled a long blade of grass in her fingertips, dabbing Josh's ear. Ken watched as Josh would swat at it, apparently thinking it was a fly. Barbara would pull her hand away as he did so, then repeat the action, and giggle to herself. Ken sighed and gazed up at the sky. Fluffy clouds languished in the blue field, metamorphosing into various Rorschach images – a dog eating a banana, a plump airplane; even a fish of some kind. The other players and spectators had gone home or off to other amusements. The field was quiet; the grass dry and warm.

Ken held a well-chewed chicken bone up to a cloud, closed an eye and tried to fit it in somehow.

Maggie rose and wandered over to the group, Luke right behind her. "I've got things to do this afternoon. Barbara help me pack this stuff up."

Barbara didn't rise, but put a hand over her face to shade her eyes. "What do you have to do? I've got to take tickets for the matinee at four, but don't you have the night off?"

"I just need to go. Now come on."

"Fine," she groaned, holding out a hand. "Help me up."

Maggie pulled her to her feet and the boys staggered to theirs. Ken nodded to Luke. "Come here a sec, will you?"

"Sure."

Ken steered Luke away from the group and spoke in a low voice. "What are you going to do about Josh and all the fuel your boat's going through? The Navy is going to wonder what you're doing out there burning up that much fuel."

Luke glanced back at Josh, shaking dust and grass off the blanket. "Is it really that big a deal? I thought we could just explain it away. Besides, I wouldn't be surprised if some of the guys at the Customs house aren't getting a small piece from Josh."

"Do you want to bank your boat on it?"

He screwed up his face. "No, I suppose not. But what can I do? The boat's half his."

"I can stall the reports for awhile, but just get your

story straight with Josh, so at least you're singing the same song if anyone should ask."

Ken looked back. Maggie had Josh off to the side, and Barbara was folding the blanket.

Maggie over at Ken and Luke. "Look, Josh. I need a favor."

"Sure, anything."

"I need to borrow your car for the afternoon."

Josh glanced over at the other men. "Why can't you borrow Luke's car? I need mine tonight."

She, too, looked at Luke. "I just can't, all right? Just do this for me please." She gave him her best forlorn look.

He sighed and looked into her eyes. "I guess I could borrow Luke's. But it seems silly for me to borrow his so you can take mine."

Maggie leaned over and gave him a wet kiss on the cheek. "Thanks. I'll get it back to you later."

She started to turn back to Barbara, but Josh caught her sleeve. "Wait. Just drive to the boat with me and pick me back up at midnight. Then I won't need the car."

She nodded. "That'll work. Sure, I can do that."

Luke picked up the basket and headed toward them. "Come on, Mags. Let's get you home."

A wisp of breeze swept dust from the track and blew it around their ankles. The poplar trees at the edge of the field swayed briefly, then fell still again.

She took Luke's free hand and strolled toward the cars. "I'm going to catch a ride with Josh. You don't mind, do you?"

He slowed down. "Yes. I do mind a bit."

"Come on, it's nothing. He's just doing me a favor."

Luke looked toward Josh. "What kind of favor?"

Maggie slapped his arm. "Don't worry, it's nothing. Really!"

"Okay. But I'm still not happy about it. It's Friday night for cripes sake. We should be doing something."

She smiled at him. "Tomorrow, I promise."

He squeezed her hand. "Tomorrow. Sure."

Luke handed Josh the basket and he placed it in the trunk and then opened the door for Maggie. She sank low into the thick tan seats of the Packard. Josh fired up the engine, shoved the stick into first, and Maggie's hair blew back as they pulled away from the lot and onto the open road. She turned in her seat for a last glimpse of Luke as his Hudson turned off into town.

Josh continuously stole quick glances from the road to Maggie's face. Her hair waved in the wind and pulled away from her neck. The collar of her sundress flittered and pressed tight to her flesh.

They were well past West Lubec on route 189, before Maggie spoke. "So are you just going to keep looking at me or are you going to say something?"

Josh tightened his grip on the wheel. "I figured if it was any of my business, you'd tell me. Otherwise, I wasn't going to ask."

She sat quiet for a moment, then turned toward him, her hair blowing across her face. "Well, how about you? When are you going to stop all this foolish smuggling? You know that's how Emma Mean's husband got killed back in '31."

"That was during Prohibition. Things were different."

"What's different now?"

"That was all run by gangs from Boston and New York. This is just local stuff. Nobody's going to get hurt."

"Then what about the law? Aren't you worried you might get caught?"

He smiled. "Those Customs boys aren't going to leave their little huts beside the road to chase the likes of me. Besides, their wives like the sugar and flour I give them, and I'm sure the fellas would miss all those cakes and pies in their lunch pails."

"You're awfully sure of yourself."

He turned the car onto the dirt entry road to the boat yard. "Is there a reason I shouldn't be?"

He pulled the car in front of the boat ramp, where the Sea Swirl sat tethered to the dock.

With the tide out, the docks were a good ten feet below the level of the yard. Leaving the keys in the ignition and the motor running, Josh hopped out and flipped the seat forward. Reaching behind it, he removed a short lever action hunting rifle and a box of cartridges.

Maggie's eyes widened. What's that for?"

"Insurance. So I don't end up like Mr. Means."

"But you said it wasn't dangerous."

"No, I said it was different." He turned and headed for the boat. "Remember, be here at midnight. I'm counting on you."

Chapter Nine

Ken shifted into second gear and the Jeep lurched as he merged west onto Route One. He flipped the visor down and sat higher in the seat to avoid looking into the lazy afternoon sun. The rush of air over the windscreen dried the perspiration from his face and uniform. His left wrist hung loose over his knee, and he steered with his right. He sped along the coast, occasionally catching a fleeting image of a car or truck heading in the other direction. The stores were winding down for the afternoon and in a few hours, they'd be closed and deserted. The remaining shoppers would have gone home to supper and even the stray dog that hung out near the barbershop would find somewhere more interesting to be.

At the post, he saluted the sailor at the gate, pulled the Jeep close to the door of the office, and wandered inside. The room was quiet and dull, long shadows draping the walls. He tossed the Jeep keys on his desk and loosened his tie. He'd just sunk into his chair when Petty Officer Durning rushed in and snapped a quick salute.

"Sir, Major Smith from Brunswick Naval called this

afternoon. He wanted to speak to you directly. But I wasn't able to locate you."

Ken propped his feet on the desk and leaned back. "That's because I didn't want to be found." He paused and let his eyes drift over Durning. "So? Did he leave a message?"

"Yes, Sir. He said the fly boys down there took some aerial photos of Howard Cove. There's a group of three buildings on a dock they want us to inspect."

"There aren't any buildings in Howard Cove. I grew up down that way. They probably took pictures of Buck's Harbor."

"Nevertheless, he wants us to inspect them."

"Fine. We'll go 'round tomorrow after breakfast. I'm going to run in town and visit my folks for a while." Durning remained standing. Ken raised a brow. "Was there something else?"

"Begging you pardon, Sir, but I think he wanted you to do it today and then call him back."

Ken looked at his watch. Three-thirty. "All right, we can be back before dark. But you're coming with me on this fool's errand. I'm telling you, there aren't any buildings down there."

Durning headed for the back. "I'll get your sidearm and a carbine from the rack."

"Whoa there, sailor. We won't need firearms. This is Machias, Maine, not the O.K. Corral. We'd end up scaring some old lady hanging sheets on the line and send her into fits."

"Sir, regulations require an officer to carry a sidearm

at all times when investigating a suspicious site during time of war."

"If it makes you feel better, get my forty-five, but not the rifle."

"Yes, Sir. Right away."

Ken started for the door, almost glad to have something to do, even a wild goose chase. "Meet me in the Jeep," he called over his shoulder.

Pulling himself into the seat, he fired up the engine and stared at the gray office door. Why did everything in the Navy have to be gray? And why did every little errand become urgent? Maybe he could swing by the mess and get a sandwich before heading out.

William bustled out the door, then stopped to lock it to keep out God knows what. He turned to the Jeep and stopped. "Sir, it wouldn't be proper for you to drive me."

"Just get in."

"Sir?"

"Do I have to make it an order? You probably drive like an old lady. Besides, I know the roads and want to get back in time to have chow while it's still warm."

Durning reluctantly climbed into the passenger seat and set the pistol belt and spare ammo clip pouches on the back seat. Ken didn't wait for him to get settled. He shoved the stick into gear, stomped on the accelerator, and spun gravel under the tires as the Jeep swung toward the main road.

Petty Officer Durning clamped his right hand onto the side of the window and gripped the seat with his left hand. Ken rocketed through Machiasport, catching a shocked stare from the Hardings as they crossed the road. A few minutes later, they shot past old Fort O'Brien, barely missing the cars parked near the entrance. Ken didn't slow down around Bucks Harbor; the Jeeps tires screeched around the corners. Finally, he reached the road leading to the Howard Mountain access lane, braked hard, and skidded to a stop in front of the entrance.

Petty officer Durning sat rigid in his seat, his black-rimmed Navy issue glasses glued straight ahead. "Sir, should I call the tower and tell them we've landed?"

Ken sat forward in his seat, looking over the steering wheel at the lane. The dirt road wound into the thick alders and scrub cedar. A bent, rusty gate guarded the road.

"No one likes a smart ass. Besides, what makes you think we've landed?"

Ken stomped on the accelerator, pulling the Jeep back onto the road, tilting the vehicle hard toward the passenger side before it could straighten out.

The Jeep decelerated as Ken braked hard again. His neck was stretched out like a goose's, his head swivelled on top. "The Heald family lives on the backside of the cove. That woman's got spunk. Her husband died and left her with five kids. Not one of them over the age of ten," He turned his head and searched the edge of the road for a break in the trees. "I remember an old access road here some place. Keep a sharp eye out."

They crept along the edge of the road, and occasionally Ken swung the Jeep into the oncoming lane to get a better look at the left hand side. Durning would cringe and stare up the road each time, as though expecting heavy traffic. Thus they traveled until they reached the Howard mountain turn-off.

Ken pushed back in his seat. "That's strange. We must've missed the lane. I know it's about a half mile before this."

He pulled a U-turn in the center of the road and inched back the way he'd come, keeping one wheel on the road and letting the other drop into the gavel shoulder. They both stared into the dense stand of evergreens.

"There!" Durning pointed.

Ken braked. "I don't see anything."

"There. See the blow down? I think those are tire ruts below the cedar top."

Ken backed the Jeep and turned it onto the gravel skirt of the old logging road. After setting the parking brake, he jumped out and inspected the tree. "This isn't a blow down. It was cut and placed here. See the drag marks? I can still smell the freshly-cut trunk"

Ken slapped a mosquito as it tried to bite his neck. "I see the French air force is here."

The narrow road dropped down the gradual slope toward the cove. A grouse drummed its wings, deeper in.

Durning slid the black-rimmed glasses up on his nose with one finger. "That's curious."

They dragged the cedar tree off the road and returned to the Jeep. Ken reached into the back seat, retrieved his pistol, strapped it to his waist, and snapped the extra clips to the webbing.

Durning pushed his glasses back up again. "Maybe I should've brought the carbine."

"Well, we're not going back to get it, so hop in."

The Jeep bounced down the old road, tires dropping into water-filled potholes and hollows. Tree branches scraped the paint on the sides and hit against the windscreen. The branches hadn't been trimmed in some time, yet several had recent breaks. Durning ducked as a stiff alder that hung over the road sprang over the top of the glass and knocked his spectacles askew.

The acrid smell of salt, mud, and rot filled Ken's nose. The tide must be out and the cove close at hand.

The road turned to the right and ran down a low grade toward the water. Another turn, and the trail widened into a grassy path, the trees falling away from its sides. The road terminated at the cove, a hundred yards further.

A long dock ran out into the water with three wooden sheds attached along one side, near the shore. The buildings were huddled together, eaves almost touching.

Ken whistled. "Those shouldn't be here. Damn if those flyboys weren't right."

Ken parked the Jeep in front of the closest building and dismounted. The round pylons holding the dock in place leaned at odd angles, having been loosened by years of flooding and ebbing tides. The boards on the planking were old and grayed from salt air and water. The rough-sawn lumber on the sheds was almost new, its golden hue not yet dulled by the elements.

Ken walked up to the front of the first building, where a heavy padlock held the door in place. He put a hand to the window beside the door and pressed his face to the glass, peering in.

"Just a bunch of fishing gear. Nets, lines, buoys, and the like."

Durning walked past him and looked into the second building. "Same here, but also a bunch of old motor parts and tools."

Ken arched his back and tried to work out the tightness from hovering over third base all morning from his muscles. The sun was still high enough to make it hot and he unbuttoned the top of his shirt.

"What about the other one?" Durning asked.

Ken's dress shoes clicked on the heavy weathered planking as he headed for the last building. "Look at this, will you? The windows are painted black."

Durning followed him out to the last structure. "Maybe the fishermen work in there at night and didn't want to have blackout curtains made."

Ken reached up and bounced his hand against the wire mesh covering the window. "That might explain the paint, but what about this chicken wire over the glass? They don't want anyone to break it and look in, either."

Ken adjusted his pistol belt and made a slow turn, looking over the area around the end of the dock and road. The water lapped around the pylons, but there wasn't a single boat in the cove. He could barely make out the black shingles atop the Heald's house piercing the trees that covered the point. Behind them, opposite the shed and dock, a low grassy hill ran along the far side, its top covered with brambles and raspberry vines. The thick vegetation shielded a view of the water that lay behind it. In his youth, Ken had dug clams on the flats that lay beyond. Although the water was shallow, a boat could be hidden on the far side if it hung close to shore.

Ken ran his hand across the golden wood of the door. "Get the tire iron out of the Jeep. We're going to have a look inside."

Durning headed back to the vehicle as Ken searched the ground around the buildings and dock. He noticed faint tire marks on the grass, but nothing recent. A line hung from a cleat on the dock, the coils white and clean. Fresh rub marks showed where a fender had held a boat away from the dock.

"I found a mallet in the back as well, Sir. Maybe we can use it." Ken watched Durning lift the thick mallet from behind the seat, wondering if the kid's skinny arms were strong enough to carry it. But William loped back, his back arched over with poor posture.

Ken turned toward to face the shed, took the tire iron, and placed the pointed end on the lock. "Hold this here while I hit it with the hammer."

Durning started to pass him the hammer. "Why don't you hold it and I'll give it a whack?"

"The silver on my epaulets says I'll be the one doing the whacking."

Durning grabbed the tire iron and stepped back, holding it low on the shaft and screwing up his face.

Ken moved back a half step, lined up the hammer, and took a couple of slow practice swings to assure firm contact.

A gunshot rang out.

A furrow of planking tore up between Ken's feet,

splintering the wood and spraying against the side of the building.

Durning dropped the iron and sprinted for the Jeep. Ken registered the gunshot half a second late, but caught up with Durning and dove headfirst behind the Jeep, sliding into place like Josh at home plate, and taking cover behind the tires. Durning crouched beside him, breathing hard. Ken tugged at the holster and managed to wrestle the Colt semi-automatic out. Holding the barrel skyward, he rested his head back against the rubber.

"Damn it! Who the hell's shooting at us?"

Durning pulled his legs close to his body and wrapped his stringy arms around them. He kept his eyes locked straight ahead and didn't answer.

"It wouldn't be fisherman. Too much risk. Has to be a smuggler." He gazed at Durning, frozen in place. "You all right?"

Durning didn't answer, but his head bobbed up and down.

Ken shuffled toward the rear, laid his pistol hand on the side of the Jeep, and very slowly, like a turtle coming out of its shell, raised his head to see the embankment. The grass and brambles were still and thick. White clouds, far over the rise, were the only thing moving. He couldn't see anything remotely human. He turned and slumped back against the wheel.

Ken took a deep breath and rested the pistol on his chest. "You want to try and sneak into the trees and get around behind him?" Ken looked at Durning, who still didn't move; then he gauged the distance to the trees. "No, probably not. It's too far in the open."

"Do you think he missed, or was he just trying to scare us?" Ken kept staring at Durning, but the man didn't respond. "Yeah, that's what I thought, too."

Ken's breathing slowed after a few minutes. The ground felt hot beneath him, and the lugnuts jabbed into his back. He placed the pistol on the ground and stared at the side of the building. The thick rough-sawed boards had water stains near the bottom, and a line of dark brown rose up through the center of one, extending up to a knot in the wood at eye level. The knot was about the size of a quarter, with a soft fuzzy center. Ken craned his neck and leaned over, taking another look up the hill. Still nothing.

"I guess we should just wait here awhile."

They sat fully exposed in the afternoon sun. It beat down on them unmercifully; sweat beaded on Ken's forehead and soon began to wet the front of his tan shirt and underarms.

His gaze returned to the knot on the side of the shed. He stared at it for fifteen minutes. The sun continued to melt them into the dirt and within a few more minutes, he'd splayed his legs out flat and slumped heavily against the Jeep.

This just wasn't right. A lot of the fellas around here might unload a charge of rocksalt at you for snooping around their building, but a rifle? He couldn't figure it out.

Scooping up a handful of small stones, he began tossing them one at a time at the knot. They struck the board all around the knot with a little thump, ricocheted off, and bounced onto the ground. He began keeping score of how many times he hit the knot.

As the sun touched the tops of the trees, the two men slumped against the tires. Their shirts were stained under the arms and along the seams, front and back, from the summer heat. Ken was running out of stones to throw, holding a few in his left hand and occasionally lobbing one at the wall.

"Screw this!" He dropped the stones and stood up.

He wobbled at first, the sudden change of posture making him temporarily woozy. The sensation quickly passed.

He looked at the hill in front of them. "You still up there?"

Silence. A light gust off the water swirled the tops of the grass.

"Here I am! Come on out and show yourself!" He looked around, listening, then turned to Durning. "Get up. He's gone." He leaned over, picked up the pistol, and shoved it into the holster.

William released his knees and adjusted his glasses. "Does that mean we can go?"

"No. That means we can look in the shed."

"I don't think that's such a good idea, Sir."

Ken started toward the shed, with William several paces behind, walking sideways to keep an eye on the underbrush. Ken moved deliberately. He already had the tire iron in place and held it out to Durning by the time he caught up with him. He took another glance at the brambles and then slowly grasped the iron.

Ken stepped back and lined up with the iron.

Bang! Another shot.

Another rut in the planking materialized at their feet, inches from the first.

The hammer and tire iron seemed to hang in midair for a second, then clanked down on the planking as the men abandoned them and sprinted for the Jeep. Ken landed in the front seat, his hand reaching the keys in the ignition about the same time his butt hit the seat. Durning dove into the back and stuck his head down behind the driver's seat.

The tires spun in the gravel, spraying rocks in small pinwheels through the air and onto the dock. The Jeep thumped backward into a ditch and Ken ground the gears as he slammed the stick into drive. The Jeep bucked and leapt out of the hollow. After weaving back and forth a few times, the tires found the ruts and tore west into the trees.

Ken didn't slow down, cracking the windshield as it struck another low-hanging alder branch along the way. When rubber hit asphalt, Durning stuck his head up and climbed into the font seat.

"I didn't sign on for this. I'm a clerk, for Christ's sake."

"If he'd wanted to hit us, we'd be dead." Ken thought about the two divots in the planking, and a tiny smile crept onto his face. "Pretty darn good shooting, too."

"This ain't funny, Sir." Durning said.

"Certainly livened up the afternoon, though."

"What now?"

Ken sped along the road toward Machias, swerving

into the opposite lane to pass slower vehicles. "We're going back to the post and calling for the MPs."

"Good. Let them handle it."

Ken grunted. "Oh, we'll be going back with them. But this time you can bring the carbine."

It was dark when the headlights of the Jeep projected on the gray office door. The tinny sound of a radio wafted up from the mess hall and crickets chirped in the long grass around the water. Leaving the motor running and the lights on, Ken fished the door key from his pocket.

"Mr. Durning, head over to the mess and rustle up sandwiches and coffee. I'm going to call Brunswick. This could end up being a long night." The latch clicked and the door swung open. He reached around the corner and snapped the switch to the lights. "Oh, and turn off the Jeep, too. Leave the keys in it."

So much for visiting my parents, he thought.

Durning headed for the mess, Ken for the telephone. He sat on the corner of the Petty Officer's desk, turned the telephone toward him, then lifted the black receiver and dialed the number for Brunswick Naval Air, printed on a sheet taped to the desk.

"Brunswick, Duty Officer McDaniels." a voice at the other end said.

"Lieutenant JG Mitchell from Machias for Major Smith."

"Sorry, Sir, the Major is over at the photo lab."

"Well, send someone over to get him and have him call me back."

"Will you be in the office there?"

"Yes, I'll wait right here in the office until I hear back. Thanks"

Ken hung up the telephone, went back to his bunk area, flipped on the overhead light and removed the key to the gun locker. He unhooked the main lock and slid the cable out of the trigger guards to the rifles. He laid one carbine and a Thompson machine gun on the foot of the bed, then fished out a bandoleer of clips for each weapon.

Chapter Ten

Friday, June 30, 1944:
Entrance to Machias Bay - Night

The drone of the single port diesel vibrated the deck of the conning tower, climbed up through the open watertight hatch, passed the two men hunched over in the dark, and escaped into the night. Its freedom was short-lived for it bounced off the rocky shore of Cross island and returned as an echo.

The night sky gave birth to a full moon, its bright-white contents stretching and pushing, trying to take it out of shape. The air had cooled over the water, forming bands of low fog around the islands, masking the points, and juts of the mainland. In an hour or so, it would blanket the bay and fill most of the Gulf of Maine.

The Kapitan peered into the darkness. "Mr. Werner, plot our course accurately. This fog is getting thicker."

"Yes, Kapitan." Werner looked over the silver path in the water that ran toward the moon, the edges of the light slipping into the gray fluff. "It was my hope to see America. We're so close, yet it remains hidden."

The Kapitan leaned down in front of the compass, sighted over the dome, and slid the swiveling sighting fin to take a relative bearing on Cross Island. "What lies behind that fog is but one state of forty-eight pieces of their country, and that state alone is almost a quarter the size of our homeland."

Mr. Werner stared at the creases under the Kapitan's eyes. They appeared darker and deeper in the moonlight. "You don't sound confident, Kapitan."

He glanced down the tube to the control room. "Confidence I have plenty of – that's not the issue. It's allowing my confidence to override my intellect I'm having trouble with."

Werner moved closer to the Kapitan. "I'm sorry, Sir. Do you mean you have doubts?"

He ran his fingers over the sides of his binoculars. "Now... our forces are too few and too scattered, with America in the war."

"What's the point then?"

He looked up into the heavens, where stars were still visible above the bed of fog. "The point is, it's our duty to do as we're ordered."

"But if we know we're going to lose, why should we continue to fight and die?"

"Because we're officers and we do as we're told." He lowered the optics. "Turn the boat to two, nine, zero degrees magnetic."

"Just because we're officers doesn't mean we shouldn't have opinions," Werner said.

The Kapitan turned to look him in the eye. "That's precisely what it means."

Werner cleared his throat. "Two, nine, zero, aye. Do you want to go in on the electric motor?"

"No. I want to keep the batteries on full charge in case of trouble. We'll switch over at the last moment." He nodded toward the hatch. "Why don't you go below and tell our guests it will be about twenty minutes before they depart?" He pulled a piece of paper from his pocket and handed it to Werner. "These are the bearings and the amount of time on each leg to the dock. Tell the helmsman to keep the boat at three knots and follow this exactly."

Werner stared silently at the sheet. The Kapitan sensed the question on his mind. "Our agent on shore provided the coordinates." He looked at his watch, then toward Cross Island. "Have him make the initial turn in exactly two minutes, if you please."

"Aye, Kapitan." Werner turned and slid down the ladder into the control room.

Below, the air was fouled by the diesel fumes, the stench of men in close confines coupled with damp surfaces and mold. But it was the diesel fumes that sickened Werner the most. They hung to his clothes and even fouled his food. He knew they would fade the longer he was below deck, but the brief time outside had brought them back to him like a sharp slap to his face. He handed the paper to the steering *matrose* and relayed the Kapitan's orders before heading toward the stern. He shivered at the sudden drop in temperature in the damp bowels of the boat.

The *Abwehr* agents were still in their alcove, buttoning

long woolen dress coats over thick woolen slacks, white shirts, and conservative ties. They were silent as they dressed. The racket from the diesel engine was noise enough.

Mr. Franks picked up the bundle containing the radio and a worn tan leather attaché case; Mr. Schuch clutched a darker cordovan suitcase.

"Well, how do we look, Mr. Werner?" Schuch asked.

"As I'd expect an American to appear, I suppose. I'm not one to judge, never having been here, but aren't you dressed a bit warm for summer?"

Mr. Franks took a nervous glance at Mr. Schuch. "When this mission was planned, we expected to be here in early spring. I guess since the boat's so chilly and moist, I didn't think about it. We don't have anything else to wear, so this will have to do." Mr. Franks rubbed the toe of his shiny black shoe on the back of his pant leg to buff out a scuff. "Is it a dark night?"

Werner studied the two men. They would look fine once they reached the train station, but their long coats and leather shoes seemed too dressy for rural Maine. "Unfortunately, no. But the fog's rolling in and should provide adequate cover."

"Should we wait here, go into the control room, or on deck?"

Werner thought for a second. "The entrance to the control room would be best. You'll be out of the way and able to hear what's going on. You'll be near the tube to the tower so you can get out quickly."

Werner turned and the agents trailed behind him. They stopped at the hatch to the control room, while he continued topside. The crew in the control room kept an inquisitive eye on the two agents.

In a matter of minutes these men would walk among the enemy.

The fog had closed in, covering the extreme ends of the boat, and filling in above, hiding the stars. As U-233 sliced through it, the single diesel engine echoed louder in the confines of the white haze.

Werner tilted his head. "Is that another engine?"

Kapitan Steiner stared into the fog. "No, just the echo of ours off the mountain and ridges."

"It is so much louder than off the island. Anyone for miles will be able to hear us." Werner looked over his shoulder and around the boat. "Why couldn't our agent bring the parts out to us?"

"He could have, but it would be just as dangerous to lie on the surface waiting for him. Besides what if he didn't bring exactly what we needed? We would we have to repeat the whole affair, doubling our risk."

Werner could see nothing but fog, yet the engine echo was close. "I suddenly have lost my urge to see America."

"Relax, I only plan to be at the dock long enough to get the parts we require and drop off the agents." He placed both hands on the metal plates of the half-wall shields, feeling the vibrations of he engine. "Pass the word. No voices above a whisper. And double the bow watch."

"Aye, Kapitan."

The drab, olive-green walls of the office reflected the

light of shadeless bulbs from the ceiling, which glistened in places and faded into the corners. A single, outdated picture of President Roosevelt hung beside Ken's desk, and an old calendar from a farm implement company opposite, both bequeathed to them from previously occupants.

Ken sat at his desk rechecking the action on the Thompson when Petty Officer Durning returned with coffee and sandwiches. William placed the heavy white plate stacked with thick breaded sandwiches on his desk, poured coffee from a metal pitcher into the mugs he'd brought, and set one in front of Ken.

"We have grenades in the storage building, Sir. Do you want me to get them?"

"No. This should be plenty."

"Begging your pardon, but that's what you said about the carbine."

Ken looked up from the Thompson, and almost smiled. "Is that disrespect I hear?"

Durning snapped up straight. "No, Sir. Sorry, Sir."

Ken smiled. "No, I kind of like it. As you were."

Durning relaxed. "Sir, have you heard from Brunswick?" He took a sandwich from the plate and passed it to Ken. "It's tuna."

"Yes. Major Smith is on his way up with a couple of his Marines." He glanced at his watch. "They should be here within an hour."

The telephone rang. Petty Officer Durning set down his sandwich, reached for the telephone, chewed a couple of times, and swallowed hard. "Machias Coastal Watch. Petty Officer Durning."

There was a pause. "Yes, Ma'am. Just a moment, please." He covered the receiver with his hand. "Sir, it's a Mrs. Heald up on Howard Point. She says she's hearing a diesel engine and it sounds too loud to be a fishing boat."

Ken took another bite of his sandwich, chewed slowly, but didn't move. "I'll talk with her."

He stepped over to Durning's desk, swallowed, and placed the telephone to his ear. "Good evening, Mrs. Heald. Now tell me what you're hearing."

Her voice was strong and firm over the crackling line. "There's a loud Diesel boat coming into the harbor."

"And what makes that so suspicious?"

Ken listened to the excited children's voices in the background before she responded. "Are you dull-witted? Fishermen don't come home in the dead of night through thick fog."

"Yes, I agree most fishermen around here are smart enough not to go out in fog like this, but one could have misjudged how quickly it would set in."

She interrupted him. "Listen for yourself. I'll stick the telephone out the window."

"What's that? No, I don't need to hear for myself." He rolled his eyes and looked at William. "No don't hang the telephone out the window. Mrs. Heald... Mrs. Heald?"

Ken's brows rose as he listened. The telephone banged and clanked; the children's voices dimmed, replaced by a low, drone.

The telephone clanked again. "Hear what I'm talking about?"

"Yes, Ma'am. We'll be out directly... thank you. Goodbye now."

He hung up the telephone.

"What is it, Sir?"

"I don't know, but she's right. That's no fishing boat."

Durning set the half-eaten sandwich on the corner of his desk and swallowed hard. "How long did you say until Major Smith arrives?"

Kapitan Steiner pressed his body against the solid front of the conning tower, leaning over and listening. Fine water droplets beaded up on the shoulders of his black sweater and cap. The diesel engine drowned out most of the sounds from the boat. Visibility had dropped, as well. They could no longer see the men standing on the bow of the boat.

"Mr. Werner," he whispered. "Switch to the electric. If we can't see the dock, we'll drive her right through it when we get there."

Werner knelt beside the open hatch, steadying himself on the steel rim of the tube. "Cut the diesel and transfer to the electric. Ahead dead slow and be prepared to reverse thrust." He rose to stand beside the Kapitan. "Perhaps a few more men on the bow with lines and maybe a crew to the anchor locker?"

The Kapitan nodded. "Get more men on the bow and issue them weapons. They can stand watch while we get the parts." He rubbed the stubble on his chin. "Don't bother with the anchor. We'd never be able to deploy it fast enough."

Werner relayed the order and returned just as the diesel went silent. He cocked his head and listened to the night: The surge of the tide on the rocks to the west, a car in the distance traveling on a roadway, and a school of squid breaking the surface near the bow.

The Kapitan switched on the signal light and gave it a few flicks with the louvers. The light reflected off the fog, unable to penetrate the water-filled air.

No reply.

Twenty seconds later, he repeated the signal.

Again, no reply.

He looked at his stopwatch. "Do you have two minutes since the last turn?"

Werner had forgotten to click his watch at the turn, but glanced at it anyway. "Uh... yes... two minutes."

Kapitan Steiner flicked the signal light again. This time, a dull glow responded two points off the port bow. "Five degrees to port, dead slow after the correction."

Werner dropped to his knees and relayed the orders. The two agents had crept into the control room and were now facing up into the tube, noses pointed toward the fresh air. Two crewmen pushed by them and climbed the ladder, rifles slung in front of their chests so as not to foul in the escape trunk.

The Kapitan climbed down the ladder to the deck and followed the crewmen to the bow. Werner stayed on the conning tower to relay orders below.

The boat continued forward, momentum carrying it toward the dock. The light from a single lantern emerged from the haze; then the tall, crooked pylons, and lastly, a dark figure in a long slicker with a hat pulled low, hiding his face. He set the lantern on the end of the dock and backed into the mist as the boat slipped in next to the planking.

"All back, left full rudder," the Kapitan said aloud.

"Aye, Sir. Left full, all back," Werner relayed.

The boat slowed, then stopped. The incoming tide edged it up to the dock.

Ten seconds later: "All stop! Secure the lines!"

The two men with rifles leapt to the dock and caught the small lines tossed to them by the bow watches. They hauled these over, along with the heavier lines attached to the ends of the smaller ones. After the men on dock looped the heavy lines over the pylons, the men still aboard tightened the lines, then moved to mid-ship where they repeated the procedure. Within minutes the boat was successfully tethered to the dock with half its length extending into the cove.

Kapitan Steiner jumped down onto the planking. His knees gave out from the force of landing onto the springy surface, and he fell to all fours. The figure on the dock, his face hidden by the bright lantern, held out a hand. Kapitan Steiner took it and rose to his feet.

The figure kept the light in the Kapitan's face, then handed it to a seaman as he walked by. "Everything you need is in the first shed. Take whatever you can use," The man's voice sounded high-pitched, yet rough.

"Your voice? Is something wrong?"

"No. Just a precaution. Should you be captured, it would be better for me if you couldn't identify me or my voice."

"Very well. What should I call you?"

The man hesitated. "Ohren. Call me Ohren."

"Ears?" The Kapitan asked, but the man just shrugged. "Fine. I have a couple of men to deliver to you."

Ohren looked toward the shore, without answering. The lantern disappeared into the shed and illuminated the doorway for a moment, a yellow glow in the still, moist air.

"Mr. Werner, bring them up."

"Wait." Ohren jerked his head back toward the Kapitan. "It isn't safe. This spot's been compromised."

"What?" The Kapitan looked about with quick movements of his head. "How?"

"I'm not sure how, but the Navy showed up earlier and they'll be back."

"What? A ship?"

"No, two men. They looked over the sheds and tried to break into them."

"Did they see the supplies?"

"No." Ohren's head swivelled back and forth.

"Then why would they be back?"

The man's voice crept up the side of the boat. "Unless the Navy has a new policy about ignoring getting shot at, they'll be back."

The *Abwehr* agents had just reached the conning tower when the Kapitan turned his attention back to the boat. "Hold up a minute."

Werner touched Mr. Franks' shoulder, then looked down at the tops of the heads of the men on the dock. "Wait. What is it, Kapitan?" He tried to see under the hat and view the man's features, but all he could make out was a slender, dark jaw line.

Kapitan Steiner looked back at Ohren. "What's our next move then?"

"How long will it take you to make repairs?"

The Kapitan scratched the short bristles on his face. "Perhaps a day if the weather remains good."

"Hancock Point is just west of here. It has deep water and good road access. Drop the agents there in two nights. I'll signal you with a swinging lantern."

"I know the Point. I saw it on the charts. Where, exactly?"

"Bring me the chart and I'll show you."

Chapter Eleven

The fog drifted in front of the headlights. It came from the dark, swirled delicately across the light beam, then slipped back into the darkness of the night. Route One was visible for only twenty feet ahead; then the blacktop faded out of focus and was swallowed up. Ken shifted his weight in the seat of the parked Jeep. The air was still and a sailor's radio from the guard shack twanged out an Elton Britt country song, "There's a Star Spangled Banner Waving Somewhere."

Durning sat upright, his back not touching the seat, the butt of his carbine on the floorboards of the Jeep with the barrel pointing skyward. Ken slouched in the driver's side. His Thompson rested across the back seat, along with the ammo bandoleers.

"They could be a while. You may as well relax," Ken said.

Durning pushed the glasses up on his nose. "I am relaxed, Sir. What makes you think I'm not relaxed?"

Ken rolled his eyes. "Oh, no reason."

The headlights of a car brightened the road, like a sundog on the horizon at sea. The engine gathered volume and lowered in pitch as it approached, moving fast considering the poor visibility. The headlights refracted off the cracked glass in the windshield, casting shadowy cobwebs.

"This has to be them," Durning said.

The car didn't slow, but sped past them, swerving toward the midline, sagging on worn leaf springs. The driver blared his horn when he spotted them.

Ken swivelled his head and watched it disappear into the fog. He slouched back in his seat. He usually avoided learning too much about people, but something about Durning chipped at his curiosity.

"So your parents were strict?" Ken asked.

"No, Sir. Disciplined. Exacting. Demanding and giving respect."

Okay, you've started. You may as well continue, he decided. "Did you always want to be a sailor?"

Durning tightened his grip on the carbine. "No, Sir. But my marks weren't good enough to get into a regular college. My father thought this would do me good." He hesitated for an instant, then his shoulders rose as he had another thought. "I did get accepted to Rochester Community College."

"So why didn't you go?"

His shoulders lowered again. "My father said it wasn't good enough. He figured the Navy would be better than a second-rate community college. He thought I might even get into Officer Candidate School."

"Well, was he right about it doing you some good?" Ken picked at the steering wheel with his fingernail.

"My applications for Officer school kept getting

turned down and well… we didn't have boats when I was a kid, so I didn't know it, but I get real seasick." He pushed his glasses back up his nose.

There was a faint roar of engines and then more lights ahead, muted by the fog. The lights approached quickly, and one vehicle had a lower pitch than the other. Two vehicles, the lights of the second lighting up the rear of the first one. Dark solid figures planted in the seats. The engines, each now distinct, drowned out the radio from the guard shack. The Jeeps pulled up adjacent to Ken and Durning.

Durning leapt from his seat and stood at attention, his carbine smartly over his shoulder. Ken stepped out of the Jeep and casually walked around. A Marine Major, fifteen years older than Ken, sat in the passenger's seat; the driver a tough-looking Master Chief who gripped the wheel with meaty hands. A Thompson hung over his knee by the strap. A brute of a sailor perched in the back jump seat, holding a carbine. The Jeep behind contained two more behemoth Marine MPs.

The Major remained seated and returned their salutes. "So I hear you boys found a bit of trouble." He spoke in a thick New Jersey accent.

Ken noticed the name tag above the officer's pocket. "We appreciate you coming so quickly, Major Smith. It's probably nothing but smugglers or an overprotective lobsterman, but we appreciate the reinforcements."

Major Smith eyed Durning's skinny figure. "I bet you do. Doesn't look like your man could subdue a wet noodle." He looked back at Ken. "So, where's this dock anyway?'

"Just below Machiasport. You'll never find it without us. Perhaps you should follow our Jeep?"

"I'm in a hurry to see what's so damn valuable that someone was willing to shoot at a Naval officer to protect. So if you don't drive like my auntie Alice, then lead on."

Ken saluted and hopped back into the Jeep. He ground the gears, popped it into first gear, and muttered, "Auntie Alice? We'll see who drives like what. Frippin' cops – they're all the same."

The tires spun, kicking up loose sand. Ken floored the accelerator and pulled into the southbound lane on the opposite side of the highway. The rear tires gripped the asphalt, slinging Ken and Durning to the right and then back into their seats as the Jeep accelerated. He was passing the lead Jeep when a speeding truck came at them over the rise. Ken slipped in front of the Major's Jeep seconds before the truck could hit them.

Durning dropped the carbine into his lap and grabbed the window frame with a death grip. "No disrespect, Sir, but you definitely ain't any aunt of mine."

Ken kept the accelerator at the floor until the Jeep hit fifty. The road disappeared under the front bumper faster than the railroad ties under a hurtling train. Driving more from memory than sight, Ken oscillated across the centerline, guessing at the twists and turns of the road, spending as much time in the opposite lane as his own.

Durning squinted into the fog. "Sir? What if there's a deer in the road?"

"Then the cook will be happy. Now be quiet and let me drive."

The Master Chief stayed right on their bumper. Ken

could see the occupants in the rearview mirror better than he could see the road ahead. The dark heads behind them swayed back and forth as the vehicles rocketed down the road.

Seeing those military policemen, Ken couldn't help thinking about old Sheriff Haskell, and how he would torment Josh unmercifully. What did he have against him? He'd hide his stacks of newspapers in the bushes so Josh would have difficulty delivering them. He'd stop him on the street and try to humiliate him in front of his friends. That sheriff must've been mean even as a kid, and then the town gave him a poor paying, frustrating job, thought Ken. A poor paying job with power. He always treated Josh like a criminal. Maybe that's why Josh doesn't mind working the other side of the line now. "Cops, frippin' cops." he repeated himself.

Street lights lit the inside of the Jeep as they shot through Machias, the moviegoers just a blur in line in front of the theater. Barbara was cloaked in the glow from the yellow bulbs in the ticket booth; it lit the fog and surrounded her cubby with fluffy mist.

They twisted and wove south, past Scott's Point where the British were fought off in the Revolutionary War by Jerry O'Brien and his mob; then around Sanborn cove, where the fog thickened.

Ken hit the bottom of Munjoy hill, shoved the stick into fourth, and floored it. The Jeep rose into the mist and shot onward.

"That hairpin turn should be anytime now," Durning reminded him.

The road ahead turned to gravel. Ken slammed on the

brakes and cranked the wheel hard to the right. The back end of the Jeep slid onto the entrance to Kennebec Road, then bounced into a shallow ditch and finally bounded back onto the pavement. Durning bounced forward and his forehead grazed the windshield. He sat back, stunned but unhurt. The two Jeeps behind him nearly collided with each other as they braked and slid on the gravel, coming to rest on Kennebec Road. They backed up to make the turn and then followed, their lights far back in the mist.

Ken's body pulsed with adrenaline. "Now this is how I please my superiors." He didn't wait for them to close the gap, but swung the Jeep right past the entrance to Buck's Harbor into the gully surrounding the mountain. "No boring duty roster. No siree."

When the road climbed toward the Howard Mountain turn-off, Ken slowed and looked for the cedar top they'd pulled out of the road earlier. Major Smith's Jeep swung in front of them and stopped.

Smith jumped out and ran over, shouting. "What the hell's wrong with you? Are you a lunatic or do you just want to get killed on one of those turns?"

Ken didn't have room between the Jeep and Major Smith to get out, so he sat up straight and answered, "Neither, Sir. Just some good ol' Maine driving, Sir. Isn't that what you requested?" He nodded toward the dirt road. "By the way, Sir, you might want to lower your voice. The dock is just a quarter mile down that path."

Major Smith pulled down his gun belt and straightened it. "You boys follow us in and do exactly as you're told." His eyes narrowed. "Understand?"

Ken nodded. "Yes, Sir."

The lantern sat on the planking, casting light onto the boat. The shiny surfaces refracted light off the inky paint, reflecting it like a setting sun on black water. The Kapitan stood at the seaward end of the dock beside the cloaked man. Sailors passed wooden crates and pasteboard boxes from the dock to the deck; sailors then handed them into the escape hatch at the base of the conning tower. Two sentries watched from the dark at the edge of the woods, peering into the night.

Ohren's voice was now raspy as it flowed out from under the southwester. "You may as well take everything. If not, the Navy will have it by morning."

The Kapitan folded his arms across his chest. "We don't have room to take it all, but these parts are scarce at home. Are you certain you can't move them to another location?"

The man turned his head toward land. "Quite certain. Yes." The figure's eyes fell on the Kapitan's epaulets. "My father was in the Kriegsmarine in the first war."

The Kapitan tried to see through the darkness and make out the man's features. "Really? What rank?"

"KorvettenKapitan.   KorvettenKapitan   Friedrich Hoffman."

The Kapitan cocked his head. "Hoffman was your father? He was a brilliant tactician. His methods of hunting and attack are legendary." He touched the man's arm. "I wish I'd had the pleasure of meeting him."

Ohren paused. "Ah, yeah."

"Fritz Hoffman's child – now that makes sense." He looked on deck at Werner. "I've never had any children, but I'm getting an introduction to the responsibility that goes with it."

Ohren must have realized that he'd said too much and lowered his voice. "We shouldn't talk about such things."

The two sentries broke away from their post and came down the dock at a dead run. They skirted the men on the dock, sidestepped around the crates, and stopped in front of the Kapitan. "Sir, we heard voices in the woods."

"How far away?"

The taller of the two leaned over to catch his breath. "At least a third of a kilometer."

Ohren turned toward the shed. "That would be at the main road. You'd best get loaded."

"Do you think they are coming down here?" the Kapitan asked.

"There is nothing else on this road for miles. I'm certain they're coming here."

"What about you?" the Kapitan asked.

"Don't worry about me. I'll be fine. Just meet me where and when I said." He looked toward the tree line where the fog around the treetops was beginning to brighten. "I've rigged the shed. The fuse is only a minute-and-a-half long so you'd best not dilly dally."

The Kapitan nodded and turned away. "Load those last two crates. Mr. Werner, get the diesel on line and prepare to cast off those lines."

"Aye, Kapitan." Werner leaned over the hatch cover. "Start the diesel and plot our exit course from the instructions I gave you before."

KorvettenKapitan Hoffman's son left the lantern on

the end of the dock and faded into the dark toward the shed. Kapitan Steiner climbed back aboard and barked orders to the crew. "Cast off those lines. Engage the screw. One third astern." Moving quickly, the bow crew unhooked the lines from the wooden cleats and coiled them into the lockers. The two sentries knelt on the bow, rifles pointed into the dark at the tree line as it brightened with the headlights of the oncoming vehicles.

Headlights broke through the forest and into the fog surrounding the grassy road. Individual beams were now visible.

The Kapitan leaned over and shouted, "All back full on the diesel!"

U-233's mass held her in place against the single screw; then she began to slip away from the dock, ever so slowly, sliding back along the wharf toward the fog and night.

The headlights from the Jeeps danced in the mist. Ken gripped the wheel as the front wheels skidded off the sides of the ruts in the road and jostled the front of the Jeep. The low alder branch that had claimed his windshield bounced off the glass of the Jeep ahead and nearly clipped the Marines in the jump seat. They ducked and banged their heads together. The road jounced the tires more than during the day because the drivers couldn't see the ruts, large rocks and obstructions.

Ken stifled a laugh. "I probably should've mentioned that tree branch."

"You've got a mean streak, Sir," Durning said.

"No, I just hate Johnny law. And these MPs give me an itch that needs a good scratch."

The first Jeep broke out of the woods and tore down the path toward the water. The vehicles fish-tailed in the damp grass and Durning swung wildly in the front seat, his head almost hitting Ken one second, and the next, almost falling from the Jeep. The Major's two Jeeps halted near the dock. Ken pulled up beside them. Over the hum of the Jeep engines came the pulse of another motor louder and deeper: the deep guttural sound of a diesel engine inside a hollow tube. A light glowed in the mist toward the end of the dock.

The Major was first out, barking orders. He pointed to the two men in the middle Jeep. "Protect our rear and right flank!" Then he pointed to Ken and Petty Officer Durning. "You two stay with the Jeeps and watch the left flank!" He waved to the Master Chief and the other man in his Jeep. "You're with me!"

The Master Chief racked the bolt on his Thompson and stepped beside the Major. The other Marine handed the Major a carbine, leapt from the backseat, and the three disappeared into the fog toward the sound of the diesel engine and the dock Ken knew lay beyond.

Durning hunched over and duck walked around in front of the Jeep. Ken stepped to the left and moved a few feet into the fog. The diesel was loud and guttural, rumbling through the night like a freight train.

He nodded at Durning. "If you're going to duck, you should probably get out of the headlights."

"Sorry, Sir." He stepped toward Ken. "What is it, Sir?"

Voices, then excited shouts from the dock.

"Halt! Stop or we'll fire!"

Then muffled voices. Ken tried to make out the words, but they didn't make sense.

Gunfire. The Thompson, followed by both carbines.

The fog sparked and flashed beyond the sheds, near the glow of the lantern. More shouts.

A larger gun. Something really big, and evidently facing them. The ground between the two Jeeps ripped up as a gun at least the size of a 30-caliber laid a strip of fire. The next burst cut into the center Jeep, blowing out the passenger side tire and headlight, then pleating a curved row of holes through the hood and into the front seat.

Ken and Durning dove to the ground. Ken pointed his Thompson toward the dark, hidden hill, Durning aimed his carbine toward the dock.

"Don't fire unless you're sure what your shooting at! Our men are over there!"

Suddenly an explosion erupted from the water like a grenade thrown into a lake, followed by more gunfire, big and small mixed together. Ken could discern definite bursts from the stout .45 caliber Thompson and the higher-pitched twang of the carbines. The rumbling of the diesel engine changed pitch and deepened.

Black ghostly figures periodically loomed up in the light of the gunfire, then vanished into the darkness.

"Sir, should we go and help them at the dock?"

Ken wanted to rush down there, but resisted. "No. They know we're here and they'll call for us if they need help." Ken rose into a low squat. "I can't see a damn thing."

At that instant, the whole yard lit up. The furthest shed exploded into a bright flash of yellow and orange. The night turned into a hazy, ghostlike white day. The sudden shock halted Ken in his tracks and he dropped to one knee. Debris flew high into the sky, up and outward.

Four figures emerged from the night, three far out on the dock and one close to the Major's Jeep. All still just shadows, but discernable. The ear-splitting roar flung shrapnel in every direction, and for a fraction of a second, daylight had come. The figures on the dock lifted off their feet and fell like hay bales into the water. Chunks of lumber and metal rained all around them, splashing into the water, plunking off the vehicles, and thudding into the gravel. The figure by the Jeep moved toward the hill.

The bright light from the explosion vanished and Ken stared into a night that seemed much darker than before.

Ken leapt to his feet as the debris continued falling. "You stay here! Watch the left flank! I'll be right back!"

He clutched the Thompson, his hands moist against the wooden stock and forearm; then he slipped behind his Jeep and stared at the treeline. Where were those other two Marines? Was the figure he saw one of them?

Footsteps. Moving fast. Dead ahead.

He caught a deep breath and sprinted into the darkness.

His own steps masked those of the other man, but he ran in a direction just ahead of where he guessed the guy was headed. His feet felt light and awkward touching down at odd angles on the dark, uneven ground.

A sound to his left distracted him. He raised the Thompson as he ran.

Wham!

On a full run, he'd collided with something. He struck it full on the left side of his body. His feet went out from under him. The Thompson slid from his grasp and chattered on the gravel as it skidded away. He landed on his left shoulder, and right hand; the hard ground bit into his skin and came up to meet his temple.

The sharp thwack to the temple slowed the motion around him. He lay writhing on the ground, having come to a stop on his right side, facing the water. The glow from the burning sheds lit up the mist over the Jeeps. He tried to breathe deeply, but could only manage short gasps.

A dark mass wriggled on the ground ten feet away from the spot of the collision, it was the man he'd run into.

Ken tried to form words. His mouth was working, but no sound came from his lips. "St..." he coughed, "...P!" His palm and fingers stung from smacking the gravel.

The figure staggered to all fours, then slowly rose and replaced the hat on his head. The light was at his back, but his silhouette included a rifle. He wore a long draping coat that masked his features, with a hood over his face.

Ken searched the ground with his hands for the Thompson, but it wasn't there. The man stood for a moment and stared at him. Ken tried to push to his feet. He still couldn't get a full breath and his arms felt heavy.

He lowered himself back down and awkwardly fumbled with his holster, trying to get his forty-five, but his skinned hand didn't respond as quickly as it should have.

Was he going to die like this, lying on the gravel near the cove he'd fished as a kid? "Get that gun out," he screamed into his brain.

Instead of raising the rifle, the man turned and ran into the mist. He disappeared as fast as he had come. Footsteps on the gravel faded quickly into the night.

Ken finally managed to free the pistol, racked the slide with his good hand, and then fell onto his back, still attempting to suck air into his deflated lungs. He slowly lowered the pistol until it rested on his breast.

"What the hell just happened?" He whispered.

It was several minutes before he felt able to get to his feet. His shoulder throbbed and a trickle of blood flowed from his knee, under the torn pant leg. He staggered around in the haze of the fire and fog, managing to locate his Thompson, and limped back to the Jeep.

Durning still lay on the ground in front of the vehicle. He clutched the carbine tightly to his shoulder, his glasses pressed firmly against the stock, pointing it toward the dock. "Come on. Follow me," Ken croaked.

Durning, startled, snapped around, and pointed his carbine at Ken.

Ken ducked down behind the fender. "Whoa, sailor! It's me."

"Oh! Sorry, Sir," Durning said, turning the rifle barrel away.

"Jesus. I've had enough already. Now get up and let's check on the others."

Durning hopped to his feet, held the carbine in front of him, and slumped his slender body into a crooked question mark as they headed for the dock.

The flames had spread up the wall of the second shed and were lapping at its eaves. The building furthest out was blown completely apart – nothing remained but the planking of the dock the building had sat on, and a few burning crates. Large-caliber bullet holes covered the dock and had shredded much of the planking. Ken stepped carefully around the splintered boards.

The sound of the diesel engine had faded into the distance, off the point.

Durning scratched his head. "Sir, what happened to the Major and his men?"

Ken paused and listened. He heard faint splashing sounds ahead near the end of the dock.

"Major?" Ken stepped forward, and his foot broke through one of the weakened boards. He dropped through up to his knee, cutting it across the front. "Damn it!" His head ached and his lungs still ached from the previous jolt, now his knee stung as well.

Durning grabbed his arm and pulled him back to his feet.

Ken peered into the dark. "Major?"

Footsteps behind them.

They swung around as the other two Marines hurried onto the dock near the burning shed. They ducked away from the heat as they ran passed.

"Where's the Major?" One asked.

Ken looked toward the water. "Down there, I think. Get back on the shore, pull the two undamaged Jeeps down to the edge, and shine the headlights out. We'll see if we can see anyone."

The Marines turned and headed back. The flames were growing on the middle shed and had climbed up onto the roof, turning the fog black in the light from the fire. A moment later, the motors turned over and the headlights cast onto the bay beside the dock. White reflected off the water as one man broke the surface, swimming toward shore. Another man stood waist-high in the water, close to the beach. It was the Major.

"Where's the other one?" Ken squinted into the haze.

"I don't see him, either." Durning moved toward the edge of the planking.

The two Marines waded into the water and helped the Major out, then returned to get the other man as he reached the shallow water.

"There!" Durning shouted and pointed.

Ken strained to look seaward in the direction Petty Officer Durning was pointing. Just a slight swirl in the water. Then a black spot. A head bobbed and an arm flailed at the surface.

Ken shoved the Thompson into Durning's chest. "Take this," He stripped off his shoes, dropped them on the dock, then unfastened his gun-belt "I'll get him."

Ken let the belt thud to the deck. The drop to the water was far less than at the quarry, but he didn't know the water depth and that was foremost on his mind as its surface rose up at him. Cold New England sea water engulfed him, all light disappeared, and his uniform clung to his skin. His stockinged feet didn't touch bottom, but his head plunged four feet below the surface.

He clawed at the water and kicked back to the surface, slightly disoriented by the sudden shock of the cold. The frigid water filled his already aching head with racking pain. He rotated in the water to see the headlights, then turned his back to them and looked seaward.

Nothing.

"Where is he?" Ken shouted.

"He's fifteen yards out and to your left!" Durning responded.

The salt water bit into the cuts on his knee and hand, but he kicked hard and swung his body into an overhead crawl. He took six hard strokes and popped his head up. This time, he could see a disturbance in the water.

"He's just ahead!" Durning shouted.

"I see him!"

Ken took short, choppy breast strokes as he approached. The Master Chief's face rose out of the water just enough to catch a breath; his right arm doggedly rotated in a dog paddle.

"Don't worry, Chief. I'll get you."

"Help me!" The Master Chief grabbed at Ken's arm, his beefy mitt slapping the water.

Ken stayed just out of reach. "Relax, Chief. I can't help you if you take me down."

The Chief lunged at him again.

Ken took a stroke away. The Chief was in a state of panic.

Ken took a deep breath, then dove under water. He swam downward for five or six strokes, leveled out, swam seaward, and then back to the surface. He broke through directly behind the Chief. Not giving the man time to turn, he grabbed the collar of his shirt and began swimming backwards toward shore. The chief's right arm flailed at first, as he tried to turn. Then he calmed down, realizing Ken would keep his face out of the water.

Ken made a short semicircle and headed for shore, swimming sidestroke with his left arm. The sheer bulk of the man made progress slow, yet the extra weight kept him buoyant.

"I've got ya. Relax."

The Chief sputtered. "My left arm's broke. Maybe my leg, too."

Ken labored to catch his breath. "Don't worry about that now. Let's just get to shore."

The Marines were back in the water when they reached the end of the dock area. Strong arms grabbed the Master Chief and dragged him onto shore. He grunted in pain as his twisted left leg hit the rocks on the beach.

The Major squatted down beside the Chief, ripped his pant leg open to the crotch, and surveyed the damage. The left leg jutted at an odd angle just below the knee.

"It's busted all right. Both bones below the knee, I'd say, but they didn't punch through the skin." He moved up to the arm and ripped the sleeve away. The shoulder was swollen and already black with blood from the bruising.

The Chief coughed up a mouthful of water. "How bad?"

"You won't be walking on that leg anytime soon."

The Major swiped a hand over his hair, then spoke

to one of the Marines. "Get me a couple of boards from those buildings before they completely burn up so we can splint that leg." He sat back so he wouldn't drip cold water onto the Chief. "Tear some strips of cloth from our shirts to bind them."

Ken sloshed through the ankle-deep water and sank onto a rock, letting the cold water drain off his body. "This didn't turn out like I expected. What the hell's going on here?" he asked the Major.

The Major locked eyes with Ken. "It ain't over yet. We've got to tend to the Master Chief and then start looking for clues. That was a German U-boat out there, and we need to find it."

Ken nodded. "And the man on shore who was helping it."

The Major's eyebrow went up. "What man?"

Chapter Twelve

The fog settled in, enveloping everything, snugging in close to the docks, weaving around the boats on stands, and brushing against the sides of buildings at the marina. The headlights from the Packard hit the wall-like fog, unable to penetrate the dense shield more than halfway out to the empty floating dock. A light burned above the sign to the office of the boatyard, casting a pale yellow glow on the yard.

Maggie turned off the lights, then the ignition. The night blossomed around her. Seabirds squawked from their nests to the north on Dudley Island. Light waves lapped the shore, shushing the birds back toward sleep. The sound of a motor from a car on the far side of the bay traveled up toward the customs house.

She settled deep into the seat, pulling her loose-fitting, button-down sweater over her shoulders. Although the night was warm, she shivered a bit as she snuggled her chin deep into the woolen collar. What had she done? She'd ruined all the plans her and Luke had made. How could she face him after this? What could she possibly say?

She'd be ostracized. Everything she had become would be lost.

The faint hum of a low-powered diesel crept through the curtain, increasing as it invisibly rounded the point in the fog and gained speed.

Maggie opened the car door and stepped onto the gravel drive, then paused to turn on the car lights before she walked toward the dock, her path illuminated by the headlights.

The lights cast a halo around her from behind, her thin, long shadow widened by the heavy sweater. The sound of the motor grew louder and she expected it to jump out of the fog at any instant, but another full minute passed before the bow sliced into the light beam.

The green hull appeared black in the night. Josh leaned out the side of the wheelhouse and steered toward the dock. He pushed the throttles to neutral, then into reverse, allowing the stern to back up to the planking. Again placing it in neutral, he hopped off the stern with a line attached to a brass boat cleat. Dropping to one knee, he lashed the line around the wooden cleat on the dock.

Maggie glanced at her watch; the silver reflected in the light from the car. Midnight, exactly.

Josh walked to the bow, attached another line, then added a spring line from the bow to the stern. "Look who's the reliable one."

Maggie walked down the slanted ramp, keeping her shoes solidly on the horizontal cleats to keep from sliding on the damp surface. "Come on, let's go. I don't like being out here this late."

Josh stepped back aboard and cut the engine. "Damn fuel pump. I almost didn't make it back."

Maggie crossed her arms and looked over her shoulder. "Well, you did. So let's go."

He turned, bent over and lifted a small crate onto the rail. Then a second as well. Stepping back onto the dock, he set one on the planking and carried the other toward the ramp. "Sure. Open the trunk for me."

She turned, retraced her steps, removed the keys from the ignition and opened the trunk.

Something clanked behind her. She spun, staring toward the side of the boatyard office.

Movement.

She pulled her sweater tighter around her shoulders.

More movement.

A gray and black striped tiger cat stepped out from the shadows and rubbed against the corner of the building.

Josh stomped up the ramp and then came around the side of the car. "You look worried."

She shrugged off a shiver and watched him set the unmarked crate into the trunk. "What do you have tonight?"

He grunted as he pushed it forward. "Nothing you need be concerned with. The less you know, the better." He paused. "In case we get stopped."

She walked around and slid into the passenger's side. Josh returned to the boat for the second crate. He staggered up the ramp, the second box apparently heavier than the first. The springs of the car bounced when he dropped the crate into the trunk beside the first one. He returned to the boat one more time and came back with the level action rifle. Maggie eyed it as he slid it behind the seat.

"I hope that wasn't needed."

He winked. "Of course not! Just insurance."

He slid in next to her, adjusting the seat to accommodate his legs. "Let's get you home. Shall we?"

She glanced back at the corner of the office. "Yeah. It's been a long day. I'd really like to get home."

The whitewalls of the Packard convertible splashed through a puddle at the entrance to the boatyard, then caught traction on the asphalt "I need to make a quick stop along the way." He paused. "I just want to drop off these crates. I don't like driving around with them this late at night."

Maggie leaned against the door, turning toward him. Her hair flicked in front of her face from the breeze. "Where?"

"I've got a little barn in Whiting. It's real close to the road and right on the way."

Maggie relaxed as Josh cautiously steered the car west. He crept along at twenty-five miles an hour and leaned toward the windshield, trying to see further ahead in the haze. She slouched in her seat and rubbed her fingers on her sweater above her breasts, feeling the hard lump underneath – a small, gold oval locket Luke had given her for Christmas.

The road swept under the front of the car, disappearing quickly behind them. Maggie rested her head back on the seat and stared at the sky. Streaks of wispy brume raced by overhead. She continued to fondle the locket through the veil of clothes and tried to put her mind elsewhere.

Anywhere.

The war in Europe was so far away. Yet she could imagine streaks of red in the vapor. Blood-red flashes in the spindles of twisted water suspended in the sky, getting brighter and closer.

"Damn it!" Josh said.

She sat up. "What?"

"Police. Up ahead."

The red rotating beacon atop the car blinked at them through the night. A man stood beside it swinging a flashlight, to and fro.

Maggie felt the blood rush from her face. "What're we going to do? He'll find the crates."

Josh sat up straight, glanced at his face in the mirror, then combed his hair back with his fingers. "Just let me do the talking. You don't know anything, no matter what." He paused and made eye contact with her as he began to brake. "Understand?"

She nodded and clenched both hands in her lap.

The officer stood in the middle of the opposite lane, signaling them to pull over behind his police car that blocked their lane. He swung the heavy metal light horizontally, allowing the twelve-volt battery attached below it to act like a pendulum. His badge reflected in the light from the car, but his face was hidden in the shadow behind the electric lantern. The man was tall and slim, a low-slung revolver on his right hip.

Josh braked harder and the Packard crept to a stop, the drums squeaking the last few feet.

The officer walked toward the car, shining the light beam in Josh's face as he approached. He swung the light to Maggie as he reached the car, then back in Josh's face.

"So, where have you two been tonight?"

"Just over to Calais to a dance," Josh said.

"Then why are you over here on 189? You should be back on Route One." He paused briefly, and then added, "Besides, Maggie, I thought you were dating Luke Johnson."

The officer lowered the light, allowing them to see the narrow cheekbones of Ray Foster, the sheriff from Machias.

"Ray. What got you out here in the middle of the night?" Maggie asked.

He nodded up the road past the patrol car. "Log truck hit a moose. The driver got hurt, but he's already at the hospital. I'm just trying to keep people from running into the back of the truck until we can get it moved."

Ray ran his light around the inside of the car. "You two haven't been drinkin' or anything?"

Josh and Maggie both shook their heads. "No, Sir. Just heading home."

His eyes narrowed. "Yeah, that's right. From Calais, wasn't it?"

Josh back peddled. "Well, we ran over to check on the boat. I've been worried about her seeping around the engine seals."

Ray nodded. "Aya. Them engine seals are tricky things." He paused. "I'd be willing to bet it's nothing a few pounds of sugar delivered to the back door of the hospital wouldn't cure."

Josh shot a glance at Maggie.

"That might just seal these lips when it comes to telling Luke who I ran into tonight, as well."

Josh started to look at Maggie, then stopped and turned his attention back to Ray. "That's not necessary. Luke knows we're out here tonight."

Ray tilted his head and stared at Maggie. "Okay, maybe it's me that's jumping to conclusions. I'll just stay out of it anyway." Again he paused. "The hospital could still use that sugar."

"I might know where I could find a bit," Josh said.

Maggie smiled. "Thanks, Ray. And, hey, stop by the diner real soon."

He stepped back and waved them through. "I'll do that."

Josh inched the Packard forward, pulled into the opposite lane, and crept down the road past the truck. The front passenger side fender was pushed in and a cow moose lay on her side under the front left wheel, her right leg wrapped up over her neck. Blood, black in the night, pooled on the road around her and ran into the sand on the shoulder. Maggie turned her head as they rolled by.

"That's awful. The poor thing. I hope it didn't suffer."

"I'm sure it'll end up in the pots of the needy. Ray's good that way."

Maggie remained quiet for a few moments, letting some distance build up between them and the accident.

"Josh... do you think Luke is going to ask me to marry him?"

Josh kneaded the steering column with his hands. "Sometime, sure... maybe next spring?"

"Why not now? I mean, it might help keep him out of the draft. You know, if the war goes on for a long time."

"Luke's all set with his father's blueberry crops. They can't take him away from a farm." He looked into the rearview mirror, then back at the road ahead. "Besides, what's all this talk of marriage all of a sudden? I thought you were the one who wasn't interested in getting tied down too early. That's what Luke led me to believe."

She leaned back and looked over the doorframe and out the open window. "Yeah, I'm just being silly, I guess. Forget I asked."

Josh rolled his eyes. "Sure. Whatever you say."

Maggie crossed her arms, sank down in the seat, and swung her head toward the road. The sand shoulder streamed by, light beach type sand and gravel, with the occasional stick or discarded beer bottle flashing in the headlights. The obstacles appeared and disappeared as fast as she could register them. They passed a few drive-ways and then the fog lightened as the car went under a street light.

Josh slowed the Packard and leaned over the wheel, eyes darting. More braking and a sudden right turn. The wheels ground heavy on the smooth, sandy drive. Trees appeared overhead close to the open top of the car. Maggie reached up and tried to catch a leaf as they crept down the path. The trail swung to the left and Josh stopped. The headlights shone on the faded red peeling paint of a small barn door. A twisted dome light hung overhead, with a single bulb screwed into the receptacle.

Josh turned off the ignition, but kept the headlights on.

"You can sit tight if you want."

Maggie sat up and fondled the door handle with the fingers of her right hand momentarily before jerking it back and giving the door a shove with her shoulder. "No. I'm coming."

Josh wandered around the front of the car, looked over his shoulder, listened for a few seconds, then retrieved a key from under a rock beside the building and unlocked the door. The shiny new padlock clicked open. He hung it on the open hasp and leaned against the door. It creaked and resisted his efforts at first, then began to slide.

He pushed harder until the sliding door finally opened. The headlights of the Packard lit the barn's interior. Maggie stepped around in front of the car and looked inside.

The barn was small, slightly deeper than wide, perhaps twenty-by-twenty-four. The floor was dirt and the walls hewn planks. The spaces between the planks were filled with smaller pieces of board to prevent prying eyes from looking in. She stepped inside. The timbers were cracked and held together with wooden pins. Congealed lumps of hay or straw mixed with bird droppings, coated the rafters. Entering, her cheek brushed a cobweb and it stuck to her face like fine strands of sticky cotton candy. She attempted to brush it away, but it wrapped around her hand as her eyes fell on two piles of crates on opposite sides of the barn.

The Packard's trunk clicked open behind her.

The crates sat off the floor on split scraps of lumber, their sides plain and unmarked.

Josh entered behind her with the heavier of the two boxes. He marched past her and plunked it on the stack on the right.

"What's in them?"

Josh shrugged. "Anything and everything. All the things people want, but aren't supposed to have in these times of 'sacrifice,' yet are willing to pay for if their neighbors don't know about it."

"That's a pretty crass attitude. Our boys are dying in Europe. We're not supposed to have it easy here."

"Who says? It's not like there's really a shortage of this stuff. If I can get all I want, most other people could do the same. I think they just feel better about themselves if they save a bit of tin or rubber in public, and then go on their merry way and do what they want."

"You can't really believe people are that uncaring."

"Uncaring? No. But I don't think the war is close enough to home really. If they were battling it out on the lawn in front of the Capitol, then you'd see sacrifice."

Josh went to the back of the car, removed the second crate, and returned, passing close to Maggie. "Do you need anything?"

She looked at the piles of boxes, thought of the diner, and rubbed her palms together. "No, I'm fine."

Josh thumped the second crate down on top of the first. "It's already here. You might as well have it as a family down the street from you."

Chapter Thirteen

Oberleutnant Zur Se Werner leaned on the open hatch cover in the engine room. Sea water streamed in around the main seal to the starboard shaft, into the small space at the compartment's aft portion. The chill of metal surrounded by cold water radiated inward, and sank into his bones. The turning shaft of the port electric motor spun beneath the caged lights, at chest level. The massive diesel sat on the other side of the electric motor attached to the same shaft. A duplicate set up was behind him. Franz, the engineer, a short burly man, squatted on the grates above the bilge pumps and poked at the water below the grates with a stick.

Franz, the scruffy Chief mechanic, glanced up at Werner "The pumps seem to be keeping up, but we're not lowering the water level."

"How long before you can re-pack those bearings and stop the leak?"

Franz pulled the stick out of the bilge and tapped it against the grate. "We'll have to make the repair on the surface. The divers will need to stem the flow from the outside, then we'll repair from the inside. Otherwise we'll never hold back the water and work in the packing and grease."

Werner tried to visualize how to keep the water from pouring in when they removed the gasket. "Did you get everything you needed while we were at the dock?"

Franz nodded. "Yes. But again, we can't pull out the old seal until we get some kind of a temporary seal on the outside. Nothing but that seal stands between the engine compartment and the sea. The bigger problem will be to re-tap the threads on the packing gland, and I can't do that until we get them off."

"Understood." Werner turned and headed to the control room a few meters away. "Fine. I'll inform the Kapitan."

Kapitan Steiner was speaking with Abwer agent, Oscar Schuch when Werner swung through the portal onto the control room deck. Steiner's face was hard and resolute. Schuch stood with his back to Werner, but his shoulders rose and fell with his animated hand movements. Steiner gripped the chart table much as he had when the depth charges hit.

"This whole affair has been mishandled from the start. You had no right to endanger our mission by firing on that convoy. That action led directly to the reason we're still aboard."

The Kapitan shook his head. "No. You won't put that on me. The rendezvous point had been compromised by an act of fate. It had nothing to do with the damage this boat suffered."

Schuch slapped his hand on the chart table. "Yes, but if we hadn't been damaged, we would've made the drop-off point a day or two earlier. Before the position was compromised."

"You don't know what fate had in store for us. We might've run into a group of battle hardened ships if we were here sooner. You have no idea what might have happened."

The Kapitan turned his attention to Werner. "Are the repairs as we thought?"

Werner continued to stare at Schuch's back. "Yes. Exactly as you were told previously. No changes, Sir."

Schuch tossed up his hands and stormed past Werner. "We'll see what Berlin has to say about this when we make our first report home."

The Kapitan put both hands to his eyes, slowly rubbed them with his fingers, and spoke softly to himself. "With any luck, they'll just shoot me and get it over with." Then he dropped his hands and spoke louder. "So, what would be your plan, Werner?"

Werner moved to the chart table, lifted off the top chart, and looked at the one underneath. "Since we need to meet der Falke in two nights on Hancock Point, I'd take us out into the deep water here." He pointed to the chart. "Off Mt. Desert Island for the repairs. That way, we'll be in position to head straight in and out again, yet have plenty of maneuvering room. Besides, we'll find less fishing traffic in the deeper water, so less chance of being spotted."

The Kapitan nodded. "Very good. Pick a suitable position and head in that direction. Stay on the surface if you can to keep the batteries charged. I'm going to my berth. I haven't slept in two days."

"As you wish, Sir."

Kapitan Steiner turned and moved toward the forward hatch and his bunk. "And no one is to use the radio without my direct consent. Is that clear?"

"Very clear, Sir."

A light breeze rose with the morning sun, stripping away the fog like layers of an onion. The bright blue of the sky merged with the orange glow of the remaining mist, and then reappeared as blue water reflected the dissipated light from the east. A single sentry stood at the end of the dock facing the rising sun, his rifle slung over his right shoulder. The only other Marine was stationed near the woods, the rest of the men having taken the Master Chief to the Machias hospital

Ken sat slouched in the driver's seat of his Jeep, the Major beside him. Ken had removed his wet shirts and wriggled into an undershirt donated by Petty Officer Durning. It was a tight fit, but at least it was dry. He'd removed his wet socks, but put his soggy shoes back on over his bare feet. The Major unbuttoned his uniform, yet kept the wet garment on.

Major Smith fished a pack of Lucky Strikes from his pocket, attempted to remove one of the soggy sticks, then gave up and squished the pack in his hand. Brown water gushed out and ran over his fist and down his arm. He tossed the pack on the ground.

He gazed at the empty space where his Jeep had been parked a few hours before. "Is that doctor of yours in Machias going to take good care of my Master Chief?"

"Yes, Sir. Doc Hanson owns the Machias hospital. He's as good as they come."

"Well, so's the Master Chief. If he doesn't get the best care, I'll have that doc's liver for supper."

Ken swung his legs out of the Jeep and pushed himself upright, leaving a puddle of sea water in the seat.

"What do you say about looking over what's left in the sheds, Sir? I think the fire's pretty well burned out."

Major Smith rotated his head toward the smoldering piles at the end of the dock and then swung his feet out. "Seems light enough now. Why not?"

Ken paused in front of the Major's Jeep. The less fortunate vehicle beside him slumped to one side, seeming to wink at him with the one intact light, its guts having spilled their vital fluids onto the soil underneath.

"I don't think you're going to be driving that back to Brunswick."

Major Smith slid out of his seat. Water ran out of his shoes as they settled on the ground. "When we're done here, you'll have to give us a ride back to town. We can check on the Master Chief and I'll meet up with the rest of my men."

The sun climbed above the haze on the horizon and radiated onto their wet bodies. Ken paused on his way over to the sheds, stretched as he faced into the rays, and wiggled his stiff knee, willing it to loosen.

The Major stepped into the remnants of the third shed. Heavy looking piles of metal were partially covered with ash and charred timbers. Sections of chicken fence and electrical wire had collapsed onto the debris.

The Major pointed to a heavy metal lathe that had

been situated just inside the door. "The charge must've been over here. Look how it blasted outward, taking the walls and a lot of the contents with it." He nodded toward the water. "The lathe acted like a blast shield, pushing the explosion in that direction."

"Why would they put the charge behind the lathe?" Ken asked. "It would actually protect the people entering. Wouldn't they want to cause as much carnage as possible?"

"Hmm. You'd think. Perhaps they were more interested in hiding the evidence than killing."

Ken placed his feet carefully on the charred decking, where loose boards and holes had him testing their integrity. The water directly under the sheds was shallow, but falling fifteen feet would be painful, if not fatal. He kicked a metal bucket near his right foot, and as it flipped over he noticed a small box underneath. It had been protected by the metal covering and was still intact.

He picked it up and peeled away the wrapping to reveal a fuel tank cover. Rolling it over in his hands, he saw that it was stamped on the outside with an eagle perched above a Nazi swastika.

"Look at this!" Ken tossed it to the Major.

Catching the cover, the Major twisted it around in his hands and cleared his throat. "I figured they were either dropping off operatives or getting replacement parts. I guess we know for sure now."

"Where do you think they're heading?"

The Major stuffed the cap into a trouser pocket. "Either Portland or St. John. Those are the two most active ports."

"Are they here to sink our transports?"

"Yes, but not directly." He paused and looked seaward. "I noticed just before the explosion tossed me in the drink, the boat didn't have bow tubes. That would make her a mine layer. A class VII if the intelligence reports that pass over my desk are accurate. Of course, that means she won't be hunting, so she'll be harder to locate."

Ken looked out at the sentry on the end of the dock and repeated the Major's words *of course*. "This is Machias, for Christ sake. The war's not supposed to be here."

The Major turned and headed back to the Jeep. "I'm sure that's the attitude they're counting on."

Leaving the two Marines to watch over the site, they drove off in Ken's Jeep.

Ken navigated back toward the post. He drove cautiously even though the road was mostly clear, with patches of fog only in the low-lying areas. They passed several delivery trucks out on morning rounds and the occasional passenger car. The Major appeared lost in thought and kept his head turned toward the side of the road.

"Sir, what's the next step?"

The Major turned back toward Ken. "What? Oh… Let's see. I'll contact Portland and get the investigation started. They'll probably send out a team of investigators immediately." He bobbled his head. "Next, they'll issue a warning to all the ships in the area, as well as to the fishing fleets, to keep a sharp eye out and report anything suspicious."

"What about whoever helped them? The person I ran into."

"They'll try to find out who that was, but it won't be easy." He rubbed his chin. "You know these people. Maybe you can find out something we can't. Talk to everyone, but don't tell them too much. Just enough to get them interested. See what they might give you for information. The smallest detail could be the most revealing."

Ken nodded. "Details won't be the problem. Around here, that's what people live for."

The Major turned to face him. "The sleepy offshoots in the world are appealing to these people. Don't let your guard down. A lax attitude can get you killed."

Chapter Fourteen

Court Street appeared deserted. Tall elms along the street muted the sunlight, casting wavy shadows across the lawns each time the gentle breeze swayed the branches. Bert Varnum's milk truck sat in front of Dr. Hanson's white Victorian. Ken and the Major turned the corner, heading for the hospital. Bert had set out four bottles next to the potted azalia on the front step, and little Sally Anne Hanson was already at the door to pick them up.

The white-sided hospital stood two stories high. Its windows lined the front like a double decker bus and were accented with a door at either end. The Major's Jeep was parked out front with one wheel up on the curb. Ken pulled in behind and kept the motor running.

"Head straight on in. The front office staff doesn't start work until eight, but the Master Chief will be in one of the treatment rooms on your left."

"Thanks. I'll swing by the post when I get done here."

"If you would, Sir. Send Petty Officer Durning out so I can take him back with me." Ken dropped one hand onto his thigh and felt his wet trousers. "I'll send over some dry clothes for you fellas."

The Major looked down at his uniform. "Yeah, thanks. Do that."

Major Smith left a wet spot on the seat when he got out. The door closed behind him and Ken was left alone in front of the hospital, where he was born twenty-seven years before. The rising sun glinted through and off the cracked windshield. Ken smiled. The report to requisition a new one should make better reading than the duty rosters.

Petty Officer Durning appeared in the doorway, paused, looked back over his shoulder, waved to someone inside, then came out, then shuffled down the steps to the Jeep, and hopped into the front seat.

"What now, Sir?"

Ken popped the stick into first and pulled away from the curb. "How's the Master Chief?"

"He'll be fine. Just a busted arm and leg. He'll be good as new in a month or so."

Ken nodded. "Good."

The milk truck had moved down the street and Ken waved as he passed by. The milkman's hands were full of bottles, but he looked up and raised his chin in greeting.

"We're going to head back and get some dry uniforms for the Major's men and myself. Then you're going to start making up some alert posters. I want to see every window and telephone pole within thirty miles of here with an information flyer and our telephone number on it."

"What are you going to do next?"

Ken slowed down as they reached the end of the street; he didn't stop, but eased through the intersection in front of the town hall. "It's Saturday and the town office won't be open, but I'm going to call the town clerk, Alice Williams, at home and see if she can open it up and we can find out who owns that pier."

"What do you want the fliers to say?"

Ken accelerated onto Route One. "We don't want to panic anyone. So perhaps something along the lines of a general cautionary message. You know the 'Heads up, watch out for strangers and report suspicious activity' type of thing."

Durning nodded. "Sure, I can do that, Sir."

Alice was standing on the front step of the town hall when Ken parked at the curb. She clutched her white pocketbook with both hands in front of her long plain dress. Her gray tight curls crept out from under her round blue cap, and a string of fake pearls adorned her neckline. She was Ken's second cousin's mother-in-law on his father's side. Ken glanced across the street at the plaque on the stone in front of the Burnham tavern, commemorating the original sixteen families that settled there in 1765; most everyone in the town was related in some fashion to that lineage.

Ken walked up to Alice, who was sporting a wide smile, and gave her a peck on the check. "Thanks for meeting me. I know you were probably busy at home."

"Aya. But I don't need much of an excuse to help out family." She turned toward the town hall and started up the steps. "What's this all about? Is it some kind of Navy thing?"

Alice wasn't the person you wanted to tell something, unless you wanted it all over town. "You know the government. They need all the dots and crosses."

"Something important?"

"No, it's nothing important. I just need to get this for a report that's due on Monday."

"Now you said you needed the name of someone?"

Ken began to follow. "Yes, that's right. I need to know who owns the land on the east side of Buck's Harbor."

She stopped. "Well, why didn't you say so on the telephone? That information ain't here. It would be in the records down in Machiasport."

Great! Ken sighed. "Who do I need to talk with then?"

"That would be Mildred Brownlee. I'll give her a call and tell her to expect you."

Ken touched her shoulder. "Thanks. Tell her I'll meet her at the office."

Alice stood on one step up from Ken in order to look him in the eye. "What's really going on? I hear there's a Marine in the hospital and there was some kinda fracas last night, down there where you're asking about. So don't go and tell me no stories. Besides, you've been in town for two days now and haven't been over to see your parents. Something has got you pretty busy."

"Nothing, really!" Ken shrugged.

"Kenneth Mitchell, you lie like a Methodist preacher."

Ken raised a brow. "Geez, maybe we should put you

on the payroll." He paused and tightened his jaw, while he looked at the queen-bee of gossip. "We're looking for someone. You don't know of any strangers around, do you?"

"Strangers." She thought a moment. "There is that new hand over on the Wilson farm. According to Bill Wilson he speaks mighty good English, but probably isn't American."

"How long has he been there?"

"A month or more I guess."

Ken thought a moment. "Why doesn't Bill think he's American?"

Alice shrugged . "Didn't ask him that."

"Thanks, Alice. I'll tell Mother I ran into you."

She smiled. "You have to see her first, before you can tell her anything. Being an only child I'd think you wouldn't be so cavalier about getting by to see them."

Ken took a deep breath. Perhaps he could swing by the house on his way back from Machiasport. He was going to get a skinning if he didn't get over there soon.

Alice started back up the steps as Ken returned to the Jeep and her voice trailed off behind him. "You're a good boy, so I know you'll head right over to the house. When you see you ma, tell her I've got the recipe to that cobbler she was asking about, if she wants to stop by."

"I'll do that."

The Jeep seemed to steer itself toward Machiasport. This was the third time in two days Ken had been down the same road. Elm Street crossed Libby Brook and then bent south toward Mill Creek and the small hamlet of

Machiasport. Bill Wilson's farm was off Elm Street, just before the bridge to town. Maybe he should swing in and check on that new hired hand? No, he could do it after seeing Mildred. She might be waiting for him.

He rolled over the bridge, past the boat launch on his left, where the road dropped into town. A simple cluster of buildings stood in a hollow, with docks on the river side and the stately homes of seafaring men of years past scattered alongside other houses in serious disrepair. A simple church with plain windows sat opposite the dock, and another smaller and more decorative, a quarter-mile further on the far hill. Hard to believe this hamlet could fund two churches.

The Machiasport town hall was located in the front room of an old, single-story house that rose up from the street and clung to the side of the hill behind it.

The steps were empty and the windows dark; apparently, Mildred hadn't arrived yet. Ken parked the Jeep in front on the street facing south. The docks lay to his left; solid structures with fishing boats tied to their sides. Classic lobster boats with stiff, turned up-bows and flat long sterns. The lines periodically slapped the pot pulling arms with the heavy clank of metal pulleys on wood as the gentle waves rolled them back and forth.

The road extended on ahead past the docks, doglegged to the right, and rose up the hill out of town. Birch Point was just visible over the docks, a mile and a half out along the west side of the bay. Ken knew Buck's Harbor and the two Marine sentries lay two miles further, on the other side of that piece of quiet real estate. He imagined them standing on the charred dock staring back at him.

"Mr. Mitchell?" A light, soft voice sprang from behind the Jeep.

Ken turned. A woman who appeared to be in her early thirties, wearing a pale yellow sundress, stood beside the rear bumper. Ken leapt from the Jeep and came around the back, extending a hand. "That's right. Kenneth Mitchell."

She took the offering in her white-gloved hand. "Mildred Brownlee. So you're Emily's boy?"

"One and the same." He paused. " Brownlee... not Tommy's older sister?"

"Not that much older."

Ken bit the inside of his lip. "Sorry. Yeah, I played against him in high school. He played right field and hit lefty."

She nodded. "That's him." She studied Ken's face. "Alice tells me you need information." A dark wisp of hair crept out of the tightly woven nest on top of her scalp and hung over her forehead.

"Yes, I need to find out who owns the land around Howard's Cove."

"That shouldn't be too hard a task. What area exactly?" she asked.

Ken moved to the front step of the town hall and she followed. "Shouldn't we go inside so you can look things up as we talk?"

Mildred dusted off the painted wooden step and sat down, pushing her legs tightly together and spaying her pointed white shoes, inward. "It's a beautiful morning. Let's stay outside and enjoy the weather. I can probably tell you anything you want to know from memory."

Ken sat beside her, keeping a respectable space between them. Her knees were smooth and solid, but not muscled. "I need to know who owns the land around the docks on the northwest side of the cove."

Her eyebrows wrinkled. "There aren't any docks there."

"That's what I said yesterday, only to find I was wrong."

She frowned. "The Larrabees own most of the west side, all the way to the point."

"Yes, I know they own that portion, but what about on this side of the stream, to the jut of land that extends into the cove?"

"Well, that would be town land. The town acquired that piece before the war when they traded some of the peat land near Shagadee Mountain to the Larrabees."

"So who built the docks?"

She shook her head. "Like I said. What docks?"

Ken stood and reached out a hand to her. "I appreciate you coming out to meet me."

She rose, then straightened the front of her dress with her gloved hands. "Not a problem. Is that all you wanted?"

Ken looked back toward the docks. "Maybe one of the fishermen will know something. They pass by there all the time."

Mildred swayed at the hips and shuffled her feet. "Do you want some company?"

Ken's eyes fell over her thin sundress and the curves it hid. "No, that's all right. I'd best go by myself. Thanks for the help."

She tucked in her chin, folded her hands in front of her, and continued to sway gently. "If you need anything else, give me a call. My number is Machiasport 2 4 2 3."

"Thanks." Ken turned and took a couple of steps, then swung back around. Mildred was still there, watching him. "You wouldn't happen to know anything about the new hand over at the Wilson's place, would you?"

She shrugged. "I've seen him in town a couple of times. Seems nice enough."

Ken waved. "Thanks again." He crossed the street and ambled down the grade toward the docks. The warm breeze lifting off the bay was as fulfilling in his lungs as the gulls cry to his ears.

A short access road swung off the main drag and dead-ended at the main wharf. The tide had ebbed, almost grounding the fishing fleet on the dirty banks of the river. Nubs of abandoned pylons dotted the mud flats above the dock. They sat in rows, extending to the waterline a few inches above the muck, soon to slip below the surface of the water when the tide returned.

The docks appeared deserted, except for a crizzled old man perched on a wooden crate at the stern of a battered lobster boat. The faded white hull had scrapes and gouges to the heart wood of the lap boards, its deck worn to ruts in the areas of heaviest traffic. A chipped and peeling rectangular name plate was screwed to the side of the wheelhouse: 'Miss Jenny.'

The old man clenched a cherrywood pipe in his teeth. It bobbed up and down while his hands worked on the trap propped in front of him. In his right hand, he clasped a seine-making tool, nimbly working it in a circular fashion as he fed line into the netting.

Ken walked out onto the dock. It creaked and protested his weight as he went. He wondered how old the boards were and whether it was sound.

"Excuse me," Ken said, stepping to the side of the boat.

The man didn't look up.

Perhaps he was hard of hearing. "Sir? Excuse me. May I have a word with you?"

The man looked up from his work, resting his hands in his lap, and scanned Ken's uniform. "What can I do for you, sonny?"

"Sorry to bother you, but I have a question. Do you know anything about the docks in Howard's Cove?"

He thought for an instant. "Yep." He bowed his head and stuck a finger through the hole in the trap's netting, then began to tie on a new piece of line.

Ken waited for more, but nothing came. "Could you tell me about it?"

His hands dropped again. This time, he removed the pipe and rested it on his knee. "I thought you only had one question?"

"Well, maybe I thought of another one."

"Such as?"

"I'm trying to find out about some docks most people don't know about."

The man leaned forward and tapped out his pipe against the side of the rail. "What do you want to know for? How people get by these days ain't no concern of the Navy."

"Sir, this isn't about fishing or smuggling. Believe me, I could care less about that. This is about the war. This is important."

"Always is with you fellas." He reached into his pocket and pulled out a flimsy leather pouch with a broken zipper. "I've seen a boat going in there from time to time. Didn't recognize the boat nor the color of it's buoys. He sure don't fish Machias bay."

"Did the boat have a name?"

He stuffed the pipe into the bag and filled it with shredded leaf, packing the bowl tightly with his finger. "You ain't very good at this questioning thing are ya? Of course it had a name, but I didn't see it."

"Do you know who built the docks?"

"The fellow in the boat, I guess. Never had a reason to ask."

Ken looked up at a tall pylon with a gull sitting on top, preening its feathers. "Is there anyone else around who might know something?"

He struck a wooden match on the side of the hull and held it over the bowl, sucking inward in short gasps. The leaf caught, and smoke rolled out his chapped lips and curled around his face. "Don't rightly know what they might know, but most are either still out fishin' or home waitin' for cooler weather."

"Thanks for your help." Ken turned to leave. Big help he was. What a waste of time!

"Green."

Ken stopped and turned. "What?"

"Green. The boat was green. Sounded like it could use a good tune-up, too."

Chapter Fifteen

Maggie leaned on her elbow and swirled her fingers in tiny circles on the Formica counter. Her coffee sat untouched in front of her, a ring of foam from the dollop of ice cream clinging to the rim, the tiny bubbles occasionally bursting and disappearing into the muddy liquid. Juliana rattled dishes in the kitchen, then clanked a pan on the stove.

The bell above the door jingled behind Maggie. She didn't look up. Warm hands slipped over her eyes.

"How's my girl today?"

Maggie sat up straight and placed her hands over Luke's. "I don't know. All right, I guess."

He slipped his hands down onto her shoulders and sat on the stool beside her. "Just all right. Just all right? It's a beautiful day out there. Why don't you play hooky and we'll go to the shore and have a picnic?"

"I don't feel like a picnic," she said.

"You? You always want to go on a picnic."

Her hand followed his to her shoulder; she tightened her grip on his fingers, then stood and strode around behind the counter. "Go have a seat in the far booth and I'll bring over some coffee."

Luke leaned against one of the stools and stared at her for a moment before he heeded her request and wandered to the far corner of the empty diner.

Maggie poured a cup for him and grabbed her cup of coffee on the way by. She set Luke's coffee in front of him and slid in close. Leaving one hand on her cup, she took his right hand in her left, intertwining their fingers.

He set his jaw. "You're scaring me, Mags. What's going on?"

She squeezed his hand and stared at his fingernails. "I've just got a lot on my mind."

"Like what?"

"I've been doing some thinking." She continued to knead his fingers. "About us."

He turned his body toward hers. "You aren't breaking up with me, are you?"

She snapped her face toward his. "No. God, no. Nothing like that."

"Then what's making you act so strange?"

"I'm worried about things."

"Things? What kind of things?"

"You know. Like where we'll live. When we'll get married. Things like that."

Luke pulled his hand away and turned sideways. "This isn't like you. You aren't the type to worry. What's really wrong?"

She stared at the tabletop.

"Come on, Mags."

She lifted her head and blurted out. "It's everything. It's this war. It's this damned diner. It's us." Her lower lip began to quiver. "It's everything."

Luke squeezed her shoulder, then began gently massaging the back of her neck. "I know things seem a bit up in the air, but we've got our whole lives ahead. We can get married next Spring and move into the cottage in the orchard. The boat's doing well. It can support us."

Maggie jerked her shoulder away, and pushed at his leg as she moved to the edge of the bench. "No. You're a fool to think it will be that simple. You've always been a fool... no, I've been the fool. Yeah, me. What an idiot I've been!"

Luke reached out to her, but she slapped away his hand. "Mags! What in Christ's name is going on?"

She glanced toward the door and the empty diner, then back at Luke. Dipping her head, she half-whispered. "I'm pregnant."

Luke froze. His face went slack. Slowly, he reached out and straightened the spoon beside the coffee cup. "Wow!" His hand moved toward the cup, then retreated. "I wasn't expecting that."

She slid back, toward the edge of the booth. "I can't even think straight. What are people going to say? My father. God, this will kill him."

Luke reached out, grasped her hands, and placed them together in his. He pulled her close. "We'll go away. I've got some money saved. We'll leave town."

"We can't just leave."

"Why not? Josh can buy the other half of the boat. He'll send us the money. We can go anywhere and start over. No one would know us or when we got married. California maybe. That would be far enough."

Her lips lifted a bit and she repeated his words.

"California. Maybe." Her voice was soft. "No one would know us. That's true."

"We can pack today and be on the road by dark. There's nothing to stop us. This is great. This is just what I need, too."

Maggie lifted her head and gazed around the diner. "I can't."

"What? Of course you can. Why not?"

"Look. Look around. My father, the diner. I can't leave him. He doesn't have anyone else."

"But what about us? We have to think of us and the baby, too."

She shook her head. "No, I won't leave. I can't."

"Listen to me. Yes, you can. You have to. You know people around here. They won't let it go. Ever." She continued shaking her head. "We could even get married before we go."

Maggie sniffled and wiped her face with the back of her hand. "Maybe."

Luke pulled a paper napkin from the chrome dispenser and blotted her eyes. "We'll figure this out."

The bell above the door jingled again. Their heads moved in unison toward the sound. Josh stepped in, waved, smiled, and wandered toward them.

Maggie grabbed the tissue from Luke and slid out of the seat. Covering her tears, she rushed toward the kitchen, pushing past Josh on the way. He stopped and watched her go, then sat down opposite Luke.

"What have you done now?"

Dust kicked up behind the Jeep as it bounced down

the lane toward the Wilson farm. The road was sand-
wiched in between a peat bog and a gentle hill that rose
into blueberry fields. The air hung heavy with the scent
of mud and berry blossoms. The back tires lost traction
and slid sideways on the washboard road. Ken compen-
sated, turning into the skid. His father taught him about
driving when he was only twelve. He'd learned to drive
out on Cathance lake in the middle of December: Dad
always said if you could drive on ice, he could drive on
anything.

The road rose out of the bog and angled to the left.
Weathered fence posts lined the road on the right, strung
with rusted barbed wire and clogged with weeds and low
brush. Cattle paths rutted the perimeter of the pasture
and the grass was chewed short at its center. A small apple
orchard lay beyond and climbed the hill on the opposite side. The field under the trees had been meticulously
mowed.

The weathered side of the barn came into view as Ken
rounded the corner. Mismatched black shingles covered
the roof, patched in over the years. The barn sat high on
a stone foundation. Boards and equipment lay protected
underneath. The vertical boards shimmered as the sunlight
radiated through the spaces between them. The house lay
just beyond at the end of a circular drive – a rectangular
two-story with white clapboard siding adorned with black
shutters that shagged away from the windows like the
wings of a tired bird. The tidy yard and grounds were a
contrast to the dilapidated buildings. The yard reminded
him of his grandfather; he'd go out and mow the fields
on the hottest of days, but the rain would have to dampen

his bed before Gram could get him to repair the roof. Green, cropped grass filled the center of the circle topped off with a brighter green Oliver 70 tractor. Its twin front tires pigeon toed in, metal engine shield removed, leaning against a large rear tire.

A sturdy, balding man dressed in coveralls stood on the far side, wiping his hands on a faded red rag.

Ken stopped at the first bend of the circle, facing the disheveled white house. A red-bordered flag hung in the front window with two blue stars on a bright, white rectangle. The window boxes were full of short-stalked plants with wilted white blossoms.

The man swung an elbow over the rear wheel of the tractor as Ken approached. "Mr. Wilson?"

The gent tipped his head, then ran the same rag over his balding scalp. "What can I do for you?"

"I heard you have a new man on the farm. I wanted to meet him if I could."

Wilson stuffed the rag into the rear pocket of his denim coveralls. "Ain't here. Took off a few days ago."

Ken unbuttoned his shirt pocket and removed a small pad and a pencil. "Really. Did he give a reason?"

Mr. Wilson eyed the pencil and then Ken. "Not so much as you'd know. Left in the middle of the night from what I can tell. Didn't say so much as a word before he left."

"Do you know where he went?"

"What's your interest in him?"

Ken glanced back at the window. "You have two boys in the military? What branch?"

Mr. Wilson didn't turn toward the house. "Any darn

fool can see the stars on the flag. That don't make you the clever one, nor does it make us friends." He removed a small clear-glass bottle from his chest pocket, pulled the stopper and took a sip, then replaced the cork and slipped it back into his pocket.

This man was just like his grandfather. "I'm not trying to patronize you. I was just being friendly."

"Why don't you be real friendly and send my boys home? I need them here. They've got no business over there in France."

"You know I don't have anything to do with that. I'm just a junior grade nobody." Ken glanced back at the tractor and Ken thought of the many times a roving preacher would stop by the family farm and want to save his grandfather's soul in exchange for a good meal. His grandfather hated lazy people. He would always offer the man a chance to clean out the cow barn instead. Funny how it never got clean. "Can I give you a hand?"

The man snorted. "Now that's what I need, help from a sailor. Shoot boy, you wouldn't know the starter from the fuel pump."

Ken pointed to the cream-colored wheel rims. "I know this tractor was originally sold in Canada because the ones here in the states have red rims. Looks like you're tightening the 9-inch single plate clutch, and I'd guess by the cloudberries in the window boxes, you're sipping on "the water of life" from that little bottle in your pocket." Ken paused for a moment. "And if you were to give me a sip of your aquavit, I'd be happy to give you a hand."

Wilson snorted again, louder this time, then shook his head, reached into his pocket, and handed the little oval bottle to Ken. "Grab that large flathead and hold back on the spring while I tighten the nut."

He leaned in beside Ken and slid the wrench over the screwhead. "Even though he had a social security card, I think he spent a lot of time in Canada."

"Why do you think that?"

Wilson's wrist rhythmically tightened the nut. "He spoke English well enough, but he had difficulty figuring out how much things cost." He paused, then added another thought. "And he ate mayonnaise on everything."

"What was his name?"

"That's another reason I thought he was Canadien. It was Paul Leveque."

"What did he look like?"

"Average enough. Black hair, thin and wiry. He could scale up to the loft of the barn quick enough. Maybe thirty, dark eyes. I don't recall the color."

Ken removed the flathead as Mr. Wilson took the final twist. "Any idea where he went?"

"He talked about having a sister down around Wiscasset. But I don't know for sure."

"Didn't mention her name, did he?"

Wilson leaned back against the tire. "Hmm, no can't say he did."

"What about habits, friends? Anything else stand out?"

"No. Nothing."

"Ken lifted up the flat engine cowling and set it in place, tightening the screws to keep it fast. "I appreciate the talk. Thank you."

"You're welcome to come in for lunch. Just some boiled meat and potatoes, but it'll tide you over."

"That's generous, but I should get back."

Ken turned and headed for the Jeep. Mr. Wilson called to him. "He always wore a dark overcoat and carried a bag, sort of like you sailors do."

Ken stopped and faced him. "A sea bag?"

"Yeah, something like that."

Luke and Josh had parked their cars at opposite ends of the diner. Ken pulled the Jeep in between them and took a few moments to button the top of his uniform and straighten his tie. After stepping from the Jeep, he hiked up the gun belt, thought about removing it, then decided not to leave it unattended in the vehicle.

The bell above the door announced his arrival and Luke looked up from the far booth. Josh's back was to him. Two patrons sat at the counter. Dave Parks' full attention was on his lemon meringue pie and William Nettles had his face buried in the 'Calais Advertiser.' Ken passed by, thought about saying hello, then decided not to disturb them. Seeing two cups in front of Luke, he slid in beside Josh.

Josh shoved over as Ken nudged him in the hip. "Watch out! Wyatt Earp's in town."

Ken leered at Josh. "I'm required to carry the thing. But if you keep up with the rhetoric, I might find a use for it."

"You wouldn't shoot a poor defenseless lobster fisherman, would you?"

Ken smiled. "No. But I'd beat a low-down smuggler like a wicked stepchild."

"Hey, I take offense to that. I'm no low-down, smuggler... I'm the best there is."

Ken glanced at Luke, who stared out the window, ignoring the banter. "What's with you? Dog eat your prize rabbit or something?"

Josh nudged Ken, and half-whispered, "He and Maggie are on the outs."

Luke's head snapped around. "We're not on the outs. We're just trying to figure some stuff out is all."

Ken placed his elbows on the table, a surge of excited interest welling up from inside. "Anything we can do?"

Luke leaned back and slouched. "No. Just leave it be."

"Are you sure?" Ken asked.

"Positive."

He filed away his fanciful thoughts of Maggie for the moment. "In that case, I need your help." Ken spent the next fifteen minutes filling them in on the previous day and a half. They listened intently, occasionally asking a question, then listening again. When Ken finished, they were all leaning on the table, heads close together.

"So you didn't hear a boat leave?" Josh asked.

"No. I figure the fellow must've had a car stashed down on the road – the lane that leads up to the Heald place."

"What about the guy at the Wilson farm? He could walk from there," Luke added.

Ken bobbed his head. "He could, but he'd have to walk along the main road and it would take half the night."

"But that would account for a lot of things," Luke said.

"True, but what about the boat that's been spotted in the cove?" Ken asked.

"Could be just a fisherman," Josh said.

Luke nodded. "Or the guy could have a boat stashed some place. Lot's of good places around there to hide a boat."

"They could hide a boat, but they'd still need fuel if they are running parts out to U-boats." Ken ran the flat of his palm on his chin. "I think that's where we need to start." He thought about the stack of fuel reports he'd received over the past few days, and muttered under his breath. "Who'd ever guess the Navy might have a good idea?"

What's that?" Josh asked.

Ken realized he'd been mumbling to himself aloud. "I said, do you want to tag along? I should start as far east as I can and then work my way back."

"Why me?" Josh asked.

"You know everyone in the Marina and they know what you do outside the law, so they'll be more likely to talk in front of you."

Josh massaged the table with his fingertips. "All right. But I need to be back by late afternoon, so I'll take my own car."

"That's fine. I need to run by the post and get the fuel reports and then I'll meet you there." Ken paused. "Why do you need to get back? Got a date or something?"

Josh looked out the window toward the river. "Or something."

Chapter Sixteen

Joel Cox's rusted-out Ford flat-bed sat in front of the marina's office. With its right rear wheel in a pothole, the truck sat almost level. Josh's Packard was parked near the dock and Ken swerved the Jeep in next to it. The Sea Swirl lay quiet at the dock, the sunshine baking the gray, weathered decking. Josh didn't appear to be aboard.

Ken reached for the stack of papers in the seat. As he leaned over, he spotted Josh at the far end of the gravel yard, deep in conversation with a fisherman. He leaned against the Jeep and watched them talk, then Josh turned and headed toward him. Josh seemed to spot the Jeep, stutter-stepped, then waved and continued along. Ken put the papers in his left hand and wandered around the Jeep as Josh approached.

"I've spoken to a couple of the fellas. No one seems to know anything about strangers or boats they don't recognize," said Josh.

"Why didn't you wait for me? I might've wanted to hear what they said directly."

Josh shrugged. "Like you said, I thought they might talk more freely to me."

"Have you talked to Joel yet?"

Josh turned toward the office shack. "No. I haven't"

Ken kicked a rock with his toe and looked back at the fisherman working around his boat. "Well, let's go then."

The shack stood on the far side of the parking area, machine parts rusting next to it. Red paint peeling from the cracked wooden door; revealed older gray paint underneath. The door handle had multiple colors of paint sticking to it.

The door stuck at the bottom, then lurched open as Josh leaned his weight against it. A pile of boxes sat inside the door; engine parts were strewn around the room in piles. A power head lay in the corner, half-cannibalized for parts. A metal desk on the far side held mounds of papers and greasy cogs and sprockets. Motor oil and grease filled the air and smelled as if it impregnated everything. Joel occupied a wooden swivel chair, nearly hidden behind the clutter. He didn't look up from the small part he was tinkering with. His black matted hair hug over a steep widow's peak and climbed to a cow-lick on top. It was difficult to tell where his sideburns stopped and his coarse unshaven stubble began.

"Hey, Joel. how's it going?" Josh asked.

Joel's sharp, knowing eyes darted up from the task. Without tilting his head, he looked back at the cog and gave the screwdriver a few more twists before setting the part aside. "Josh, wicked good to see ya." He stood and extended a soiled hand. "What can I do for you fellas?"

Josh took his hand, shook it, then subtly wiped his

hand on his pant leg. "This is my buddy, Ken Mitchell. He's got a few questions for you."

Joel picked up a filthy-looking rag from the desk and wiped his hands on it. "What kinda questions?"

Ken stepped forward. "Just about fuel usage and the like. Pretty routine stuff." He glanced at Josh and continued. "I was interested in having you go over some of these boats and their owners with me."

Joel looked at Josh, his eyes bright behind the weathered face. "I sent in my report as I'm supposed to. I don't know what else I can tell you."

Josh picked up a stack of newspapers off a stool near the desk, set them on the floor and sat down. "It's all right. We're all friends here. Ken's a pal from Machias. Tell him what he wants to know."

Joel sat back down, leaning back in the chair. "Fire away. I'll tell ya what I can."

Ken leaned on the boxes by the door, lifted the reports, and started reading the names, beginning with number three on the list. "Mike McPherson. What kind of guy is he?"

The questions and answers went back and forth for half an hour. Most of the men were locals; some second and third generation mariners who still lived in the houses their grandparents had built. The lower-usage boats were just passing through or berthed at other marinas farther down the coast and only came in occasionally to refuel. Joel was able to shed little light on them.

Ken reached the end of the list. He flipped over the

last page, looking for more information that didn't exist. "I guess that's all I have."

Joel rocked gently in the chair, shifting his gaze between the two men. "I notice you didn't ask about your friend here."

Ken straightened the stack of papers on his knee. "I think we both know about that."

Joel rocked a few more times and eyed Ken and Josh; then his brow raised and he bolted from the chair. "Hey, I just remembered. I finally found a fuel pump for you, Josh. It's not new, but it seems to be in good shape." He hunched over a pile of metal and twisted hoses next to the desk.

"Great. It only took six months."

"I knew yours wouldn't last much longer. I traded a guy down in Bucksport a pair of props and some barely used plugs for it. You owe me a wicked favor." Joel pulled the black canister from the pile and handed it to Josh.

Ken rose. "I'll give you a hand putting it on."

Josh rolled the greasy part in his hand. "No, I can do it later."

Ken offered a hand to Joel. "Thanks for the information."

Joel took the hand and nodded. "Any time."

Ken headed for the door, with Josh at his heels. "Come on, Josh. The day's almost gone. We may as well put on the pump."

Josh gazed up at the sun, hanging low in the sky. "I've got things to do. I can put it on later."

Ken ignored him and continued across the boatyard. "It's a fifteen minute job. I can do it if you want to leave."

Josh again looked at the sky. "I'll do it. You don't need to get your uniform dirty."

The boat's hull was dry and warm from basking in the sun. They hopped aboard. Ken stripped off his gun belt and placed it behind the steering wheel, then removed his uniform shirt and hung it over the wheel. After setting the pump on the deck, Josh went inside the berth to get his tools.

Ken lifted the top off the engine compartment and looked at the pump. "We'll need a three-eighth wrench and a flathead."

"Just stay put. I'll be there in a second," Josh shouted from the berth.

Ken leaned closer to the pump. It was clean and didn't have the layer of grime over it the rest of the engine did, except for the very top. He ran his fingers over the surface. Black grease lifted off, revealing deep deliberate scratches. He wiped off a bit more. The scratches appeared to be obscuring the manufacturer's emblem. Ken looked about for a rag. He reached into a small waste bucket on the stern and pulled a cloth out of it. As he did, a pasteboard carton the size of the fuel pump flopped on the deck. Ken picked it up and stared at it.

Josh emerged from the berth. "Stand aside! I've got the tools. Let me have at it."

Ken remained squatted down next to the barrel, holding the package. His head slowly rose to look at Josh. "You?"

Josh looked puzzled. "Me, what?"

"How could it be you?"

Josh remained frozen near the hatch to the berth. "You're not making any sense. What about me?"

Ken staggered to his feet, turning the box toward Josh. The emblem, a black eagle above swastika and the words *Deutchland*, was clearly visible.

Josh's face drained of color. "You don't think..." He raised a hand. "Wait just a God damned minute."

"No wonder you didn't want to change the pump. You already did it."

Josh stood quiet, shaking his head. "You're wrong."

"Now it makes sense why you didn't shoot me at the dock." Ken's voice was getting louder. "I thought there was something familiar about the figure who ran into the fog. It was you!"

Josh continued shaking his head. "You're wrong. All wrong."

Ken glanced at the pistol behind the wheel. Josh's eyes followed his.

Still clutching the toolbox to his chest, Josh said. "Just hold on. We need to talk about this."

Ken stepped forward and dropped the box to the deck. "Yes we do. Back at the post with Major Smith."

Josh shifted toward the dock, putting his body between Ken and the pistol. "You've known me most of my life. Do you think I'm capable of this?"

Ken's mind flashed back for just an instant. A time at the beach, a trip to Camden with his class, then it was back on Josh. "I don't know, but it needs to be explained."

As Ken took another step closer, Josh tilted his head.

"I'm not going in with you. I didn't do nothing and I'm not going to pay for it."

"Set down the toolbox and let's go in as friends. If need be, I can get you a good lawyer and things will work out."

Josh snorted. "Lawyer? What good's a lawyer? You know how the friggin' judges around here work. If I'm accused, I'm guilty."

Ken slowly moved up the side of the boat, closer to the pistol. "This has gone far enough. Now set down the box."

"Sorry. Can't do that." Josh's arms shot out, flinging the toolbox at Ken. Ken tried to dodge the projectile, but it dealt him a glancing blow to the shoulder and cheek. He spun toward the rail, attempting to regain his balance. Josh was there in a second, and gave him a shove. Ken's knees thudded against the rail and his weight projected him forward. He tumbled off the boat.

Not again! The cold water instantly reminded him of the night before. He floundered beneath the surface for several seconds, then managed to turn over and kick his way back up. He broke out of the water and gasped for breath. Josh was looking over the side of the boat. Ken wiped the water from his eyes and tried to focus on Josh.

"Sorry about that," Josh said. "I need time to sort some things out." He disappeared from view.

Ken spun around in the water looking for a way out. The retaining wall bulged out fifty feet to the south. As Ken swam for it, he heard tires spinning on gravel.

Maggie looked up from wiping the counter as the

front door burst open, nearly knocking the bell off its tether. Josh stepped in, his eyes wild, and stood in the center of the room, staring at the empty tables. His eyes settled on Maggie and he rushed toward her.

"Where's Luke?"

Maggie folded the rag and began wiping the counter. "Come have a seat. What's the hurry?"

Barbara came out of the kitchen and stared at them. "What's going on?"

Josh pointed at Maggie. "Where the hell's your boyfriend?"

Maggie stopped wiping. "You're scaring me, Josh. What's going on?"

Josh glanced around the empty diner again, then bent over and looked up the road. "Nothing. I just need to find Luke."

Barbara gave Maggie a nervous look. "Just settle down and tell us what's going on. Maybe we can help."

His voice dropped. "I don't have time for that. When did you see him last?"

Maggie thought for a moment. "Right after you left with Ken. He was going to go over to his father's farm to fetch something."

Josh leaned over the counter. "Was he coming back?"

She shrugged. "No, I don't think so. Wait. He said he was going to Ellsworth to pick up some baling twine for the hay-baler."

Josh shot a glance back out the window and up the road. "Give me a pencil. I need to leave a note for Ken."

Maggie handed him a pencil and her order pad. He

scribbled a quick note, tore it off the pad, folded it in half twice, and held it out to her. She tried to take the note, but he didn't release his grip.

"Can I trust you not to read this and give it to Ken?"

She started to pull it away.

"I'm serious. You can't read this."

Her eyes narrowed and she cocked her head. "If it's that gall darned important to you, sure. I can do that."

"It is. Thanks." He leaned over the counter and gave her a peck on the cheek, then headed for the door.

Barbara gave Maggie a frantic hands-up gesture and ran out the door behind Josh.

Josh reached the front of the car at the same time Barbara reached the passenger's side. She flung open the door and plopped into the front seat.

"What the hell are you doing?"

She looked straight ahead. "I'm going with you."

He shook his head and opened his own door. "The hell you are! Now get out."

She folded her arms and stared ahead.

"I don't have time for your foolishness. Get out!"

She didn't budge. Josh looked up the road and heard tires squeal on the corner coming off Route One. He jumped in and fired up the engine. "Fine, but don't say I didn't warn you."

The cloud of dust from Josh's departure was settling on the glass of the theater across the street when Ken skidded into the driveway. The Jeep bucked over the corner of the curb and rocked to a stop in front of the door. Ken jumped out and sprinted inside.

Maggie was still at the counter and might have laughed at his soggy pants and shoes if she wasn't still in shock.

"Have you seen Josh?" He blurted.

"Yeah." She nodded toward the road. "He just left with Barbara."

Ken cocked his head. "With Barbara?"

"Yeah. They left just a second ago. Josh was looking for Luke."

Ken spun on his heels, ran out the door, and jumped into the Jeep. His tires were spinning on the pavement before Maggie remembered the note. She rushed for the door, flung it open, and held the paper above her head. She waved and hollered to Ken. He didn't hear her, rounded the corner, and disappeared behind the town office building.

She stared at the empty parking area, then slowly closed the door and returned to the counter. Sitting on one of the stools, she placed the folded note on the Formica in front of her, and stared at it. She flicked the edge with her finger, peeking at the words inside, then slammed the flat of her hand down over the paper hiding it.

The diner was empty. The bright lights over the counter glared off her hand. She stared at the back of her hand for a moment, then sighed and removed it. Plucking the note off the counter, she quickly unfolded it.

She read slowly at first, her eyes moving faster as they took in the words.

Chapter Seventeen

Frenchman's Bay, two miles
Southeast of Mt. Desert Rock:

Seawater trickled down the gray paint on the pressure hull. Metallic clanks and muffled voices drifted into the control room from the passageways. Werner pulled at the collar of his damp, smelly wool sweater and kept his eyes on the Kapitan.

Kapitan Steiner drummed his fingers on the chart table, head tilted down, staring at the far bulkhead with his eyes glossy and far away. The diving mate and the steering *matrose* eyed each other nervously while seated at their stations, hands firm on the wheels in front of them.

The Kapitan's fingers stopped. He lifted his head from the periscope. "Surface the boat."

Werner reached for the red speaking tube, leaned into it, and gave the order. "All hands to stations. Surface the boat." He released his grasp, and spun the wheels beside the diving mate. "Positive buoyancy on all ballast tanks. Dive planes full up."

The Kapitan moved to the periscope. "Call out our depth."

Werner peered at the depth gauge. "Passing fifteen meters."

Kapitan Steiner put his face back to the scope. His feet shuffled in a circular motion in a slow dance with the periscope. He completed two rotations by the time the boat breached the surface, her nose lifting out at a twenty degree angle before settling level in the water.

"Secure the electric and start the diesel. I want a full charge on the batteries." He pushed the handles up and secured them. "Mr. Werner, place lookouts on the conning tower and man the two gun platforms. I don't want to get caught with my butt exposed while we repair the shaft seal."

"Sir." He turned and barked orders into the passageway. "Two-man crews on the twenty and thirty caliber. Two men on the tower and one on the bow."

The Kapitan turned toward the stern. "I'm going to check with the engineer. You supervise the tower and I'll be up shortly."

"Aye, aye, Sir."

Werner moved to the hatch and climbed the wet, slippery ladder. The wheel resisted his effort, but he leaned his weight into it and it released, spinning free. He remembered the water around the escape trunk too late and it poured down on him, soaking his already damp clothes. It was the first time he'd been asked to go on deck first and he was so eager to reach the fresh air, he'd forgotten to put on a rain slicker.

The afternoon air greeted him like an old love, warm

and familiar, yet fresh and exciting. Sunlight sparkled on the trunk and he squinted as he climbed into the sun's embrace. The mechanical racket of the boat faded beneath his feet, replaced by the wind pushing the surface of the water, the water breaking over the bow of the boat, and the boat's protective grates thumping in the slosh.

Men filed out of the trunk behind him and hurried to their stations, removing the canvas from the guns on the platforms in front of him and behind. They pressed up to the rails and lifted binoculars to their eyes. The bow watch scrambled over the tops of the seven mine release ports, a safety line in his hands.

"Lookouts report!"

"All clear." They reported in sequence.

Werner turned his back to the steel rail and the open ocean, his attention landward. Mt. Desert Rock loomed up to the north, its brown head protruding out of the white surf's collar and disappearing into the cloak of blue. The mainland was a distant dark streak on the horizon.

The Kapitan climbed out of the hatch, breathing hard, and nodded toward the stern. "I don't think a temporary seal will work. We'll have to lower the bow in the water and try to raise the stern to keep from flooding the boat while we make the repairs."

"Should we flood the forward compartments and move everyone into the bow?"

He pursed his lips. "Yes, but that won't lift the stern high enough. We'll need to turn the boat into the current and drop the hook. If we can attach to something solid, we might be able to winch the bow down enough to work on the shaft."

Werner rung some of the water out of his sweater. "The boat's in sixty meters of water and the depth soundings aren't very promising. The bottom appears solid, but doesn't have any big outcrops of rock to latch onto."

Kapitan Steiner shrugged, then leaned over the open hatch. "All stop! Drop the anchor and pay out five times the depth in scope!" He then turned back to Werner. "We'll just have to find something solid. Let's drag the hook."

"Aye, Sir." came the reply from below.

A muffled clunk emanated from below the bow decking, then the rat-a-tat of chain splaying over the metal guides. The screw stopped turning at the same time and the boat began to swing in the current. The bow edged to the starboard, being pushed by the waves. The boat gently rocked in the swells that increased in size as she exposed more of her beam to the wind and current.

The bow watch clipped his safety line to the radio antenna support cable and knelt down to keep from toppling overboard. The heavy anchor line behind the chain continued to pay out as the boat turned full broadside to the waves.

"How much time do they need for repair?" Werner asked.

"Not long. Maybe half an hour, but unless we get it out of the water, we can't do anything without flooding the boat."

The anchor chain stopped, then began lifting out of the water as it came taut. When the bow swung into the current, the anchor had skipped across the bottom, causing the chain to jerk up and down in the water as the hook caught and released.

Werner put a hand on the bulkhead to steady himself, then turned to look at the Kapitan. The Kapitan stared at the chain, but didn't speak. The bow and chain continued to jerk and tug, like a huge fish nibbling at the hook.

Suddenly, the chain lifted clear of the water and the bow dipped and dove. The stern swung, pushed by the ebbing tide, wind, and waves. The bow dropped lower in the water, but not by more than a few degrees.

The Kapitan shouted to the control room. "Start the port diesel and take us back dead slow!"

The single screw began turning and the boat inched backward. The single engine pulled the boat, unevenly, turning the stern.

"Compensate for the swing with five degrees of right rudder!" the Kapitan shouted.

The boat straightened and the bow dipped as the engine whined against the strain of the chain.

"She's holding," Werner whispered.

The anchor lost its grip.

The chain went slack and the bow snapped out of the water flinging the men to the deck and rails. Werner nearly tumbled into the open hatch. The Kapitan grabbed him by the sweater, and – at the same time grabbed the rail with his free hand, preventing Werner from disappearing below.

The anchor caught once more and the bow dipped again, lurching the crew in the opposite direction. The bow watch was flung to the deck and lay spread eagled on the grating, hanging onto the mine bay doors, while the boat steadied itself.

The engine droned on, but the boat remained stationary in the water. Then her nose dipped, and the waves broke over her bow and washed up the deck. The bow watch crawled backward on all fours to escape the onslaught of water.

"We've hooked something solid. Secure the port engine and reel in the anchor! Do it slow and steady!" the Kapitan shouted.

Werner clung to the steel armored plates surrounding the tower and wiped his forehead on the upper arm of his sweater. "Do you think she'll hold?"

"We won't know until we try," the Kapitan said.

The line fed into the housing, disappearing into the bow of the boat as she moved forward and infinitesimally lower in the water with each turn of the windlass.

The Kapitain straightened his cap, standing shoulder to shoulder with Werner. "The windlass wasn't designed for this. The force of the boat could pull it from its mounting right out through the pressure hull."

Werner swallowed hard. "What then?"

"We'll find out how hard the bottom really is."

The windlass continued swallowing the anchor chain, which became steeper as it moved into the water, dragging the boat downward. The hum of the electric motor on the windlass deepened in pitch as the load increased. The strain slowed the uptake of chain and the chain occasionally popped as it slipped on the capstan.

"She won't take much more," Werner said.

"A bit more," the Kapitan replied.

The stern rose higher in the water, the tops of the screws just breaking the surface.

"Just a little more. You can do it," the Kapitan encouraged.

The chain entered the boat a centimeter at a time.

"Sir, the windlass is overheating!" a voice cried up from the trunk in the conning tower.

"Just another meter," the Kapitan urged.

A loud squeal from beneath the bow, then a clank and silence.

"Sir, the motor froze up."

"Can you fix it?"

"No, Sir. It got so hot it fused the coil. The brake will hold it, but it's under quite a strain."

The Kapitan twisted around and looked at the stern. The propellers were half out of the water, but the seal was a third of a meter away from the surface.

The Kapitan slapped his hand on the steel plates. "So close."

"Could we go into shallow water and let her ground out at low tide?" Werner asked.

"That might work, but we'd be stuck there for hours, completely exposed. We'd be better off staying with the one screw."

"There must to be a way to lift it just a little bit more," Werner said.

"You're welcome to think of something, but I'm fresh out of ideas."

"At least the winch held. I'd hate to be out there in our rubber rafts." He paused and smiled. "That's it!"

"What's it?"

"The rafts. We can use them like salvage bags to lift the stern the rest of the way."

The Kapitain appeared puzzled. "How?"

"We can attach a line to a raft, run the line under the stern of the boat and attach it to another raft and snug the line. When we inflate them, the buoyancy of the rafts will lift the boat."

The Kapitan's face brightened. "Perhaps if they were placed three quarters of the way between the tower and the shaft seal. But we'll need quite a few rafts." He nodded to Werner. "It's your plan – get to it."

Werner saluted. "Right away!"

He slid down the rails of the ladder, landing hard on the deck of the control room, and paused to gain his footing. He rushed toward the stern, where the rafts were stored in lockers near the engine room. Oscar Schuch grabbed his arm as he passed.

"Is there anything we can do?"

Werner shook off the hand. "If you can tie a decent knot, then follow me."

Schuch and Franks rolled off their bunks and clambered along behind Werner. He reached the raft storage lockers, flipped open the hasps, pulled the rubber rafts out, and tossed them onto the deck.

"Well, what are you waiting for? Get these up on deck."

Schuch hesitated. "Are we abandoning the boat?"

Werner smiled. "Not quite."

Each grabbing an armful of the smelly bundles of rubber, they headed for the hatch and piled them at the bottom of the ladder. Mr. Franks climbed to the top, Schuch to the middle, and Werner remained at the bottom to pass the individual rafts upward. The Kapitan tossed them to a gunner's mate on the rear platform and he, in turn, tossed then onto the stern decking.

Werner pointed to the diving mate. "Cut eight coils of 8mm line into twenty meter lengths and bring them topside."

The afternoon sun seemed warmer to Werner as he emerged for the second time. The day could work out after all. Not only might they repair the boat, but his idea would solve the problem.

"Fishing boat two points off the starboard bow! She's heading right at us!" a chilling voice came from the bow.

The Kapitan swivelled around, plastering his binoculars to his eyes.

"Has she spotted us?" Werner asked.

"If she hasn't, she will in a minute," the Kapitan said.

"Can we sink her?"

"She's out of range of our guns and our stern is away from her."

"Does she have a radio?" Werner asked.

The Kapitan stared through the glass, not speaking. The boat turned ten degrees away from them to pass to their east, seaward. "I can see a whip antennae above her wheelhouse. We'll have to assume we've already been reported."

Ken slammed on the brakes and skidded to a stop in front of his office. The fuel reports slid off the front seat and landed on the floor in front of the passenger seat. He rushed in to find Major Smith seated at his desk with Petty Officer Durning at his side, holding a sheaf of papers. They both looked up in unison.

He slogged across the room and gave the Major a quick salute. Before he could speak the Major said, "You could've come back and changed before setting out to investigate."

Attention drawn to his soaked pants and shoes momentarily distracted him. "I will. I mean I did." He shook his head. "It doesn't matter. I found out who the spy is."

The Major leaned forward. "I guarantee suspense will be lost on me. Who?"

Ken swallowed. "It's one of my friends. Josh Harriman."

The Major's lid fissures narrowed. "We have proof, do we?"

"Yes. No. Sort of."

"Well, what is it? Are you sure or are you just guessing?"

Ken paced in front of the desk. "Josh is..." He struggled to think of a way to talk about his friend. How to betray him. How to convince this stranger that his friend was the enemy.

"Josh has been burning a lot more fuel than he should. He could be using his smuggling business as a cover to explain the late night trips."

The Major leaned his elbows on the table. "That doesn't make him a traitor."

"I know, I know. But I found this on his boat." Ken

pulled the flattened carton out of his waistband and plunked it on the desk.

The Major leaned close; Durning recoiled as if it were a snake. "This was on his boat?"

"Yes, and the part that came out of it was attached to his engine."

The Major tilted the box toward him. "Well, then I guess I need to speak with him. Where can we find him?"

Ken laid both hands flat on the table. "That's the problem. I confronted him on his boat and well... I ended up in the water while he took off."

The Major reached for the telephone. "What does he drive? Where does he live?" He began dialing numbers. "Come on, fill me in."

Ken told him everything he thought was pertinent, though his stomach ached as he talked about his friend. He began to have doubts as he spoke, but he didn't break rhythm. The Major relayed the information to Portland as he received it, then hung up the telephone and walked over to Ken. He rested one hand on his shoulder.

"This has to be tough, finding out your friend betrayed all of us. But you did well and at the end of the day, you'll know you did right."

Ken nodded, but didn't speak.

Major Smith hung up the telephone. "The F.B.I. will be heading up the investigation, but they won't be able to mobilize from Boston until the morning. That leaves it up to us in the meantime." He tightened his grip on Ken's shoulder. "What do you say we find your friend and get him to come in without getting hurt?"

Ken looked at his wet trousers. "Yeah, I've done so well so far."

"Go on – get changed and we'll start looking."

The telephone rang.

Petty officer Durning answered and turned to Major Smith. "It's Brunswick. A fishing trawler reported seeing a U-Boat off Mt. Desert Rock. They're diverting the K-14 from its regular patrol to investigate."

"The K-14? What's that?" Ken asked.

The Major rose from his chair. "It's a dirigible out of Lakehurst."

"A dirigible? What's that supposed to do?"

"They're armed with a thirty-caliber machine gun and depth charges. They'll give the sub a run for its money."

Chapter Eighteen

Frenchman's Bay, two miles
south of Mt. Desert Rock:

Werner knelt on the stern deck, his wool cap snug over his ears. The grates covering the pressure hull bit into his knees as he leaned over to hang onto one of the rafts. It dangled against the side of the boat, the swells periodically nipping at its terminus. The raft he held was tied to a second one by a section of the eight-millimeter cord. The swells rocked it to and fro, slapping the rubber against the side of the hull with a sticky, wet kissing sound. Two divers bobbed in the water, the brown twill cotton covering their rubber suits glistening in the sun like seal pelts.

One of the divers latched onto the free end of the line, pulled it underwater, and swam it to the far side of the boat. Another seaman reached for it with a pike pole, hooking the line and holding it steady as the diver lashed the raft in place just below the surface. Four other deck hands prepared more rafts and lines on the stern in front of Mr. Werner.

Werner remained on his knees, slid to the center of the boat, lifted the stern hatch cover, and shouted down to the engineer: "Tap a high pressure hose into the line to the blow system. Then run it topside through this hatch so we can fill the rafts."

"That system has too much pressure; they'll blow the valves on the rafts," a voice replied from below.

Too much pressure. How can we modify it? "Can you splice in a regulator, maybe from one of the welding torches?"

A brief silence. Werner lowered his ear toward the opening. "Yes. I think so, but it might be easier to tie into the emergency air breathing system, it's one tenth the pressure."

"Good. Get at it – and run it up on deck when you've got it done."

He left the hatch open, rose, and moved forward. His knees were sore from the decking and the muscles in the small of his back were in spasm, causing him to walk hunched over. The men had finished lashing the rest of the rafts together and were lowering them over the side. The Kapitan had both elbows on the armored plates of the conning tower, a calm expression on his face.

"You're going to have to fill the bladders in those rafts equally or they'll slip out," Kapitan Steiner said.

Werner placed a hand over the pain in his back and headed away, mumbling under his breath. "I'm not a fool."

"What was that, Mr. Werner?"

"Yes, Sir, I'm on it."

The light was fading fast as the sun kissed the horizon.

It had turned orange, lighting up the clouds that hung on either side to almost the same brilliance, and then ran across the water to the stern of the boat.

Werner stepped quickly onto the sunlit deck. "Get that last raft attached. We're running out of light. If we don't get moving soon we'll never make the rendevous."

The diver clipped the last raft in place and Werner slid the high pressure hose over the side. "Just fill it about a quarter full and then I'll pass the air hose to the other side so we can even the lift."

The diver nodded, his glass faceplate glinting in the setting sunlight.

The Kapitan climbed down from the tower and walked out onto the stern to stand beside Werner. "It seems to be working. You've done well."

Werner passed the hose to the other side. "If the rafts don't break free or slide back, it should." He released the hose. "Maybe we should rig a second pressure line?"

"The divers will be done before the engineer could do that."

Werner straightened a kink in the hose. "So if you marry my mother, does that mean I'll have to relive this voyage anytime you have friends over to visit?"

The Kapitan smiled and stifled a laugh. "I hope you'll have a family of your own and will only have to suffer on the holidays, but that's your duty as the younger generation. To tolerate the torments of our stories, us living in the past, when we find it too boring to live in the present."

Werner continued to pass the hose back and forth as

the bladders filled and lifted the stern. "Permission to ask a personal question."

The Kapitan cocked his head. "If you're going to ask if I love your mother? I do. If not, ask away."

Werner pulled the hose up and tossed it back over the far side; it struck the diver in the shoulder as it landed. The man flinched and so did Werner. "Am I that transparent?" The Kapitan eeked out a grin. "Fine then. How about. 'What happens to my mother if the allies take repercussions on the officers and their families after the war?'"

"We won't marry until this war's over. One way or the other."

"The packing gland is out of the water!" came a call from the stern.

Werner leaned over the open hatch. "The gland is dry. Start your repairs." Then he began to coil the hose and feed it back down into the boat. A sharp clinking noise echoed through the hull and then rose up from the hatch as a hammer fell on steel. "It shouldn't be long now."

The Kapitan removed his cap and rubbed his hand over his thinning, damp hair, and turned toward the north. Darkness was descending on the hills and peaks of the islands. The horizon melded into the sky. A single oval, gray cloud stuck out from the rest. He stared at it. "Zeppelin!"

"What? Did you say Zeppelin?" Werner asked.

The Kapitan pointed at the cloud moving slowly against the wind. "There! That's a Zeppelin!" He paused. "Prepare to dive."

"Sir, we can't dive. The anchor is fast aground, the stern is out of the water, and the hull is open to the sea."

The Kapitan didn't listen; he leaned over the hatch and shouted down. "Seal up the packing gland. Don't try to finish it. You've got two minutes."

"We can't get it done that fast," came the reply.

"Two minutes and we're going down. Done or not!" He pointed to one of the crew near the base of the tower. "Get a sledge and wait at the bow to free the chain break. Don't release it until it until I give the signal."

The man saluted and rushed forward. Werner glanced at the rafts. "We'll need at least one of those to get the *Abwehr* agents ashore."

"Salvage what you can. But my first priority is the boat."

The Blimp loomed larger. It hung in the air about a hundred meters above the surface of the sea, pointed directly at the boat. Large black letters lay on her nose, "K-14 U.S. Air Force."

"Rack the guns! If you need to fire, don't bother to lead her. Shoot for the main body," the Kapitan shouted.

Werner watched her come. She crawled across the sky, her gray color turning silver in the setting sun "What does she expect to do? Our guns will shred her."

"Do you see those barrels on the side of her car?"

"I see two, no four," Werner counted.

The Kapitan touched his shoulder. "Those would be depth-charges, and they won't have to be too clever to put them on us if we're still on the surface." He paused. "One pass is all she'll need."

Werner stuck his head back into the hatch. "How long, damn it?"

"The bolts are stripped. We're re-threading them. Five more minutes."

"Thread every other one and make it two and a half," Werner shouted.

The Kapitan turned and headed toward the conning tower. "Looks like she'll get that one pass."

Werner leaned back on his haunches. "Your orders, Kapitan?"

"Release the chain once the seal is packed, we'll let the anchor pay out all the way to the weaker safety link at the end. It should shear off and leave the chain to the sea. Save a raft if you can, but watch your ass."

Werner looked up toward the blimp. "You too, Sir."

The blimp's engines droned low and steady, accented by the zing of the high-speed propellers. The barrel of a larger gun stuck out the stern of the blimp like a stinger hanging off the carapace of a bee.

Two-man teams still operated the thirty calibers on the platforms. They cast quick glances at the Kapitan as he moved passed. The gunners tightened their grips on the weapons, constantly changing the angle of the muzzles as the airship neared. The whine of the huge propellers grew as the sun continued to slip from the sky. The orange light disappeared from the decking to be replaced with a dull blue color. The divers were back on deck and doffing their gear, stuffing it through the hatches as quickly as they were able.

"Faster! Get that gear stowed!" Werner shouted.

Werner pointed to the lead diver. "Hans, get a gaff and hook one of the four-man rafts. Take out your knife and be ready to cut it free. Tell the others to do the same with the rest of the rafts. Don't worry about saving them." He took a brief look at the blimp. "After you cut them free, pull the lines out so they can't foul the screws."

"Aye, Sir," Hans responded.

A loud blast!

The bow platform gun fired.

"Hold your fire, damn it! They're out of range!" the Kapitan shouted.

"How long on that seal?" Werner yelled back.

"Almost there."

"Make it quick! All hell is about to rain down on us!"

The blimp eased over in front of the bow, making it impossible for the U-boat to use the stern gun. They were going to let the wind carry them over the boat and drop their ordinance. The boat was a target at anchor. A sitting duck.

"Fire!" Kapitan Steiner shouted from behind the metal plates of the conning tower.

The gun let loose her initial blast.

Werner watched. His brows curled as the blimp didn't react to the fire. "What the hell?" he whispered.

The blimp didn't explode, didn't fall from the sky, didn't even waver. The forward gunner continued to fire. Then the fabric of the blimp quivered just a bit as the rounds tore through the cloth and began to release the gas.

"Keep firing!" the Kapitan shouted.

"The packing is resealed as best we can with half the bolts," came a voice from below.

Werner spun on his haunches. "Cut those lines!"

The divers leaned over the sides, hanging onto the decking and sawed at the lines with their knives. The first line snapped and the raft on the far side popped to the surface like a cork out of a champagne bottle. The others followed in quick succession. The boat's stern dropped just as the forward gun went quiet.

"Verdammt!" Werner's head snapped around. The thirty-caliber had jammed. The gunners mate slapped his hand against the mechanism and shook the slide to no effect.

Out of his peripheral vision, Werner caught the diver pulling the raft aboard. "Kapitan! The seal is secure!" Then he rushed toward the bow to help with the gun.

"Release the brake to the windlass!" Kapitan Steiner shouted.

The blimp was losing altitude, but the wind had swung her stern to them and their gun opened up. The lead hit the water in front of the bow and wound a path along the anchor line and onto the bow. The first few bullets to hit the boat ripped into the decking and struck the sailor with the sledgehammer in the right hip. It spun him around and his leg landed on the deck four feet away. He teetered for an instant, dropped the sledge onto the deck and fell into the sea. His body bobbed on the surface like a discarded orange peel.

Werner tore his eyes away, forcing his thoughts to the welfare of the boat. His eyes locked on the sledge laying on the deck between the bullet holes. He rushed toward it.

With the rafts cut away, the screws were back in the

water, but just barely. "Get the diesels on line and full ahead on both engines!" the Kapitan shouted.

Werner bumped into the conning tower as he sprinted passed. The gunner had freed up the slide and it belched out another burst, hitting the car on the underbelly of the blimp. Glass shattered in the windows, and one of the crew manning the gun was knocked off his feet.

"Shoot at the cloth, damn you!" Kapitan Steiner shouted.

The far side of the conning tower fell into shadow and suddenly became much darker. The last of the sun dipped below the horizon as Werner scooped up the sledge.

On the dirigible, another man filled the fallen gunner's place and its gun opened up again. The lead landed wide of the bow and then swung in on the conning tower. The bullets thumped off the heavy metal plates and ricocheted seaward. The diesels roared to life and Werner flung back the hatch to the windlass compartment. The brake handle stuck up above the windlass between the pressure hull and the boat's skin. He dropped the head of the sledge into the space and gave the handle a wack. It didn't budge.

"There's too much strain on the chain. Keep the boat moving forward!" Werner shouted. The two opposing guns continued to exchange fire as he gave it another wack. This time the handle moved, but not enough to disengage the brake from the gear. Werner repositioned his feet Just as another blast from the K-14 ripped along the deck grates, passing centimeters from his feet. He leaned away, almost dropping the sledge.

He quickly braced his feet again and hit the handle with all his might. This time the handle clinked free easily and the force of his swing allowed the sledge to continue past the handle. It clanked into the pressure hull and flipped out of his hands.

The bow rose, flinging Werner backwards onto the hard decking; Then it swung to port with the sudden release of buoyancy. Werner didn't wait to see where it fell, instead he slammed down the hatch and secured it. The blimp had lost a hundred feet of its altitude and loomed close overhead. The propellers had caught the water and moved the boat forward, farther under the blimp so its gunner could no longer hit the boat.

Werner regained his footing and headed toward the tower, just as the blimp released the first depth charge.

The high explosive hit the water thirty meters away, amid ship, and exploded as it struck the surface. The boat rocked to the side and rose up with the force of the charge. Werner flew toward the far side of the boat, landing hard on his side and rolling over the edge.

His hand caught a recessed cleat as he tumbled over. He hung by one arm as the blimp released a second canister. He watched it fall, silent and slow. It disappeared behind the conning tower and exploded. The boat rocked forward this time, Werner's weight swinging on the wet cleat. The metal slipped from his grasp just as a strong hand grabbed his wrist.

He looked up into the eyes of the Kapitan.

"We're not ready to get rid of you yet, Mr. Werner."

The Kapitan leaned back, using his body's weight to drag Werner up. Werner scrambled against the side of the boat with his feet. Once he reached the decking, he collapsed beside the Kapitan.

"We need to get below," Werner wheezed.

Kapitan Steiner nodded toward the blimp drifting behind the boat. It looked like a soft, gray raisin. The stern had collapsed over the car, blocking the gun and preventing the release of more charges. It tipped nose up and sank with the last sliver of sunlight into the bay.

Werner climbed to his feet and looked at the distorted mushroom resting on the water. The stern gun fired into it, deflating it more.

"Halt your fire!" the Kapitan shouted. "Save your ammo. They're done for." He looked back at Werner. "You in one piece?"

Werner ran his hands over his body. "Thanks to you, yes."

"Good, because we need to get out of here."

Werner gazed back at the sinking blimp. "What's the rush now?"

"They would have reported our position to Brunswick Naval Air. They should have flying boats, fighters and destroyers headed our way by now."

"Where to?"

"It's time to play dead for awhile. We've got a good charge on the batteries. We're going to head to an area with lots of submerged ledge and put her on the bottom. We'll hide in the shadows until it's time to drop off our cargo."

"What about the men in the Zeppelin? Shouldn't we try to help them?"

Kapitan Steiner looked toward shore away from the sinking airship. "Not my worry."

Chapter Nineteen

The sun had slipped from the sky half an hour earlier and the moon was now in its full glory, catching the rays from the sun that would become tomorrow, reflecting them onto the darkened landscape. A promise for tomorrow. An inkling of possibility. A nightlight for those willing to dream.

Josh's Packard sat backed into a gravel turn-off, the lights out, and the top down. Barbara's peach sundress appeared off-white in the moonlight. The bodice seams strained to contain her; lower, the cloth billowed out in small pleats and wound over her knees, disappearing toward her feet. Josh looked at her face. She smiled at him, her pale skin accented by the black, waves of hair that curled in below her ears.

"Do you like what you see?"

Josh flushed and turned his attention to the steering column. "You know I do. That's not the problem."

She placed a hand on the seat between them. "Then what is? You know I like you. I always have."

"Yeah, I know."

"So why don't you do something about it?"

Josh turned his head away and looked up the road. "I want to, but..."

Barbara slid her hand closer and touched the side of his thigh. "Who is it this week? The new girl at the diner?"

Josh swallowed hard. "No, nothing like that."

Her eyes narrowed. "I think you want to settle down. You're not as fancy-free as you try to make people think."

Josh moved his gaze halfway back to hers. "What makes you think so?"

Her fingers crept up his leg and she placed her hand on his thigh. "When the gang isn't around, you act different around me. Kinder, gentle even. We could have a life together. A good life."

His eyes finally worked back to hers. "Yes, I'm sure we could. You certainly seem to be able to overlook my faults and shortcomings."

A smile worked up her face. "Of course. That's because we're friends first."

"There's no doubt about that. You've always been a true friend, and that's more than I can say for most people."

"What's wrong with that then?"

"There's nothing wrong with that."

"Then there's only one direction to go."

He sighed. "Perhaps you're right."

He placed his hand on hers and squeezed gently. "You are full of surprises, aren't you?"

Her smile widened. "It might be fun to find out for

yourself." She looked up the dark road. "What are we doing sitting out here anyway?"

Josh swung his attention back to the road. "Waiting for Luke."

"Luke, Why? And why here?"

Car headlights lit up the road.

Josh spun his head toward the oncoming car.

"Luke has to go this way if he's going to Ellsworth." He squinted at the approaching lights. "Is that him? Can you tell?"

"I can't tell." She shaded her eyes with her right hand. "Besides, you're assuming he's going to Ellsworth."

"Well, that's what Maggie said."

An old Plymouth sped around the curve, its right rear wheel dropping off the pavement and kicking up dust.

"Why don't you tell me why finding him is so gosh darn important?"

Josh turned toward her, tightened his grip on her hand, and locked eyes with her. "I think Luke's the spy."

Her face brightened. "Why can't you be serious?"

He continued to stare at her. "I am serious. He's the one. He's the spy."

She shook her head. "You're having fun with me."

His face remained stern.

She frowned as she watched his solemn face. "What could make you say such a hurtful thing?"

He told her about the nights he'd gone to use the boat, but found it gone. He told her about the fuel pump and his run-in with Ken. She sat quietly, listening, shaking her head.

"It could've been Joel. He has access to the boat and could start it without a key."

Josh hadn't considered that. He thought for a moment, then shook his head. "No, it's Luke."

"You just want it to be Luke. That would make you feel superior. You've always been jealous of him."

He spoke softly. "I don't want it to be him. I just know it is him."

"Fine. Believe what you want, but you're wrong. We'll talk to him. I'm sure he can straighten things out. Just promise me you won't do anything stupid until we have a chance to hear his side. "

Another car approached, moving fast. The engine whined in the distance, its headlights dancing on the road as it bounced along.

"That looks like a Hudson."

Josh leaned forward and started the engine. The car sped by without slowing. "That's him. That's his car."

Josh flipped on the headlamps and shifted into gear. Gravel spun from under the tires as he swung the wheel and climbed onto the road, following Luke.

The moonlight flowed over the stern, washed over the Kapitan and Werner leaning on the armored plates of the conning tower, and illuminated the boat's path toward Hancock Point. The wind had subsided with the setting sun, allowing moonlight to flicker on the undulating surface, creating a pockmarked water road.

"Do you think any of the men in the Zeppelin survived?" Werner asked.

Kapitan Steiner hid his hands under his arms. "I told you. That's not my concern."

"We could have at least stayed long enough to see if they reached the rafts we cut free."

"That might have been all the time the Americans needed to get a fighter plane on top of us. No, we had to leave them."

Werner rubbed the top of the steel plates. "It seems cruel."

"That's what war is. Those who don't realize that and act accordingly won't survive."

"I think you can do your duty and act with compassion and some sense of fairness at the same time."

"Is that what they taught you at University? Fairness? Compassion?" He twisted his head, stretching his neck. "I've been on one boat or another for four years. Believe me, there's no room for classroom ethics. We do whatever needs to be done to accomplish the mission and get home with as many men still alive as possible. Nothing less."

"But what if it didn't compromise the mission? What if you could save lives and still do what you came to do?"

"Not possible. You can't save your enemy to fight you another day, and you know we can't bring prisoners aboard this boat."

The faint silhouette of a high-sided, slow-moving ship edged along the shore, its shape revealed by the lights of the town behind it.

"Sir, do you see the ship?"

"Yes. Yes, I do." He removed his hands and grabbed the steel in front of him. "This will be a good lesson for you."

Werner looked out at the ship, then back at the Kapitan. "What kind of lesson? That's a small civilian passenger ship."

"When a fox wants to raid the hen house, he doesn't knock on the door and ask the farmer's permission." He turned toward the hatch. "Lookouts below! Prepare to submerge the boat!"

Werner followed the Kapitan and slid down the ladder after him, pausing to secure the watertight hatch behind. The darkness of night was replaced by the red lamps in the control room that protected the crews' scotopic vision. Mr. Franks milled about at the entrance to the control room, but stayed out. He wore a long wool coat, buttoned to the neck, his collar up to protect him from the cold, moist, metal hull of the boat.

"Take the boat to periscope depth, Mr. Werner."

"Aye, Kapitan." Werner turned toward the diving mate. "Flood the ballast tanks, half down on the dive planes, and make your depth twenty meters."

"Twenty meters, aye," came the reply.

"Our heading, Sir?" Werner asked.

The Kapitan drew a straight line with a grease pencil against the parallel rules he'd laid on the chart. "Heading of three, three, zero magnetic. Full ahead on the port electric, let's not put a strain on the other one yet." He drew a small circle on the chart. "That makes our heading zero, six, five after the attack."

Werner's neck snapped around. "Attack? What attack?"

"The Yanks have every asset they can spare up there

looking for us. I'm going to give them something else to do for a while."

"But they're civilians, Sir."

"I prefer to think of them as the foundation of their army. They make the war possible with their little jobs back home. Building tanks and guns, paying their taxes to the government. Breeding soldiers for the cause. No, they're not just civilians – there's no such thing in war."

Werner turned his back to the Kapitan. The diving mate and steering *matrose* stole nervous glances at each other. The Kapitan replaced his wool cap with a waterproof rain hat, then lifted the periscope. Streams of water rushed down the sides, over his hands and splattered on the deck at his feet. He put his eyes to the optics and swivelled the scope.

"One-half kilometer and then we put our stern to her." He leaned back. "I'd like you to take the shot, Mr. Werner."

Werner didn't move. "I'd rather not, if it's all the same to you, Sir."

"It's not all the same to me. You're the second on this boat. If you expect to reap the bounty of the Fatherland, you must first plunge your hands into the soil to plant the seed." He nodded toward Werner. "Come on – this is no different than sinking a merchant ship. I'd prefer to sink a troop carrier, but this is what we've been given."

Werner moved toward the periscope. The Kapitan removed his oilskin hat and stuck it on Werner's head. "Oberleutnant Werner has the con."

Werner adjusted the hat and held onto the handles, paused, then leaned forward to place his eyes on the scope. He clicked the magnification and took a relative bearing on the target. "Gradual one-eighty turn, slow to headway speed."

"Aye, dead slow, change heading to one, five, zero magnetic," came the response.

"Easy on the turn. We don't want to create a wake!" Werner snapped.

"Yes, Sir. Sorry, Sir," the steering *matrose* responded.

The boat continued to swing, and Werner rotated with it until his body faced the stern, his eyes still glued to the optics. "All stop on the electric. Prepare to back toward the target."

The Kapitan leaned on the table and watched his future son in-law orient the boat. Werner kept his head to the scope, and turned enough to see a faint smile on the Kapitan's face.

"Load the stern tubes." Werner said.

The Kapitan walked to the speaking tube and passed on the order.

"Target estimated at one thousand meters. We'll send two fish with a five-degree spread on my command."

"That ship's unarmed. Send one torpedo and keep the other in reserve," the Kapitan corrected.

Werner turned to look at the Kapitan. "Aren't you afraid I'll miss?"

"If you do, I'll have the back-up tube for the second shot. Besides, if she's hit only once, she'll sink slower and will have more time to send distress calls."

Werner put his eyes back to the periscope and whispered to himself, "We haven't salted my mother's shoes yet."

Kneading his hands on the periscope handles, Werner forced a blink to clear his eyes. "Electric, dead slow astern."

"Dead slow, aye."

The boat lurched as the shaft engaged and they eased backward. The ship before them appeared to be some type of bulky high-sided ferry. A ramp had been fitted to its bow and stern to off-load cars and trucks, but it had an enclosed cabin above the auto deck. In the light of the moon, he couldn't read her name. Lights dotted the windows and shadowy figures moved inside.

Werner pulled the stopwatch from under his sweater and grasped it in one hand as he adjusted the focus with his other. "Prepare to fire. Hold. Hold." His raised the watch higher with each word. "Hold. Now! Fire tube one."

The Kapitan relayed the order and the tube hissed. Werner clicked the stopwatch and pinned his eyes to the periscope.

"Surface the boat, and be ready to start the diesel," the Kapitan commanded.

Werner spun around. "What?"

"We're going topside to see this." The Kapitan pushed past, plucking the hat from Werner's head and tossing it on the chart table as he went. He shoved a pair of binoculars against Werner's chest. "Come on."

"What if I miss?"

The Kapitan was already at the ladder and the boat leveling at the surface. "We can shoot the second one from the tower if necessary."

Werner looked at the watch, then hurried up the

ladder onto the conning tower. His eyes adjusted quickly, having been in the red light. The civilian ship's engine droned in the distance. Voices, faint and soft, drifted over the water. He put the binoculars to his eyes. The ship was close. Much closer than it appeared in the scope. He could see details through the windows. Men and women, hats, a man smoking a pipe.

He froze as he watched another man lift a small infant in the air over his head and set it on his shoulders.

The sky exploded in brilliant light. The sound rocked the ship a second later. The torpedo tore into the stern section, sending water and bright light in all directions. The ship's windows were momentarily hidden by the flash.

The night swallowed up the explosion, and darkness returned. Screams. High pitched wails of terror streaked across the water. Werner searched for the man with the infant, but couldn't find him. Debris landed in the water, splashing within fifty meters of the U-boat. Some of it floated and bobbed on the surface; most disappeared into the deep.

Alarms, warning alarms, then a loud speaker. "Abandon ship! Abandon ship! All crew members aid with loading the lifeboats."

"Good shot, Werner. You hit her in the engine room. She'll lose steerage and power, but the batteries should let her get off a distress call."

Werner didn't respond. Instead, he kept searching the decks. Three crew members struggled with a wooden lifeboat, but it appeared the cables had fouled and they couldn't lower it. The ship was already taking on a significant list to its port side, lifting the far rail into view. Cars began to side across the lower deck and smash into each other. People dodged the carnage and clung to rails and bulkheads. A few on the upper deck had tan, bulky life vests on, but most did not.

The lights in the windows flickered, then went out. A multitude of voices rose in unified panic as the lights extinguished. Then their voices merged in chaotic chatter.

"All ahead full on the diesel. Make our course zero, six, five." the Kapitan shouted into the hatch.

The U-boat pulled away from the ship as people leapt from her sides into the chilly Maine water. No life rafts had been put in the water. Even though it was summer, Werner knew they wouldn't last long in the water.

The Kapitan grasped Werner's shoulder. "Time to get below. We have a delivery to make."

Chapter Twenty

Petty Officer Durning leaned over his desk and picked up the phone on the first ring. "Machias Shore Patrol." He paused. "I'll get him, Sir, stand by."

Ken slipped off the corner of his desk and headed for the telephone. Who the hell was calling now?

"It isn't for you, Sir. It's for the Major."

Ken stopped in mid-stride.

Major Smith dropped his feet off the desk and stepped around Ken to the phone. "Major Smith… I see. Any men lost? Where exactly? Yes, I know the spot." His face tightened and his eyes darted toward Ken. "Do you have any ships in the area? Yes that makes sense to me, too. I'll do that." He handed the telephone back to the Petty Officer.

Ken leaned back on the corner of his desk. "Anything we should know about?"

"The K-14 reported a U-boat sighting just before dark. They were going to engage it and haven't been heard from since."

"Son of a bitch!" Ken's chin dropped. Things are

getting out of hand, he thought. "Do you think they got her?"

The Major didn't answer.

"I heard you ask about ships. Do we have any in the area?" Durning asked.

The Major seemed lost in thought. "What? No. That's not what I was interested in. The U-boat apparently attacked a Nova Scotian passenger ship somewhere near Southwest Harbor."

Ken rose from the desk. His legs felt detached, far away, yet his brain started spinning faster. "What do they hear from her?"

"They received an initial distress call and nothing since. Boats are on the way, but who knows when they'll get there."

Ken's brain shifted into overdrive. He leaned over his desk, pulled open the bottom drawer, and withdrew a folded navigational chart. He spread it out on the table as the other men stood beside him. "Did they say where the K-14 sighted the U-boat?"

The Major put his finger on the chart. "Two miles southwest of Mt. Desert Rock."

Ken moved the tips of his fingers over the chart. "The ferry routes would go through here, so the U-boat would've had a straight shot landward from the K-14 sighting."

The Major nodded. "That's right."

"Why would it be headed landward? If it was on a mine-laying mission, it should've gone south toward Portland and the shipping lanes. If it was trying to escape our vessels, it would've headed for open water. What's it doing coming toward shore?"

The Major drummed his fingers on the desk. "That's solid thinking. Why indeed?" He paused. "Perhaps it has a different mission. Something that involves your friend Josh."

"That makes more sense. They could easily head toward Port Clyde or anywhere around Bar Harbor." Ken's head snapped up. "A diversion. That's what the ship attack was about."

The Major smiled. "Sounds like you agree with the brass in Boston. They want us to start running the roads, looking for anything suspicious, and notifying the local law to keep a sharp eye on things. They'll talk to the State boys and put them on alert."

"Durning, start calling the town sheriffs. Tell them we're looking for Josh Halley and his Hudson. I'll get you the tag number. I'm going to give the Major a tour of the coast and see if we can't find him ourselves." Ken paced behind the desk, wondering what he might be forgetting.

The Major tried to tuck in the shorter shirt Durning had loaned him. "Command has cancelled all leave and put all stations on full readiness. We can check in back here when we get to Bucksport."

Ken looked at the ill-fitting shirt on the Major. He felt conflicted; they were after one of his best friends, yet the chase had his adrenaline surging. "I'd loan you one of mine, but I seem to have gone through all of them in the last day and a half."

The Major's smile wasn't dissimilar from the way Ken

felt, excited in an odd way. "Loan me a Thompson and we'll call it good."

Josh pushed his foot to the floor, pinning the accelerator to the floorboards. The Hudson fishtailed off the gravel skirt and laid a patch of rubber on the asphalt The smell of hot tires climbed into his nostrils and masked the night air. Luke's Packard was a third of a mile ahead, streaking south on Route One toward Jonesport. The needle climbed steadily past sixty, then toward seventy. I'll get you, you bastard, he thought.

The soft springs of the Packard, worn from heavy loads of smuggled goods, swayed like a low dip on the dance floor as it rounded the corners.

He nearly lost control at the first corner when the rear of his car skidded onto the shoulder. Holly crap! Josh shrieked to his brain.

"Slow down! We'll catch up." Barbara latched onto the dashboard with both hands.

I don't remember asking you along, he thought.

Josh kept his eyes straight ahead. "That Hudson of his is fast. But I'm a better driver than he is."

The needle edged to the far side of seventy as they hit the bottom of Hall's Ridge Road. The road remained dark except for the two sets of lights shooting through the darkness. The Parkard thumped into a hole, but Josh corrected, steering into the skid.

"Damn potholes!"

"Just get close to him and flash your lights. He'll stop." Barbara pleaded.

"Yeah, that's likely." I wouldn't, he thought.

Josh tried to force the pedal further, but it was already pinned. Come on, come on! You can go faster, he urged the car. Luke's Hudson cut into the left turn at the top of the hill, traveling in the oncoming lane as he rounded the curve. Josh followed, trying to shorten the distance and allow more of a margin of error should he lose traction. Barbara was pressed against the passenger's door and Josh held the wheel tight to keep from slipping out of his seat.

"Shit!" Josh gasped.

Lights. A car appeared in front of them. Josh pulled his foot from the accelerator, but didn't hit the brakes. He veered hard onto his own lane, then accelerated again to pull the car around the corner, out of the curve.

Barbara shrieked. "Let me out!"

He straightened the wheel and glanced into the rearview mirror as the taillights of the other car disappeared around the bend. "Sorry. Can't stop. I'll lose him."

"So lose him! It's better than killing us all."

Luke's bulkier Hudson had to slowdown in a short series of S turns where the road dropped down off the ridge. Josh closed the distance between them and was right on Luke's bumper. Barbara leaned over and pushed on the horn. Josh swatted her arm away.

"I can't see to drive! Stay on your own side."

"Then blow the horn. Get him to stop."

Josh obeyed, laying heavy on the horn at first, then sequentially beeping it. The horn seemed to have no effect on Luke. Josh reached down and flicked the lights on and off a few times. Luke accelerated.

"What'd I tell you?"

The road straightened for a mile before the turn across Beaver Brook. Josh floored the Packard and pulled into the lefthand lane. Luke held him off by pulling into the center of the road. Josh shot for the shoulder. His passenger tires floated on the sandy shoulder and he began losing control. He jerked the wheel back toward the far lane just as Luke swerved toward the shoulder to keep him from passing on the outside.

Josh rocked in his seat, trying to urge more speed from the car. His front bumper passed the rear of Luke's Hudson. Luke started edging over; Josh held the road, and Luke didn't bump him.

The Packard's tan fender wells inched up alongside the Hudson. Luke gripped the wheel with both hands, staring straight ahead.

Barbara cranked down her window and hung over the door screeching at him. "Stop! Stop, damn it! Stop!"

Luke ignored her.

Josh inched the Packard closer until the vehicles' fenders almost touched. He swerved out further into the opposite lane, then back to within a couple inches of the Hudson, and repeated the maneuver twice more. Still, Luke didn't look at them.

"Can you reach the rifle behind my seat?"

Barbara sat back in the seat, stiff. "Why?"

"Maybe I can get one of his tires and he'll have to stop."

The hair blowing around on her face hid her expression. "That doesn't sound like such a good idea."

"Just try it, will you?"

She twisted in the seat and scooted up on her knees, fishing behind the seat with her right arm. "I can touch it, but it's stuck."

The end of the straightaway was coming up fast.

"Give it a yank! We're almost into Jonesport."

She rocked back and forth, putting her weight behind the thrusts. Suddenly, it popped up, and the barrel struck Josh in the back of the head.

"Careful, damn it!" He tried to ease the pain by twisting his head and pressing the bump against his shoulder. "Give it to me."

"I can do it." She waved the gun barrel around the front seat wildly.

"Be careful. It's loaded." He took a hand off the wheel and pushed the barrel away. "Just jack a shell into the chamber."

She fumbled with the lever and in a jerky motion cocked the gun open, forcing the hammer back, lifting a cartridge into the mechanism from the tube magazine.

"I got it." She closed the action.

"I said, be careful. There's no safety on that…"

The Parkard hit a bump. She bounced forward, the gun hit the dashboard, and her finger came down on the trigger.

The gun fired, shattering the front windshield instantly. Glass flew back in the wind and covered them.

Josh instinctively ducked as the glass ricocheted off him and bounced in the seat.

"Shit! Be careful with that thing!"

Luke looked over at them, the muzzle flash catching his attention. He stared at Barbara, then at the rifle. He eyes returned to the road for a second; then he jerked the wheel to the left. The heavy Hudson slammed broadside into the Packard. Josh gripped the wheel and tried to hold the road, but the heavier car edged them toward the soft sand on the side and the oncoming curve.

Barbara shrieked and dropped the rifle on the floorboards, grabbing for the dash.

"What's he doing? He's going to kill us."

Josh muscled the wheel toward the centerline. The Hudson resisted, but edged over a bit. Then the cars parted. Luke had pulled away.

"Why did he pull away?" Josh asked.

Luke braked. The front of his car drifted back to the rear of Josh's as they entered the turn.

Barbara removed her hands from the dashboard. "See. I told you he doesn't want to hurt us."

Just as the words cleared her lips, Luke slammed his front bumper into the rear fender of the Packard. It crumpled instantly and pressed in on the rear tire. The tire shredded against the twisted metal and flew out over the road. Josh slammed on the brakes, but it was too late – the car was already in a spin.

They spun completely around, kicking up dirt and rocks as the rim dug into the asphalt; then the front flew into the wooden guardrail on the right side of the road. The front of the Packard splintered the railing, the car barely slowing down as it passed through. The car went airborne, cleared the high grassy ditch, and plowed into the mud and water of Beaver brook.

Barbara's head snapped forward and slammed against the dashboard. Her body kept moving through the shattered windshield and she came to rest splayed out onto the hood. Her feet dangled limply in the water that now poured in, covering the floorboards.

Josh struck the steering column, nearly snapping the top completely off. The seat broke and slammed forward, jamming his knees under the dash, pinning them. The steering column had split his forehead and he lay wedged in place, blood flowing from his forehead and running down his face.

The front of the car was completely submerged in muddy water that came halfway up the doors, and rushed in around the floorboards. The dark, muddy water inched up the sides of the interior.

Luke backed up and stopped on the side of the road until his headlights pointed at the swirling dust from the crash.

Chapter Twenty One

Ken laid two Thompson machine guns on his desk, along with a pair of canvas ammo pouches and an extra clip for his side arm. Major Smith picked up one of the wooden stocked forty five caliber weapons, racked the slide open, and inspected the action.

"Your man keeps too much oil on these Thompsons. It'll collect grit and foul the action. A light film is all you need."

Durning, giving his full attention to his work on the telephone, missed the comment. Ken adjusted the government-issued Colt on his hip and shrugged. "There's a cloth in the top drawer if you need it."

The Major opened the drawer, found the white linen rag, and ran it over the outside of the mechanized rifle. He then stuffed the rag into the action and gave it a twist. "Any thoughts on where Josh might meet the U-boat?"

Ken withdrew his Colt from the holster and ran a finger over the slide. "There's deep water access from Jonesport to Winter Harbor. They could put in there any place." He pushed in on the waffle-patterned end of the spring cap and twisted the flat slide keeper. "But that would be quite a hike from where they sank the ship. They wouldn't have much darkness left by the time they got there."

"That sounds about right. Where, then?"

Ken pulled out the cap and spring, then moved the slide forward an inch and popped the pin that held the slide. "They wouldn't go south. Too many people, lights, and activity. They'd want some place quiet, secluded, and dark. Maybe Mt. Desert Island?"

The Major pulled back the slide again and reinspected the interior.

Ken answered his own question. "No. Why take a chance on being trapped on an island with only one road off? They'd go to a point somewhere around the island, yet on the mainland side."

The Major grinned and handed Ken the oily rag. "That's good deductive reasoning. Why else might they go there?"

Ken removed the barrel and wiped the funnel-shaped feed tube. "I don't know. It would depend on their mission. There's nothing of strategic importance around that area." He wiped the saddle where the barrel sat, then returned it to the frame. "Unless you're right about them dropping people off. In that case, they'd want handy access to Route One and the main artery south to the cities."

The Major nodded. "Now you're thinking. What's our plan if we make that assumption?"

Ken dropped the spring back in place and pushed it into the space below the barrel. "Somewhere Josh knows well that's near the road. Maybe Castine or Cape Jellison."

"Why there?"

"Josh spent a summer working in Stockton Springs. He knows that shoreline well." The spring slipped from his grasp and shot across the room. Major Smith dodged it as it flew past him and landed with a metallic clank near the door.

"Sorry." Ken set the pistol on the desk and headed over to pick up the spring and cap. "That would put them pretty far up Penobscott Bay. Why would they take that risk?"

There was a knock at the door just as Ken bent over to retrieve the spring. He flinched as he rose, then opened the door. In the light of the single bulb, stood Maggie, a sentry by her side.

"Sorry to bother you, Sir, but this girl said she needs to see you. She says its urgent."

Ken waved the sentry off. "Fine. No problem. Thanks." He opened the screen door and Maggie stepped inside. Her hair was tied with a blue ribbon that crept out from underneath her tan, straw hat. Ken took a deep breath through his nose as she passed, catching the scent of soap and a hint of watermelon. "What are you doing here?"

Major Smith stood near the back desk with the Thompson still in his hands. Durning stared at her and lowered the telephone, but kept it close to his ear.

She stared at the floor, the rounded brim of her woven hat shielding her eyes. "I had to see you. Can we talk privately?"

"What's this about?"

Maggie's face stayed glued to the floor. "Luke."

Ken relaxed. "I'm not sure I have time to talk to you about your love life right now. We're in the middle of a situation here."

"No." she whispered. "It's not my love life. It's something far more important than that."

Her hand trembled as she pulled a note from her purse and raised it to Ken. "You need to read this."

Ken took the wadded paper from her soft fingers, unfolded the crumpled mass, and held it up to the light. It was a scribbled note in Josh's familiar handwriting.

Ken,
It isn't me. I swear it.
It has to be Luke. He had access to the boat, and must've replaced the fuel pump.
If it wasn't me – and it wasn't – then it had to be him.
I'm going to find him and will get the truth out of him.
Josh

"When did he give this to you?"

Maggie shrugged. "Right before I saw you at the diner. I hadn't read it then and you left so quickly, I forgot to give it to you."

"Why now? You could've brought this over hours ago."

Her eyes rose from the floor and she leaned close to his cheek, her warm breath drifting into his ear with her words. "I'm pregnant. The baby is Luke's. Don't you see the spot I'm in?"

Ken pulled her into his arms, the warmth of her body penetrating her thin sashay. He whispered, "Don't worry. We'll figure this out. You did the right thing." He pulled her tighter to his chest. "I don't care what has happened. I'll be here for you."

Ken could hear her muffle a sniffle and felt her reach up to wipe her eyes. "I know you will."

The Major laid the Thompson back on the desk with a thwack. "Is this a private party or can anyone play?"

Ken held Maggie for another instant and then unwrapped himself, walked over to the Major, and handed him the note. The Major read the crumpled message and dropped it on the desk.

"What's the probability this is right?"

Ken thought a second. "Why else would Josh bother stopping at the diner to write it? If it's him, why wouldn't he just go to the rendezvous with the U-boat?"

The Major rubbed his chin. "Why indeed? Perhaps to throw us off. Get us moving in another direction?"

Maggie chimed in, "Barbara's with him."

Ken turned to look at her. "Barbara is with Josh?"

"Yes. She insisted on going."

"He wouldn't take her along if he was the spy. That wouldn't make any sense."

"Maybe," the Major said. "But who knows how far he'd go to hide the truth."

Ken shoved the spring back into the pistol and twisted the keeper in front of the spring cap. "It really doesn't matter at this point. Neither one of them is here. They're both out there along Route One some place, so let's saddle up and get on the way."

Major Smith nodded. "Durning, stay here and finish the calls. We'll need you here to relay messages to Boston or Portland."

Durning stayed seated, still talking on the telephone, and saluted.

The Major slung the ammo clips over his shoulder and grabbed both Thompsons. Moving deliberately, he headed for the door and shoved one of the guns at Ken as he passed.

"The girl should stay here."

Ken grabbed the rifle in one hand and gave Maggie a quick hug with the other. "We'll call the second we find out anything."

He turned and headed out the door, letting the screen slam behind him. The Major was already in the driver's seat, cranking over the engine.

Maggie hurried over and grabbed Ken's hand. "I need to come, too."

Ken shook his head. "No, this is a Navy matter now."

"But I can help," she pleaded. "I know Luke better than anyone and I can talk to him if you find him. We can straighten this out together. You'll see this was a big mistake."

Ken turned toward the Major, who frowned, but nodded. "She might be right. Maybe she can help us."

Josh tried to lift his head and open his eyes. His left lid was sealed shut, but his right flickered open. Darkness and water. He tried to raise his left arm to wipe the blood from his eyes, but the arm was jammed between the door and the twisted steering column. His legs ached. Not the achy pain his bad knees gave him on cold damp days, but a solid, thudding, deep pressure pain.

Dark water swirled in front of him, and Barbara lay halfway out the windshield, draped on the hood and framed in chrome that had held the glass.

He tried to call to her, but his voice just croaked at first. He swatted at his face with his left arm. It was heavy and didn't respond. His hand dangled at the end of his forearm like a marionette on a string.

"Barbara!" His throat hurt. "Barbara. Can you hear me? Wake up!"

Water had filled most of the front seat and gurgled around the top of his chest and neck. It was warm, but he felt cold, very cold. It flowed as high as the top of the back of the seat; Barbara's dress swirled in the slow current.

Footsteps came up behind him, then a splash in the water. Luke vaulted over the trunk of the car and slipped onto the top of the seat behind Barbara.

Josh attempted to focus on Luke's face in the dark. The headlights were still on, underwater, but they afforded little light.

"You son of a bitch! Look what you've done!"

Luke dropped his feet into the water behind Barbara, reached forward, swept the matted black hair from her face, and put his fingers to her neck.

"Don't you touch her! Damn you! Get away from her!" He tried to swat at Luke with his mangled hand; instead, only splashing water in his own face.

Luke removed his fingers, closed his eyes for a few seconds, then turned to Josh.

"She's dead." He said mechanically.

Josh swung his head wildly. "No. She's not! You lying sack of shit! Get me out of here so I can help her."

"She gone. There's nothing anyone can do now."

Tears welled up in Josh's open eye, clouding his vision even more. His voice cracked as he spoke. "Why?"

"Sometimes things just boil down to family. I'm German. My father is German. My mother and twin brother died in the First World War. This is what I was raised to do."

Josh tried to shake his head. "What were we? Just props in your sick, twisted game?"

"No. You were my friends, but friendship has its limits. My father taught me that."

Josh blinked hard, attempting to clear his eye and look at Barbara. "It shouldn't."

"I'm sorry, but it does. This is what I was trained for."

"You were trained to kill your friends?"

Luke looked up toward the road and his car parked on the side. "Did you tell anyone about me?"

Josh continued staring at Barbara, her pale cheek covered with wisps of black strands. "Who would I tell? They think it's me."

"Yes, they would. A smuggler who'd do anything for money. Why not?"

Josh rested his head on the bent steering wheel. The muddy, foul water was in his nostrils. He could picture the note in Maggie's hands. So pure, so white.

Luke slipped back into the water and rested his hand on Josh's shoulder. "I really did love you all."

Luke grasped the back of Josh's head, wove his fingers

into his hair, and shoved Josh's face into the water. Josh reacted; he forced his neck back with all his might. The strong neck muscles he'd developed from sports lifted his face clear of the water. He sucked in a huge gulp of air and tried to swing his broken limb at Luke. Josh's blow bounced off Luke's body and skidded across his arm.

Josh's fingers found Luke's forearm as his face went back under water. Josh squeezed his fingers around Luke's wrist and tried to wrench free, but his broken bones wouldn't work with his muscles, and instead, his elbow slapped at the water.

His head kept bumping the steering wheel as he forced his head upwards against the pressure of Luke's hands. His right eye could see flashes of light in the brown, brackish water. Salty water and gunk got sucked up into his nostrils; then he choked on the water. Coughing, he sucked in, filling his lungs. The water was cold in his chest. He body went into spasm and bucked at the thick fluid that filled him. The car's headlights faded and he was suddenly sitting on the rocky, granite ledge above the quarry. Barbara laid her head on his shoulder and they looked out over the brilliant blue water.

Chapter Twenty Two

The light over the guard shack glinted off the spider-webbed broken windshield as the Major steered out of the gate and pulled onto the main road. Ken adjusted the Thompson between his knees and turned in his seat to look at Maggie.

"So where would he go?"

She slumped in the rear seat, her hands resting on her belly. "We had a couple of favorite spots: Schoodic Point, Crabtree Neck on Hancock Point, Lamoine Beach."

"Schoodic is too close to the post at Winter Harbor," the Major said.

"The other two are close to each other. We can check them both," Ken replied.

The warm air plowed through Ken's short-cropped hair. The night sky had brightened and moonlight cast dull shadows across the pavement from the trees lining the road. His body jounced in the seat, his stomach muscles flopping each time the vehicle hit a pothole. He chanced a look at Maggie; her slender belly bounced with his.

Ken braced himself on the backs of the seats and climbed out of the front and into the back with Maggie.

The Major made a sharp turn and Ken nearly landed on top of Maggie, but he caught his balance and settled in, staring at the back of the Major's head.

Ken leaned close to her ear. "So what now? Are you going to have the baby?"

Maggie turned and slapped his face. "What right do you have to ask such a question?"

He was momentarily stunned, sitting back, her demeanor had suddenly changed. "Because I'm your friend."

"My friend? My friend who wants to put my child's father in prison, most likely to hang."

Why was she putting this all on him? "You didn't have to come to us. You know we're right in hunting him down. Don't act innocent. Don't you dare act like you aren't part of this."

"I may be part of this, but I didn't know the whole story, and I still don't. You grew up with Luke. Do you think he could do this?" She looked at her belly. "I certainly don't."

Ken reached out and touched her cheek. He knew she was scared and lashing out. She needed time. And so did he. "I'm not absolutely certain, either, but the fact remains that he's on the loose, leaving a bunch of unanswered questions, and we need to find him, damn the consequences."

Maggie rubbed her belly and watched the dark pines whirl by. She stared at the passing trees for several moments, then said to the Major. "I'd pick Hancock Point. Luke always liked it because of the deep water and the islands that protected it from the far side. He'd say

'What a spot! High and dry, the wind dampened by the islands.'"

"Are you sure? Would there be some place else?"

"No. Nowhere else he's taken me. If there is some place else, I swear he's never talked about it or taken me there."

Lights. Numerous lights. Red lights, flashing. White ones steady. They lit up the road ahead.

Ken pulled himself forward in the seat. "What's up?"

"I don't know. Looks like an accident."

The Major slowed the vehicle and edged toward a man standing in the road holding a flashlight.

The Major applied the brakes. They ground to a stop in front of a half dozen cars – two squad cars, three civilian vehicles, and a hearse. The roadway was black, but several lights shone off to the right, down in the gully. The Major eased the Jeep ahead.

The man with the light shouted at him. "Stop! You can't go up there."

The Major continued to creep forward, inching past the two civilian cars, and pulled in behind the hearse.

The man with the flashlight ran alongside, protesting his every move. "You can't be up here! This is a police matter. Don't you park there. Move along."

The Major stepped from the Jeep. "Mr. Mitchell, hand me my Thompson."

Ken passed him the automatic rifle. The man eyed it, his eyes widened, and he backed into the darkness.

"Let's go."

Ken leapt out of the back seat, then held out a hand for

Maggie. She stepped around onto the front seat, accepted Ken's hand, and hopped onto the side of the road.

The Major led the way around a police car toward the back of the hearse. The rear of the vehicle was open and a body lay in the back under a white sheet. An attendant stood beside the open door.

"What happened?" the Major asked.

"Looks like a couple of cars were racing. They do that on this long straight stretch." He nodded back toward the road. "They must've collided and one went into the water."

The Major glanced toward the splintered guardrail. "What about the other car?"

"Didn't stay around. You can see where it stopped." The attendant pointed at tire tracks in the sand. "They must've gotten scared and took off."

Ken stepped up to the top of the bank between two broken posts. Two uniformed officers were attempting to pull a body from behind the steering wheel. Another stood on shore behind the car, holding a light for them.

Maggie moved up behind him. "How awful!"

Ken nodded. "Whoever it was, looks like the end came quick."

The officer at the rear of the car dipped his light so it reflected off the bent license plate. Ken cocked his head as he read the numbers in his head. "Shit! Stay here!"

He jumped onto the slope, his feet skidding out from beneath him. Landing on his butt and hands, he bounced down the steep incline.

Maggie shouted from behind him. "Where are you going?"

"I said, stay put. I'll be right back."

His feet hit level ground at the base of the hill, flinging him forward and back onto his feet. The rear of the car lay fifteen feet ahead, the officer partly blocking his view. He scrambled toward it, pushing past the policeman.

"Hey, where do you think you're going?"

Ken rushed forward, and plowed into the back of the Packard, slapping his hands onto the trunk to stop himself.

One of the officers stood chest deep in the water beside the open driver's door. The other crouched over a man's body from the passenger seat. Ken placed a foot on the bumper and climbed up onto the back of the seat.

The police officer in the passenger side looked up. "Just who the hell are you?"

"Is he dead?"

"I said, who are you?"

"I'm his friend, damn it! Is he dead?"

The pinned man's head flopped back and the flashlight from shore lit up the side of Josh's lifeless, muddy face."

"Yeah, he's dead. But according to his license plate, he's the one you Navy boy's, are looking for, so no big loss. Good riddance"

Ken's vision began to dim; his head felt light. He stared at the officer's smiling face, and began to tremble all over. Without thinking, he drew back and cold-cocked the officer with a right cross, then leapt on top of the man and thumped his head down onto the hood. His hands on the man's head felt good.

"Stop! Stop or I'll shoot." the other officer shouted.

Ken didn't stop.

"Last chance. Stop now."

The hammer of a pistol clicked.

A burst of machine gun fire erupted from behind the car and tore up the water around them.

"That's enough from everyone!" Major Smith shouted.

Ken's vision began to come back. The water gurgled and his eyes fell on Josh's head swaying in the current, back and forth, as if to say no. Ken released the stunned officer and slouched back into the water against the seat.

The officer with the pistol turned toward the Major. Looking into the barrel of the Thompson, he holstered his weapon.

"Was the person in the hearse a woman?" Ken asked.

The officer on the hood put a hand to his head and rolled skyward, still too stunned from the blows to answer. The other policeman nodded. "Yes. Black hair, full-figured, about thirty."

Ken closed his eyes and tried to picture her face.

A bottlenose dolphin broke the surface, arched forward, and slipped back under the dark water. It rose again seconds later to repeat the performance. Werner watched the animal swim alongside the boat as he stood in the conning tower with the Kapitan. The night was quiet; the electric motor pushed them silently toward Hancock Point. White flickered on the bow when a wave crested to nose off the boat and reflected in the moonlight, then disappeared as fast as it had come.

"I want you to go ashore with the *abwehr* agents," the Kapitan said.

"Me? Why me?"

"It'll be good experience for you."

"I don't need the experience. I should already have my own boat."

"You've had plenty of experience at sea." The Kapitan laid a hand on Werner's shoulder. "You're one of the brightest young men aboard this boat, but you lack real life experience. You don't understand the need to do certain things."

"Like killing children?"

"Sometimes, exactly that."

Werner eyed the Kapitan, suspicious of his motives. Is that why you want me to go? So something might happen to me and then you can return to my mother without me there to tell her the things you've done? "We'll see."

The Kapitan paused and removed his hand. "I've done things much worse than you've witnessed. Things only a monster would do under normal circumstances. But these aren't normal circumstances and if you don't get that through your thick skull, you will never have your own command."

Werner turned toward the Kapitan. "Is that the requirement for command? To be a brute?"

"Brutal at times, but not a brute." He looked ahead at the dark coastline rising ahead of the boat. "I'd kill every single person on that continent to save Germany and our lives."

Werner continued to stare at the side of the Kapitan's

face. "Isn't there a point when we just stop fighting and take what the rest of the world has in store for us?"

"No," the Kapitan replied.

"What do you mean no?"

"Just what I said. No. No giving up on our people. No compromise on our culture, and no sacrifice of our ideals."

"What if our ideals are wrong?"

"They're still ours, wrong or right, and we must stay true to them."

"Don't they have some flexibility? Can't we change them, make them better?"

"You're a sailor and those are not questions you have the luxury of asking." He clasped his hands together. "Now get down on the bow and help get that raft ready to launch. I'll send up the agents."

Werner stood for an instant, not moving.

The Kapitan reached under his coat and removed a Luger. He held it firmly in his hand between them, then flipped it around, holding it by the barrel, and handed it to Werner. "You might need this. I do want you to live, and you can tell your mother anything you want. She and I have spoken at length about this subject and she agrees the only important thing is getting us home alive."

He turned and climbed down the ladder to the control room. Werner stood in the dark night, still holding the pistol.

Werner rested his paddle in the bow of the raft that sat on the deck of the U-boat. His hand grazed the dry, sticky rubber. It smelled foul, like an old raincoat put away wet.

The bow of the U-boat didn't rock, but plowed through the water, diligent and steady. Land ahead filled the horizon and swept around them, leaving only a small area behind the boat for escape. Black serrated tree branches were visible against the lighter horizon above the rocky cliffs. The wash of water on rocks and shoals filled the night sky.

Westward, lights from the houses dotted the shore. To the east, a single light stood out among the trees and blanket of dark. At this hour, most people would be safe in their beds dreaming of things they never could have.

Franks and Schuch stood behind the raft. Franz, the boat's engineer, positioned himself on the opposite side from Werner. Franz had his wool cap pulled down low over his ears and held the short paddle in his left hand. Werner had selected him because he was strong and lean. He would be like a little electric motor in the bow, getting them in and out quickly. Besides, the man was accustomed to being by himself in the engine compartment and would not be prone to useless jabber.

The agents placed their watertight bundles in the center of the raft. The bundles held their shoes, socks and spare clothes.

A seaman scurried across the deck to Werner and whispered, "The Kapitan's going to lower the profile of the boat. He's going to submerge to the conning tower and hold here for you."

Werner nodded. "Get in the boat, men. Unless you want to get your feet wet."

Werner adjusted the Luger in his belt and stepped into the starboard bow position, kneeling on the rubber deck of the raft. It was hard upon his knees, as the raft was still supported by the grates of the U-boat.

The seaman disappeared behind them and Werner picked up his paddle.

The boat began to submerge. Water rushed around the side of the U-boat and the ballast tanks hissed as they released air. The deck was quickly awash and the raft lurched when the sea nudged its sides and began lifting it free.

The bottom of the raft softened and his knees dug into the squishy rubber floor.

"Paddle on the port side on my command," Werner whispered.

The raft jostled sideways as a small wave hit the bow. "Ahead on the port."

Franz and Franks dipped their paddles and pulled with short choppy strokes. The bow swung to the right, leaving the safety of the U-boat. Werner reached forward with his paddle.

"Both sides paddle. Match my cadence."

Werner dipped his paddle into the water and pulled. His right hand dunked into the seawater, the cold water wetting his wrist and the sleeve of his black wool sweater. He pulled five steady strokes and at the end of the fifth, Schuch's paddle came forward and hit his.

"I said match my pace. Pay attention," Werner hissed at the man behind him.

Schuch hesitated, missing a stroke, then started back in.

A pale white line separated the water from the trees. That had to be the beach. Werner continued paddling rhythmically. He tried to think of something with a beat to keep his mind on track, but nothing came to him.

A trickle of cool water ran down his leg and pooled around one knee.

"The raft's got a leak," Franks whispered.

"Keep paddling. It's too small to worry about."

Schuch leaned forward as he paddled. "Do you see the signal?"

Werner stopped paddling. "All stop."

He looked at his watch, then at the dark shoreline.

"It appears he's late."

Franks rested his paddle on the bladder of the raft. "Now what?"

Werner squinted into the dark. "We wait."

The raft bobbed gently in the light chop. The moonlight teased the side of the raft, flickering as the wet rubber bobbed under its touch.

"We're too exposed out here. We need to get ashore," Schuch said.

"And if we get to shore before he signals, then what? Which way do we go on shore? We could walk right away from him." Werner paused. "No, we wait. If he doesn't signal, we return to the boat and try again tomorrow."

Franz slouched over the side of the raft, his eyes searching the shoreline. Werner tried to lift his wet knee off the rubber deck, but his other knee sank in and the water shifted places and soaked the second one as well.

A light moved overhead. It was high up and quick – an airplane. Too high to see them. Almost too far up to hear the hum from its engines, but Werner concentrated and the steady whine became apparent. His chin lifted as the plane passed over, ten maybe even fifteen thousand meters. Despite the distance he couldn't help watch it.

"There!" Franz pointed toward shore.

Ahead and to starboard, a light swung back and forth for a few seconds, then vanished.

Werner took the small hand light from his pocket and flicked it on and off three times. The light on shore returned for two swings and was gone.

"All ahead with me."

The men dipped their paddles and pulled for the shore where the light had been.

A shadow of a figure loomed on the beach as the raft touched the rock-strewn shore. Werner and Franz jumped into the ankle-deep water and dragged the raft as far as they could. The agents gathered their things and hopped onto the firm, irregular ground. The man stepped closer, a rifle in one hand. He wasn't cloaked in a hooded jacket tonight, and his short-cropped hair fell onto a strong jaw line.

"We must hurry," the man said. "There has been trouble and the police will be all around tonight."

"What kind of trouble?" Werner asked as he dragged the raft further onto the shore.

"Nothing that concerns you, but something I'll have to deal with." He looked toward the wooded shore. "Please hurry."

Franks and Schuch sat on the ground, pulled foot-wear from a bag, and began to dress their feet.

Werner nodded toward them. "These are your men. They need to get to New York."

Der Falke reached for one of the parcels, and slung it over his shoulder. The Hawk adjusted the straps on the sack and eyed the dark woods.

"I've got a car up on the road that can take you to Bangor. The last train leaves in two hours. We can make it if we go now." The Hawk said.

Werner pointed to Franz. "You wait here with the raft. I'm going up to the road with the agents and Der Falke, to make sure they get off safely."

Franz nodded.

"That's not necessary. I can handle it from here. Oh, and call me Luke. I hate that stupid codename."

With their footgear in place, the agents stripped the oil cloth from their cases and tossed them into the bottom of the raft. Luke had already started up the shore. Werner followed and the agents trailed behind. Werner's feet felt unsteady on the uneven shore, but the air was clean and his lungs enjoyed the freedom from the confines of the boat.

The rocks on the shore grew larger as they angled toward the trees. A band of firm ledge separated the waterline from the soft earth beneath the pines. Werner thought of Christmas as he entered the forest.

Luke paused ten feet into the trees, squatted down, and faced the men. "Until we reach the car, no one talks unless I ask a question."

The Jeep's front tires crossed the Sullivan line when it hit a pothole and jounced Ken. His thoughts left Josh and Barbara and moved ahead of the Jeep. He hadn't realized how much of a daze he was in. Blinking forcibly, he wiped his face with his hands and looked over at the Major.

"We should've taken that last left if you wanted to go to Schoodic Point."

"Yes, but Maggie talked me into Hancock Point as being more likely."

Ken turned toward Maggie in the back seat. "When did she do that?"

She reached up and placed a hand on his shoulder. "For the last twenty minutes."

Ken rubbed both his ears at the same time. Twenty minutes, he thought. "I didn't hear you."

"Maggie thinks Hancock is more likely since it's closer to Route One. I tend to agree."

"Fine. Take the first left after the bridge." Twenty minutes he thought again.

The tires rumbled over the expansion strip and onto the steel grates of the bridge, their high-pitched whine too loud to talk above. Ken looked to the right into Taunton Bay. Several lobster boats lay moored to buoys. The outgoing tide kept them all pointing landward, and a steady stream of water trailed off the sterns, seaward. Several crab pots dotted the surface, scattered in seemingly random patterns, but Ken knew fishermen wouldn't leave things to chance alone, so the crab pots had been deliberately placed according to the bottom topography.

Hancock lay on the far side of the bridge. It was dark with only a light dotted here and there. The street lights were off as an air raid precaution. The Jeep dropped onto the asphalt at the far side of the bridge and continued down to the turn-off. The Major made the corner without further instruction, and the road narrowed along the neck.

The houses got smaller the farther they traveled from town. The sprawling, seafaring mansions of the captain's past, had been transformed into more modern single-family dwellings. The road rose and fell with the hilly terrain of the inside part of the peninsula. However, it soon straightened and flattened when they approached the point.

"What does his car look like again?" the Major asked.

"It's a brown Hudson, Maine plate 4462," Ken said.

The Major slowed down as they began to get glimpses of the water through the trees. The houses had all but disappeared in the undeveloped part of the point.

"Can you see out into the bay?" the Major asked.

"A bit, but not well," Maggie answered.

"Watch those side roads. He would try to hide his car," Ken said.

"If it was damaged from hitting Josh's car, he might not be able to get it off the road," Maggie added.

The Major slowed down even more. "This forest is dense. It's like looking into a room through a keyhole without a light inside."

"Perhaps we should stop and walk out on the point, to look around. Maybe we could spot the boat," Ken suggested.

Ken watched the back of the Major's head cock to the left several times as he thought. "No. Let's go round once and see what we find. We can always come back."

The road reached the terminus of the peninsula; they

rounded it, heading back landward, on the west side. The trees were larger here. Tall stands of pine with sparse undergrowth were separated from the road by a thin strip of sand that appeared white in the headlights of the Jeep.

"What's that?" The Major pointed as he braked.

Ken pulled himself forward onto the edge of his seat. A car sat on the shore side of the lane, pulled onto the sand and leaning toward the ditch.

Ken stiffened. "That's it! That's Luke's car."

The Major killed the lights and the engine at the same time, allowing the Jeep to coast to a stop in the road a hundred feet from the car. Setting the brake, he reached for his Thompson.

The Major slipped from his seat. "He probably won't be alone. Don't take anything for granted."

Chapter Twenty Three

Luke remained crouched, facing the three men in the dark. The toes of his shoes dug into the soft earth, releasing its musty and disagreeable sweetness. The two agents clung to their cases and took short, quick breaths. The officer appeared calmer, but had removed the Luger from his belt. He held it near his leg and pointed toward the ground.

The faint sound of a car motor farther out on the point caught Luke's attention. "Shh! Listen."

The motor drew closer. Luke turned his head with the sound, judging where the car was on the road. His head swivelled above his square shoulders, reaching the point where his car was parked. The sound stopped. "Damn it! We may have company," Luke whispered." He rose and crept forward. "Follow me, but not a sound."

The undergrowth was thin from the dense canopy of pine branches above, which, in turn, had coated the ground with a thick bed of needles, making walking easy and quiet. Luke retraced his steps from the car and soon the slope up to the road became visible. The bright line of sand in the moonlight traced the path of the asphalt, just above eye level.

They'd come to the edge of the road north of his car. Luke crouched and waved his hand, indicating he wanted the two agents to hunker down; then he pointed to the officer and waved him forward.

He leaned close to the officer's ear. "Stay near. Let's have a look."

He took a final look at the agents to assure himself they were staying put; then at a crouch, moved toward the car.

Light voices drifted in the night. He couldn't make out the words, but they were soft and hushed. He slowed down even more, each step heel to toe. Two steps, stop and listen, then two more. The outline of the car came into view. Three figures stood by the front bumper. He listened.

"Look at the damage to the driver's side. This car was definitely the one that rammed the Packard off the road," the one voice said.

"That son of a bitch killed them!"

Luke froze, his friend Ken's voice stinging in his ears. How could it be any worse than having him here? How could he have crossed his friends?

The officer crept up behind him and whispered, "There are only three of them. We can take them."

Luke nodded. "Maybe."

The officer pointed with the muzzle of his Luger. "I'll sneak over to the front of the car and you stay here. Listen for my shot and you shoot when I do."

Luke looked down at the rifle in his hands. The thick

wood around the stock suddenly became heavier. "That might work."

Then a higher pitched voice came from the area of the car. "I can't believe it. There still needs to be another explanation."

The officer began to move. Luke struck out, grabbed the officer's sleeve. "No. Stop. Let's go back."

"Why? I can get two if you take the other."

Luke thought for a second – he couldn't kill Maggie. He couldn't murder his unborn child. He'd already crossed everyone whoever cared for him. He thought for another instant, then lied. "The car doesn't work anyway. It got damaged. We can go around."

The officer pointed at the Navy Jeep on the shoulder. "What about their Jeep? We could take that."

"Now that wouldn't raise any suspicion." He tried to mock, but his voice was too soft to be effective. "Two civilians in a Navy vehicle."

The officer looked back toward the road, then at Luke. "I still think its our best option."

Luke could see the moonlight glint off Maggie's face. "No! They don't know you're here, or the agents. We should stay hidden."

Luke backed away quietly and stealthily, careful with each placement of his foot. The officer hesitated, then began to back up as well. The voices soon faded and they reached the two agents, still crouched where they'd left them.

"It's no good – you'll have to go around. I'd suggest crossing the road here, above them and continue to work north along the road for several hundred yards. After that, you can return to the road and follow it to Route One."

The older agent cocked his head. "Then what? We don't have a car."

Luke glanced back toward the road. "People are pretty trusting around here. You can catch a ride once you get to the main road."

The man shook his head. "I don't know. You were supposed to get us to Bangor and the train."

Luke reached out and grabbed his lapel. "Look. I'm more of a liability to you now. They know who I am and are looking for me. They don't know you. Just play it calm and you'll be fine."

The young officer locked eyes with Der Falke. "I think he's right. What choice do you have?"

The agent bobbed his head, then motioned for the younger man to follow, and they slipped into the darkness, moving north as instructed.

Luke rose. "Looks like I'm going with you. Let's get to the boat."

The moonlight reflected off the water, casting its haze into the tree line, and brightened their path to the shore. The engineer sat hunched over on a rock, near the bow of the inflatable, taking cover behind the boat. His head rose as Luke and Werner came out of the trees, he watched them step onto the beach.

Luke and Werner hurried over to the boat.

"What's he doing back here?" the engineer asked.

"It appears we're going to have a passenger on the return trip." Werner looked over his shoulder at the forest. "Now let's get out of here."

The engineer grabbed the bow and shoved it into the water. "You don't have to ask me twice on that one."

Werner wadded ankle deep into the water and pointed to the stern. "You take the stern on my side. Paddle in unison with me. Franz, you paddle at your own pace and I'll keep us straight."

The dark water filled Luke's shoes, soaking his socks, and pant legs up to his calves. Stepping into the raft, he knelt down in the stern as the two other men shoved it off. The sagging floor pooled all the water around his legs. He grabbed one of the short-handled paddles and took a couple of strokes as the other men climbed in, bringing more sea water with them.

A light breeze lifted off the water; it struck them in the face, evaporating the sweat from their bodies. The light wavelets, however, had coalesced into a steady series of waves that slowed their progress. Digging into the water with his paddle, Luke's hand dipped into the waves, which, in turn, splashed on the side of the rubber inflatable, and dribbled off the handle into the boat.

A black pole protruded from the water, breaking over a submerged shoal. They pulled hard on the paddles, dragging the rubber craft toward it. Luke's shoulders burned under the strain and his muscles tightened. The pole rose up as they approached. The coning tower lifted out of the water, but the boat remained submerged. They navigated the tiny craft over the bow of the U-boat. The boat then rose slowly, the water rushing off the deck and pouring back into the bay. The officer grasped the bow radio antennae to keep the raft from washing over with the flow. He stood as the raft lowered onto the firm deck, then released his grip as they settled aboard.

"Get that boat deflated and stowed. I want to get underway." The Kapitan paused and leaned over the edge of the conning tower. "Who's that with you? Who's the third man there?"

"It's Der Falke. He's been compromised and will have to catch a ride home with us." Werner said.

The Kapitan waved. "Fine. Get him below with the raft, while I get underway."

Luke shifted his weight, acclimating to the deck. The dark shores of Maine began to recede, and with it, twenty-two years of his life. He couldn't stop thinking about Maggie. What would she do? Would she still have the baby? How would the child be treated? Had he made the right choice? Maybe he should have gone to California. He could have talked Maggie into it.

He shook his head and tossed the paddle on top of the deflating raft.

It didn't matter now. The choice had already been made.

Maggie refused to stay behind. Her leather flats, giving her no support in the soft undergrowth, she remained quiet, but stumbling as she went. The Major hunched over and picked his way through the trees. Ken followed, his forty-five clenched in his right hand. The ground lightened as they broke free of the evergreen canopy, the air stirred, and the sound of water lapping the shore drifted into the trees.

The Major stopped at the edge of the forest. The

water glistened, the waves ebbing and flowing on the shore. The temperature dropped several degrees this close to the water.

"There!" The Major pointed seaward.

Maggie slipped behind Ken, her warm body grazing the back of his shoulder as he squinted in the night. A black tower rose from the water three hundred yards out at their ten o'clock. The base of the tower sloped out in a thin dark line a few feet above the water. Ken instinctively raised his pistol.

The Major pushed his arm down. "They're too far away. All you'll do is let them know we see them and give away our position. Besides, the thirty caliber guns she has can reach us."

Small figures moved on deck near the tower, then disappeared; the U-boat began to back out of the bay. Slow and silent, it slipped backwards, lowering in the water as it went. The deck was the first to go, followed by the tower, leaving a single periscope, and a V-wake trailing.

"Do you think Luke's aboard?" Maggie asked.

"That would be the smart play." Ken answered.

"Follow me," the Major said, moving out onto the beach.

Ken stepped onto the sand and followed the Major, Maggie at his heels. "Stay behind me," he whispered.

A dark, roundish shadow lay at the water's edge.

The Major clicked on the small flashlight he'd brought from the Jeep and played it over the beach. "Pay attention. You might learn something." The light stopped on a smudge in the sand, then on several smaller disruptions. "That's where the raft landed." The Major said as he squatted down, to study the hard-packed sand. He duck-walked a few steps to the north, then waddled landward ten feet. "Four came ashore, and were met here by another man." He paused and looked down the water-line. "See these other marks? Three returned, and left on the boat. That leaves two unaccounted for."

"Which way did they go?" Maggie asked.

"By the direction of the foot-prints, we must've passed them in the woods."

Ken picked up a mussel shell, rubbed his thumb on the smooth inside surface. "Either that or they had a second car and left before we even got here."

The Major rose. "Could be. In either case, we need to notify the police and the F.B.I. so they can start watching the bus and train terminals, as well as to scour the whole point for tracks."

"So what's our next move?" Ken asked.

The Major looked at Maggie. "It seems we won't be needing your help from here." He then turned to Ken. "We'll drop her off at the Ellsworth State Police Barracks and then head to Rockland."

Maggie cocked her head. "Drop me off? I don't want to be dropped off anywhere. I'm coming with you."

"Sorry, but from here the FBI can chase the two that were left ashore. It's our job to catch the U-boat."

Even in the dim light Ken could see her face sink.

The Major turned to Ken. "I've got a buddy at the coastal watch office who has a boat. We can shoot out and meet with one of the destroyer escorts patrolling Casco Bay."

Ken dropped the shell. "We don't have orders to go aboard a destroyer."

The Major winked. "We will by the time we get there."

___

The sun scratched at the eastern horizon as they reached Rockland. Maggie wasn't too happy to be left at the police barracks. She protested, but fatigue had won, and by the time they left, she was resting on a bench with a phone book under her head. One of the troopers had graciously volunteered to take her back to Machias.

Route One shot straight into the center of town, then hooked sharply right, westward out of town. They didn't take the right turn, instead bearing eastward down a short grade to the docks. Stinson's Cannery extended out on a long pier, occupying the whole north side of the harbor, it's pale, lime green buildings reflecting the first rays of light. A small office sat in front of the buildings. Ken recognized the same temporary concrete footings and gray paint of his office back in Machias.

The water in the Harbor was flat-calm. It undulated almost randomly, the sunlight bouncing off its surface like a huge signal mirror. The Major parked the Jeep in front of the building, stretched his arms and headed for the door. Ken followed.

"Doesn't look like anyone is around," Ken said.

"Oh, he's here. He hardly ever leaves."

"Who's that?"

The Major rapped hard on the door with his thick fist. "Lieutenant Aloysious Jones."

Ken grunted. "Now there's a ten dollar handle."

"His name isn't the best part – wait until you meet him."

The Major rapped again, harder this time.

Footsteps behind the door, the metallic clank of the deadbolt, and the door swung open. The unshaven face of a fifty-year-old – plus, with tousled hair stood behind the screen.

"What the Christ time is it?" He spat.

"Time for the oldest lieutenant in naval history to open the door for a friend," the Major replied.

The man's eye's brightened and he swung open the door.

"Commander Swain. What brings you to my door?" He looked at his bare wrist. "And so damn early."

"Well, if you let us in, I might just tell you."

Lieutenant Jones pushed open the screen and stepped back. Swain pushed passed into the darkened room.

Ken followed, muttering under his breath, "Commander?"

The office was a single room with a bunk in the far right corner, a desk opposite, separated by a door which Ken guessed went out to the dock. A gray file cabinet stood beside the desk and thread-bare red arm-chair sat just inside the front door. The room was a shambles, papers scattered on the desk, a dirty uniform crumpled on the floor, and a plate with a half-eaten sandwich atop the file cabinet. A single window adorned the left wall above the desk.

Lieutenant Jones didn't salute. Instead he plopped back on the rat's nest of a bunk and shoved a pillow under his head.

He yawned. "What do you need me to do this time, Sir?

"What do we have for ships in the bay?"

Jones scratched the top of his head. "There's a Hunter-Killer group patrolling off Sable Island."

The Major moved a rumpled pair of trousers off a chair and sat down. "What's it made up of?"

The Lieutenant ran a hand over the course stubble on his face. "The aircraft carrier USS Card and five destroyer escorts."

"Raise them on the radio and see which one is closest. Then arrange for us to meet them." He paused. "Oh, and we'll need a ride out there."

Jones fluffed his pillow. "Do we have time for breakfast, or is this one of your right-now things?"

"Now would be good."

Jones rolled on his side, sat up and arched his back. After a heavy sigh, he got to his feet and walked over to his desk. He dropped into his chair and swivelled, turning his back to the room. Removing his pants from atop a rectangular table that lay under the window, he slid one leg into them and picked up the microphone to the radio it had covered.

"Whiskey, Mike, Charlie, one, five niner to CVE-11. Come in, Baker." He set the microphone down and put his other leg into his pants.

The radio crackled. "Whiskey, Mike, this is one, one. Go ahead with your message."

He took his time buckling his pants before he reached for the microphone again. "One, one, I've got a priority Alpha delivery for you." He reached into the top drawer of his desk and removed a thin brown binder. Flipping through the pages, his finger stopped mid-page. "Can you rendevous at point Zulu six at zero seven thirty?"

The radio was silent, except for the pop of static. Ken looked at the Commander, who in turn, continued to stare at the box.

"No can do, Whiskey Mike. Zero eight hundred is possible. We'll send DE one niner two."

"Zero eight hundred. Roger. Whiskey Mike out."

Jones flipped off the radio and reached into his bottom drawer. He removed a half-empty bottle of Old Crow whiskey and set it on his desk. "I guess that gives us time for breakfast after all."

Chapter Twenty Four

The back door of the office opened onto a short, slanted ramp to the dock. Dew still glistened on the rails and the western surfaces. The dock's flat boards and easterly exposed surfaces were already dry from the morning sun. The water undulated with the tide, and ripples marked the surface further out in the harbor. Gulls squawked and circled near the cannery. A fishing boat, stern to, headed out of the harbor with its diesel engine droning, a thick baritone against the tenor hum of machinery in the plant.

A small sailboat, a two-masted day-sailor, was secured to the dock, starboard side in, her black hull unmoving. Her masts sharply raked, she was Bugeye-rigged with a wooden bowsprit and deadeyes forward of the main mast. Her bow rose high and dropped back sharply, giving her a wedge appearance. Although only a bit more than twenty feet in length, she had a white-sided cabin covering the main deck between the two masts.

Ken leaned on the rail and looked further up the harbor. "Where's your boat?"

Jones moved past Ken on the dock, his white canvas

sneakers untied. "Geez. She's right in front of you boy. The Seaquence."

Ken looked back at the day-sailor, and then at the recently fortified, still rumpled Lieutenant. "We're using a sailboat?"

Jones continued down the dock, speaking as he walked. "Can't put nothing past you."

The Major strode by. "One thing he does well – sailing."

Ken stared at the small boat, then looked out at the immense harbor, considering the vast Gulf of Maine. He shook his head as the Major hopped aboard and opened the hatch to the cabin.

Jones was already in the cockpit, starboard of the raised center board. "If you're coming with us, cast off the bowline, and hop aboard."

The Commander had settled into a seat just inside the cabin. "This is his boat. He gives the orders here."

This is nuts, Ken thought. One decent wave and we'll all be at the bottom. He loosened the dock line from the galvanized cleat and tossed it onto the bow. His foot lifted slowly, then he hopped onto the deck beside the cabin. Stooping to hold the top of the cabin, he stepped into the cockpit beside Jones. The boat heeled over toward the dock.

"Best be getting to the port side if you want to keep us upright."

Ken nodded, then settled onto the wooden bench seat and slung an arm onto the rail for support.

"What do you think, Commander? Do we have time

for a sailing lesson?" Jones coiled the line, wrapped it neatly, and hung it on a hook in the cockpit.

The Commander nodded. "Great idea. Let's see how clever our young officer is."

Mr. Jones turned to Ken. "So, what do we do first, sailor?"

Ken stiffened. "What do you mean? Aren't you going to sail us?"

"You're in the Navy boy. Just what do you think we do here?"

"Until yesterday – paperwork." Ken muttered.

Jones grunted and looked at the Major. "Commander, where'd you dig this one up?"

Commander Swain rubbed his knees. "He's a bit rough, but it's like this old boat – nothing a few days with a plane, sandpaper, and time won't cure."

"I'll take your word for that." He turned back to Ken and quickly pointed out a few of the main features of the boat; the main, her mizzen, and the key lines. "So, have you come up with a plan to get us underway?"

Ken shrugged. "I'd raise the sail, I guess."

Jones spat into the water. "You guess! Be decisive, boy. Make a choice and stick to it until you see a better way."

Ken lifted off the bench, his eyes searching the length of the boat. "Raise the main."

The Commander set his jaw and held on tighter.

"Raising the main, aye," Jones replied.

Jones released the ties holding the sail to the boom, and hauled on a line. A deadeye lifted and came taut. The line ran through smoothly up the height of the main, around a pulley, and back down to the furled sail. The bright white sail hoisted into the air.

That wasn't so bad, Ken thought. He reached for the tiller, and cranked it over to starboard as the gentle morning breeze began filling the sail. The boat edged away from the dock and picked up more breeze. Ken though of all the adventure books he'd read as a youth, Robinson Caruso, Moby Dick, and of course Captain's Courageous. He tried to remember the sailing terms they had used.

The boat heeled to port and headed out into the harbor. This wasn't hard at all. In fact it was kind of fun, Ken decided. They passed through the calmest part of the harbor and entered the light wavelets further out. "Raise the mizzen," Ken said with confidence.

The Commander leaned back against the bulkhead while Jones unfurled the mizzen. "This what you want boy?" He raised a brow.

The sail rose and the wind lifted the starboard side out of the water, heel harder to port.

Ken felt a shot of adrenaline rush up his chest. He turned the tiller into the wind. "No. Wait. Um..."

Jones loosened another line. The mizzen boom swung out perpendicular to the wind and luffed the sail. "Make up your mind. I don't want to be doing everything twice."

Ken looked about the boat. There had to be a way to make it more stable.

"That's right, boy. I can see the wheels turning." He waited another moment. "That thing in front of your feet ain't a foot rest."

Ken looked to the center board. Of course. He unhooked the keeper lash and lowered the board. The fin bit into the water as it lowered and righted the boat. "Now, how about that mizzen sail, Mr. Jones?"

Jones grunted, and turned toward the Commander. "Not lacking confidence, that's for certain."

The stern lifted as the sails filled. He pointed the bowsprit between the squat house of Breakwater Light and the steep cliff face of Owl's Head, then gently massaged the handle of the oak tiller. His mood shifted. Uncertainty and fear left, taking with it his worries and grief.

Gulls soared beside the main, their wings matching the angle of the sails. Whitecaps rolled the tops of the waves beyond the breakwater. The wind picked up beyond the head, but he didn't worry how the boat would react to the waves and wind, nor how he'd react to the boat. He just wanted to get to them, into them, and away.

Luke was assigned a berth vacated by one of the agents, but he tossed on the stiff mattress throughout the night. Sleep hung over him, torturing him, taunting him, but never came. The pounding of the engines was deafening. He pulled the damp wool blanket over his head breathing, the musty odor and diesel fumes, trying to muffle the noise. At least it was better smelling than everything else on this tub. The men were rank, the air putrid. God only knew what they ate.

The darkness under the blanket put him back beside Josh, his smashed body beneath the river. Barbara, sweet Barbara. He yanked away the covers.

"Can't sleep?" It was the young officer he'd been ashore with, carrying a mug. "I thought you could use some coffee."

Luke rolled over and took the mug. The cold inside the U-boat caused steam to form above the mug, even in July. The brew was the first decent smelling thing on the boat.

After taking a sip, he kept the mug close to his nose to mask the other odors. "Thanks."

The officer stuck out a hand. "Werner, Johann Sebastian Werner. I'm the second on this boat."

"Luke Morgan... ah... Hoffman." Luke shrugged. "Sorry. I haven't used that name since I was six. Sebastian, that was my twin brother's name."

"You're a twin? Where's your brother?"

Luke looked away. "Dead."

"Sorry." The officer ran his eyes over Luke. "Tell me about America. Is it great like the stories I hear?"

"I don't know what you've heard. But yeah it's all right."

"Just all right? I heard everyone is rich. Every house has inside plumbing, huge kitchens, and plenty of food in the cupboards."

Luke moved the mug closer to his nose. "I don't know about every house, but things were pleasant. Still we had to ration. You could get almost anything you wanted, but most luxury items are sold on the side. Not like in Germany."

Werner chuckled. "When did you say you were there last? Everything is in short supply – unless you have the rank to take it or the money to buy it."

Luke frowned. "That's not what my father said. He told me the German government was the greatest. They're above such things."

"All due respect to your father, but he's wrong. Things haven't been good at home for several years."

"I don't believe it. That's not possible."

Werner shrugged. "Believe what you wish, but it's true."

Luke lay his head back on the pillow. "That just can't be."

A sailor ducked passed Werner. The officer momentarily watched him move down the passage, then turned back to Luke. "What about the girls? They must be something?"

Luke kept staring at a pipe that ran above his bunk. "They're fine, I guess."

"You guess?" Werner scowled. "Was there anyone special?"

Luke set the cup of coffee on the tiny shelf at the head of the bunk. "I'm sorry, but I really should try to sleep."

Werner nodded. "That's fine. I need to get to the Kapitan's berth. We need to design a pattern and pick a location to release our mines into Casco Bay."

Chapter Twenty Five

The main fat, the mizzen tight, the little sailboat was in her glory. She danced across the open water of the Gulf of Maine, heeled on her port side, taking the head swells. She rose with the crests and curtsied with the troughs. Ken sat high on the rail, keeping his weight far out over the starboard side. He figured that should he lean any further, he'd have to swim. Commander Swain and Lieutenant Jones were jammed in beside him, holding tight to the gunwales.

This is the balls, he thought. He'd lived on the water his whole life, yet had never sailed. What a waste.

The Commander kept a close eye on him, and Lieutenant Jones an even closer eye on what Ken was doing to his baby.

Adrenaline surged through Ken's body. He looked into the wind. "Major – sorry...Commander, would it be too bold to ask for an explanation?"

"About what?" The boat dipped into a trough and water sprayed over the bow. "Oh, the name thing. Sure. Commander Bill Swain detached to Naval Security Group Command."

"Naval security – you mean the Shore Patrol?"

He winked and spoke loudly over the wind. "Not exactly. We mostly do code breaking and cipher work, but occasionally, they send us out of the office for information gathering."

"Why the secrecy?"

The boat bucked as it rose on the largest crest in the seven-wave cycle. Commander Swain and Lieutenant Jones nearly cracked heads. "Whoa there, horse!" He smiled as he rode it out. "We like to keep a low profile. Both for the civilians, and in case anyone's watching us."

Ken thought about that for a minute, then looked at Lieutenant Jones. "No disrespect to the Lieutenant, but what's up with the oldest living junior grade in the entire navy?"

Commander Swain intentionally bumped shoulders with Mr. Jones. "What, this codger? He served under me for a number of years in Europe, as my Chief Warrant officer. When the war heated up, I got him a field commission. After what he's been through, he deserved a better retirement."

The wind shifted in a quick gust and the boat lurched. Ken pulled on the tiller to keep her on course. "What kind of things have you been through?"

The Commander stole a look at the Lieutenant and grinned.

Mr. Jones tightened the line to the mizzen. "Things that ain't no never mind to you, sonny. You were in short pants and playin' with roller skates then."

The Commander glanced at the compass screwed to the cabin cover. "Time for a turn yet, Al?"

Mr. Jones looked over his shoulder at Fisherman's Island. "Hard over, Mr. Mitchell. Put us on a course of one, eight, zero magnetic."

"Dead south, yes, Sir." Ken swung the tiller and Mr. Jones released the mizzen. The boat swung into the wind, the sails luffed, and the boat slowed. Her momentum nudged her past the point of dead into the wind. The breeze caught her bow and began to swing her quickly. The main boom swung fast to the starboard side and the sail filled with a snap. All three men ducked under the swinging path of the mizzen boom and scrambled for the port side rail.

Mr. Jones reefed the mizzen and the sailboat was off on a canter.

"Tally Ho!" Jones shouted.

They held their course, steady for twenty minutes. Ken stared ahead at the open ocean. Nothing lay between him and France except wide-open water and sky. A pang of guilt crept inside; he was playing sailor here, while Americans were dying on those shores. Then again, he thought, people are dying over here, too.

"There she is! Two points ahead of the port beam." Jones pointed.

Ken turned, looking behind him. The haze and sun blinded him as he looked eastward. He raised a hand to shield his eyes. Then he saw a shape like a tower, with a fat, squarish base. It was darker than the sky and water, yet lighter than the islands, and heading straight at them. Hard to believe a ship of war with hundreds of men aboard had broken away from its duties to pick them up. His lungs swelled with cautious self-importance.

The Commander reached inside the cabin and pulled out a pair of binoculars. Facing east, he put them to his eyes and focused on the ship.

"It's a destroyer escort, Cannon Class." He adjusted the right ocular. "DE, one, nine, zero. That would be the Baker."

Ken watched her steam toward them. She was steady in the swells. The prow didn't rise and fall, but the white waves she churned off her bow did.

"She's a big mother," Ken said.

"Not so big," the Commander replied. "Three hundred feet or so, just under forty wide. Wait until you see the USS Card."

Jones luffed the mizzen on the port side and the sailboat settled into the water. "You'd best let me take her from here."

Ken bobbed his head. "I can handle her."

"You'll need to be ready to climb up the netting they'll hang over the side. You can't steer and disembark at the same time." For the first time since he was a kid, Ken felt like he wanted to pout.

Lieutenant Jones' hand replaced Ken's on the tiller. Jones kept the mizzen line in his other hand. "Loosen the main sheet. Give her about another foot of line."

Ken slipped up the side of the cabin and released the line from the cleat, let out a foot, and put a figure-eight lash back on the oak stay. By the time he looked up again, the Baker was almost on them.

He stumbled backward as he craned his neck to look high enough to see the top of her prow.

"At twenty-one knots, she sneaks up on you." Jones smiled.

The Baker cut her power and the bow dropped, yet her forward motion was still impressive. Lieutenant Jones came about and attempted to pace her, keeping out in front of her bow wake and to the Baker's windward side.

The massive bow furrowed up and pushed a large wave in front of her, one Ken doubted they could surf over – especially if they were to take it on the stern. The Baker drew closer and Jones tightened the mizzen to sneak out a bit more headway speed. The Baker continued to slow, but the wave didn't seem to diminish.

"Get on the bow and prepare to catch the netting."

Ken skirted around the cabin on decking no wider than his feet. He crawled under the main boom and squatted down, one hand on the main mast. Men aboard the Baker tossed a heavy hemp rope webbing over the side. It hung down to the water amidship. The sailors white caps were dots on pale faces in blue work shirts high above.

"I suppose this is it, Commander. I wish I were going with you." Jones stuck out his hand.

The Commander took the hand. They didn't shake, just gripped for a moment. "I'd like nothing more. Another time."

Jones nodded. "You'd best get up on the bow and chaperon your whelp."

The Commander grunted. "I'll do that. Watch your six."

"You too, Sir."

The bow wave drew near and Ken gripped the mast tighter with each passing second. If they slipped too close, the massive hull, the Baker, would crush them without even knowing it. The crest of the wave was sharp, but it didn't roll over the top. He watched it advance toward their stern. Damn it! They're still going too fast for us, he thought. The leading edge of the swell tickled the stern, lifting as the sail boat ran ahead of it like a porpoise being pushed through the water ahead of the behemoth. The top of the crest began to round, and as it did so the sail boat continued to ride up and over stern first. The boat hesitated just before the crest, and then dropped into the lee of the destroyer.

Ken looked skyward. The top of the main mast didn't reach half-way to the deck. The heavy steel plates of the Baker undulated as they ran her length. He'd expected them to be smoother. The Baker continued to slip by yet the sailboats main boom kept them from getting any closer. Lieutenant Jones kept the Seaquence as close as he could without rubbing the hull.

"Get ready!" the Commander ordered. "We're going to have to jump for the netting."

"Jump?"

The Commander smiled. "Why do you think the Navy still includes the standing broad jump in physical testing."

Ken moved close to the side, still reaching behind to steady himself on the main. The ship eased by, armored plates and rivets flowing by like a stream. Her screws were no longer turning, but the deep thud of her engines rose in his ears.

The leading edge of the net reached the Commander and he leapt from the deck of the sail boat. His right arm caught in the webbing; his left missed, but found home quickly. He wove his foot into the hemp, and looked back. "Your turn," he said as he cruised by.

Ken waited until the Commander passed, swallowed hard, then jumped.

The instant his feet left the deck, he knew he'd jumped too flat; nowhere near high enough. He caught the rope with his right hand, but his left passed through the web and smashed into the hull. His wrist doubled back and pain shot up his arm. He pulled back instinctively, repulsed by the pain, and his left-hand fell away from the netting. Ken's face ground into the coarse rope, burning into his right cheek. He bounced off the netting and fell back, facing outward away from the ship. He dangled from the line by one arm, both legs splashed into the sea up to his mid-thighs.

Adrenaline rushed his senses. The sailboat blurred further out, yet the water next to him remained clear. The water rushed by, running under his body and churning up white bubbles and foam as it passed. He had to get a hold with his other arm.

Ken swiped at the web with his left arm, but his hand wouldn't grasp. Harder, damn it! Don't wear yourself out with half efforts, he chastised himself. He swung again; this time, his arm caught. Looping his forearm through the netting, he hooked his elbow over.

Voices from above. Was it cheers or shouts? He couldn't tell. Damn, that hurt.

The netting ended at the waterline and his feet were

below, still dragging in the water. He pulled with his right arm, but couldn't drag his whole body up. Water kept rushing by, sweeping his legs toward the surface, and they bobbed up and down with the undulating swells.

Maybe if he timed it right, he could pull up with his elbow and hand at the same time, the waves helping to lift his feet. He watched his feet dance and bob, his mind trying to match the rhythm. Here goes! he shouted to himself. His feet rose and he pulled with his upper body. The right leg caught the lowest rung of the net, but his left missed.

He lay diagonally across the bottom of the net, looking skyward. The sun blocked much of the deck-rail, but he saw the Commander climb over the top to safety. Okay, your turn, he decided. His left hand was regaining feeling, but still hurt. Pull up with your right and reach up with your left, he told himself.

A strong jerk and he pulled his left elbow out, but as it came free, his swipe at the net missed and he fell back against the hull with a thud. Shit! Now dangling by one arm and one leg facing away from the net, he looked like a starfish in the net of a lobster trap.

Ken's left foot suddenly left the water. What now? The net jerked and bucked. He wasn't going to die this way. He dug down deep and lunged again, spinning his body up and toward the webbing. This time, his left hand found purchase and he grabbed on tight, his butt sagging downward.

The net continued to jerk. What the hell were they trying to do, knock him off? He glanced over his shoulder. He was now ten-feet off the water. They were pulling him up. He just had to hang on a bit longer. The net jounced and shortened; he closed his eyes and counted the jolts. Maybe sixty feet to the deck, he thought. If they pulled him up a foot at a time he had to hold on for another full minute. His arms screamed in agony as he hung onto the line and counted the jerks.

God, could he hold on? His arms were getting so weak. Twenty, he counted, gritting his teeth.

The netting felt loose in his palms and his fingers as though they were going to be pulled off his hands. Forty-five! his mind screamed.

His right foot fell free and more weight was shifted to his arms and hands. Too close. Don't let go now.

His mind hurried the last of the count, fifty-eight, fifty-nine, sixty, and he opened his eyes. The rail was just a few feet away. Strong tattooed arms in light-blue shirts dragged the net the last bit, then latched onto him. He rolled over the rail and flopped onto the deck in a mass of rope netting.

"Looks like we caught ourselves a mermaid," one voice said.

"More like a pollywog if you ask me. Maybe we should toss him back!" came another.

Laughter flowed all around him.

The netting was peeled away and two sailors lifted him to his feet. He ran his hands over his sweaty face and then looked at his feet. He'd lost one shoe and the sock on that side stuck out as if his foot were twice as long. His pants dripped water from the thighs down.

Commander Swain stood in front of a K-gun, grinning at him. "Now that was an entrance worth noting. We just can't seem to keep you dry, can we?"

Ken coughed and tucked in his shirt. "Misjudged the jump, Sir."

"I'd say that was the understatement of the year." He pointed to a hatch at the base of the tower. "If you can stay on your feet and promise not to fall overboard, we've been invited up to the bridge."

"I'll do my best."

Ken followed behind the Commander, his gate awkward with only one shoe on. The grates on the steps clung to his sock. By the time they reached the upper level, his sock had torn, and dangled half off, exposing his toes.

Commander Swain entered the bridge first; Ken followed close behind, and stood against the abaft bulkhead. Nine sixteen-inch, brass-rimmed portholes lined the forward bulkhead at eye level. Two on each side fore of the hatches and five across the front. Left of front center stood a seaman at post behind a twenty-four-inch diameter, mahogany-rimmed steering column, a compass at his twelve o'clock embedded in the steering post.

The senior officer stood between the steering mate and the executive officer. The senior officer saluted the Commander as he entered, even though the Commander still wore the uniform of Petty Officer Durning. "Commander on deck. He has the con!"

The steering mate turned toward the Commander, snapped to attention, keeping one hand on the wheel, and saluted. The Commander returned the salute. "As you were. Thank you for the courtesy, but Lieutenant Commander Hoffman retains the con."

Lieutenant Commander Hoffman nodded to the officer at attention beside him. "This is my executive officer, 'Forky,' ah... Gus Forkiotis."

The Commander returned Forky's salute.

"Forky, have the quartermaster send up a better fitting uniform with proper insignia for Commander Swain and a dry uniform for the Lieutenant."

Forky moved by them and slipped into the compartment behind them.

Ken couldn't take his eyes off the Lieutenant Commander. He was Ken's age, perhaps a year or two older. The Exec was even younger. The Lieutenant Commander still had some acne on his face and probably could have gotten by without shaving every day.

Hoffman folded his hands behind his back. "Captain Young, commander of the USS Card, informs me we have a U-boat in our waters."

The Commander stripped off his shirt and began to don the fresh one a sailor had brought him. "One I can verify personally. We sighted it at zero one hundred this morning near Hancock Point."

"I understand she's a mine layer?"

"If it's the same boat we fired on two days ago, she's a VII series with twin stern tubes and mine ports on her decks."

"Any insight as to her course or intended target?"

The Commander buttoned his shirt. "With the tides as they are, if she ran full speed on the surface she could cover about a hundred fifty-nautical miles. That could put her as far south as Brunswick or as far north as Lubec." He paused as he winced and buttoned the tight top button on his uniform. "There were replacement parts at the warehouse in Machias, so I'd guess the boat was damaged. Therefore, they must be closer. Perhaps a hundred miles from Hancock Point."

"And the target?"

"Most likely shipping, so Portland Harbor."

Lieutenant Commander Hoffman paced to the starboard porthole, stared out for a moment, then turned to the Commander. "I'll notify the Card. She and her escorts can spread out and screen from the northeast. We can move southwest under full steam. At twenty-one knots, we should catch up to her by nineteen hundred."

"If we guessed correctly," the Commander added.

"Yes, that's true." He looked at Swain's weary face. "Commander, may I offer you my cabin, and the boson will find space for your Lieutenant? Nothing much should happen for a while and you both look like you could use some shuteye."

"That's a good offer." He turned to Ken. "Meet me in the Ward room at Eighteen hundred." A wry smile crept onto his face. "Let's catch us a Sub."

Werner pulled the chart across the table and ran a finger along the line the Kapitan had drawn. The cook clanged the lid on a pot of boiled potatoes, although across the corridor it was loud, being only a meter and a half from the table. Werner flinched.

"I don't know, Sir." The Kapitan leaned against the pressure hull on the far side of the table, one leg up on the bench seat. "Why take the boat out into deeper water, only to turn back?"

"Orders are to remain in deep water whenever possible. Besides, that should put our lubber line on a course straight into the harbor."

"Why not just sneak down the coast? It would be quicker, and with the one shaft still oozing, we could use the time saved."

The Kapitan sat up straight, leaned over the table, and stared at Werner. "I broke from my orders to attack that convoy. It almost cost us the mission." He glanced at the galley and lowered his voice. "I think I was trying to impress you and to that end, your mother. Perhaps I thought you'd tell her what a great skipper I was, and it would have meant more coming from you. But orders and rules are there for a purpose. I'd do well to remember that and will try to stick to them from now on."

Werner's jaw loosened . "Your candor is... well... surprising." He stuttered and tried to think of something better. The silence felt awkward. "And refreshing. I respect that and I know my mother will."

The Kapitan waved his hand over the chart. "We'll lay a nice web of mines for them and then head for home."

Werner continued to look at the Kapitan's thick, pockmarked face. "Home. Yes, that would be good."

Franz, the engineer, appeared in the passage. "Sir, the starboard shaft has a vibration I can't fix. It must have gotten bent in the explosion."

"Is it slipping or losing thrust?"

"No, Sir, but I'm afraid it's getting worse and if it continues, we might damage the engine."

"Shut it down and do what you can. We'll use it in an emergency."

Franz nodded and slipped back down the corridor.

"Are you sure we shouldn't hug the coast?" asked Werner.

The Kapitan ran a hand over the chart. "No. I won't even bend the rules this time."

Chapter Twenty Six

Ken looked up from the book he was studying. Commander Swain stood in the frame of the Ward room hatch, sipping from a thick white mug. His uniform was rumpled around the armpits and knees, but otherwise in order, his hair neat and freshly combed.

The Commander pointed with his mug at the books and pages on the table in front of Ken. "I thought you'd be still sleeping. What are you reading?"

Ken laid a hand on one of the open books. "The Exec loaned me a manual on the ship and a stack of Incident Reports about other ships' encounters with U-boats." He placed his hand on one pile. "Some of these date back to World War One."

"Did you find anything interesting?"

He shrugged. "All of it."

"Anything that will help?"

"I don't know. Maybe. But I'm sure Lieutenant Commander Hoffman knows a lot more than I could learn in a few hours."

The Commander nodded "He seems capable enough."

"He's awfully young to be a Lieutenant Commander, isn't he?"

The Commander stepped inside the room. "Are you saying he's young for the rank or I'm too old?"

Ken stiffened. "Sorry, Sir. I meant no disrespect. I was taken by surprise is all."

The Commander pulled a chair up to the table and sat across from Ken, eyeing him. "Captain MacDaniel at the Subchaser Training Center (SCTC) in Miami turns out a fresh crop regularly, but he has a reputation for making sure they know their business." He sipped the liquid from the mug. "This war has all departments full of young men doing miraculous things. Maybe you should come and work for me."

"What, a code breaker?"

The Commander tilted his head. "That to start perhaps, and much, much more." He looked at the paperwork in front of Ken. "I'm intrigued by a man with curiosity and gumption."

"I'll have to think about it, Sir."

The "whoop, whoop" of an alarm bell sounded, followed by the loud speaker. "General Quarters. Report to your stations."

The Commander set the mug on the table and stood. "Don't take too long. Things happen fast around here." He started for the hatch, then paused. "You coming?"

The Exec leaned on the hatch frame abaft the bridge, hanging half into the control room with his feet still in the Control Information Center (CIC). Hoffman was reading what appeared to be a printout from the universal drafting machine Ken had just read about.

"The aircraft reported oil in the water twenty miles southeast of our position. Could be a leaking U-boat."

The Lieutenant Commander rubbed his chin. "I don't know, Forky, it could be a diversion, or a fishing boat cleaning out her bilge. If she was hurt, she'd hug the coastline to decrease the distance to her target area."

Ken spoke before he thought it through. "Sir, the Incident Reports Mr. Fortiotis loaned me indicated most wounded boats seek deep water for repairs."

The Lieutenant Commander's right lip curled up with the brow on the same side. "Is that what they taught you at SCTC?"

Hoffman was too young to pull off the sarcasm well, Ken thought. "No, Sir. You know I didn't go there."

"Annapolis then? Class of what?"

Ken's eyes wanted to seek the floor, but they didn't. He stared back at the Lieutenant Commander. "Not there either."

Hoffman handed the paper back to Forky. "Stay the course. Active on the sonars maximum range."

Forky saluted. "Aye, Sir."

Ken continued to stare at Hoffman as a seaman handed Forky another paper. The Exec. read it, then held it out to Hoffman. "Seems the kid was right. Aircraft from the Card spotted a swirl and dropped sonar buoys. They confirmed a boat in the water at that location."

Kid. Who's he calling a kid? Ken fumed to himself.

Hoffman's head swung around. "Who's closest?"

Forky grinned. "We are. Then the Thomas."

Commander Swain leaned to Ken's ear. "Nice call. Speak up again if the urge strikes you."

"Twenty degrees to port. Ahead full." Hoffman winked at Forky. "Radio the Card. Tell her we'll attempt to engage the enemy. Then get Lieutenant Commander Kellog on the horn and tell him to attack from the south. We'll squeeze the boat between us."

The words blurted out of Ken; he wanted to stop them, but they came anyway. "Why not head straight at them, banging away with the sonar and have the Thomas lay for them, moving slow and quiet on her electrics? You could herd the boat right to her. We used to drive deer the same way back on the farm. The deer spent so much time looking over their shoulders they didn't see what was in front of them."

Hoffman's face hardened, his lid fissures narrowing. "We have tactics aboard ship. Tried and true methods. If you want to shoot deer, go back to the farm."

Ken inched back. "Sorry, Sir."

Commander Swain leaned close again. "Tact, Ken. For God's sake, even if it's a good plan, being right isn't everything."

Hoffman heard the Commander mumble to Ken. "Sir, did you have an idea?"

Commander Swain tipped his head. "The Lieutenant was right about the boat. It sounds like a good idea."

Hoffman rocked on his toes and folded his hands behind his back. "Is that an order?"

"I may outrank you, but no. I'll defer to your judgement. This isn't my specialty."

Hoffman moved closer to the forward portholes. "Put

300 pounders in the stern tracks. Tell the men I want short bursts with the deck guns if she surfaces. Don't waste ammo. These boys are green and I don't want them spending all their ammo in a single useless stream."

━━━

"Kapitan, aircraft dropping sonar beacons in the water!" a voice shouted down the passage.

The Kapitan bolted out of the seat and rushed toward the control room. Werner rolled up the chart and followed.

Luke was sitting on the edge of the bunk when Werner rushed by. "What's the excitement?"

"Aircraft has spotted us. We need to maneuver."

Luke hopped off the bunk, landing hard on the grates. "May I come?"

Werner didn't slow, half diving through a hatch. "Sure, just stay out of the way."

Luke moved forward. Men pushed past him as they rushed to their stations. He shivered at the cold and pulled his sweater down over the top of his pants as he reached the control room. The Kapitan leaned over a chart on the far side of the periscope. The men at the steering stations were perspiring, despite the chill in the air.

"Maintain course for three minutes. Give them a good vector, then dive to sixty meters and make a circular swing to the northeast. Keep the boat in an arc until you reach one, one zero true."

"Sixty meters at one ten, aye."

Werner looked back at Luke, then moved to the speaking tube, and shouted orders to the men. The boat angled down and Luke grabbed a pipe above his head for support. His hand hesitated as he reached; there were dried smears on the pipe. It was blood.

The Commander looked at his watch, shook his wrist, then stuck it to his ear. "What time is it, Ken?"

"Seven thirty."

"1905 local. Zone plus one hour and twenty minutes for GCT," Commander Swain said under his breath.

"Right, 1905 local. Sorry, Sir."

Hoffman paced behind the portholes, from the brass throttle control, to the starboard hatch and back. "Continue the zig zag in accordance with the Cards' plan twelve." He shot a glance toward the CIC. " Forky, what are the sound conditions?"

The Exec. stuck his head through the hatch. "Sonar medium 40/11C."

"Maintain zero six six true, twelve knots for two more minutes." He stopped, gazed out one of the portholes and rocked on his toes. "She's out there, but which way did she go?"

Ken leaned toward the Commander and whispered, "If she saw the sonar buoys dropped, she'd figure we'd anticipate her heading for Portland. Then they might go north instead to lose us. That would put her right about here."

"That's not a bad guess. But you said she'd run for open water if she was hurt."

"Not if she knows we spotted her."

There was a commotion in the CIC. "Sonar contact!" Forky shouted. "Bearing one one zero, range 2200 yards."

Hoffman moved to the center of the control room. "Where do we stand in relation to the Card?"

Forky's voice came from the CIC. Two hundred and seventy-degrees relative, distance ten miles."

"And the Thomas?"

"Three miles and closing."

Commander Swain leaned toward Ken. "Okay, you've got my attention. Got any good tips on race horses?"

Ken shuffled his feet, but kept his eyes on Hoffman. "Just lucky, Sir."

Commander Swain leaned away. "Sure. Luck. Face it, son, you've got an aptitude for this."

"Forky, do you have a depth on them yet?" Hoffman asked.

There was a whir of tiny electric motors, clicks and bleeps from the CIC. "No, Sir. Inconclusive."

Hoffman cleared his throat and coughed. "Change the stern tracks to mark eights a pattern of five. If we set them deep, then the magnetic impulse detonators may fire if she's running shallow." He paused, then rocked on his toes again. "Make it a full pattern of thirteen. Stream the Foxer. Report when ready."

"Aye, Sir."

Ken stuck his hands in his pockets. "How close do we need to get them to sink her?"

"With the three hundred pounders, ten yards to breach the hull, thirty to damage her," Commander Swain replied.

"Gun crews manned, tracks loaded!" Forky shouted.

"Come right twenty, speed standard." Hoffman locked eyes with Ken. "Range and bearing movement?"

There was silence. Hoffman continued to stare at him, and Ken wondered if he was supposed to answer.

"Four hundred yards, but the target angle is too high. I can't get relative bearing drift."

"Hold course. Let me know when you've got it."

The Baker sped forward. Ken felt uneasy with Hoffman's eyes on him and moved to the hatch on the port side, adding distance between them. Gray water ahead. Nothing to indicate the danger that lay below.

"Now, Forky! I need that information now!"

The gunners hunched over their weapons. Round, smooth helmets protruded up out of bulky life vests, surrounded by armor plating and anxiety.

"Appears to be left to right." Forky's voice pitched lower. "No, wait. Right to left."

"Are you sure?"

"I think so. Yeah, I'm sure." came the reply.

"Con left with full rudder. Straighten her out after twenty degrees and fire the pattern!"

Ken stepped out the port hatch onto the observation platform to watch the canisters roll off the tracks and splash into the water. The boat held steady for thirty seconds as the pattern was launched. The first explosion followed the deployment of the fifth charge. A plume of water shot into the sky like a geyser, turning the sea white at the base of the spout. The spray landed on the surface just as the second explosion sounded. Eleven more in rapid succession.

"Con left and get me a sonar report!" Hoffman shouted.

"Splashes!" the sonar operator yelled from the alcove in front of the control room.

Luke moved away from the pressure hull. His father had told him about situations like this, but being here was different than hearing about it in the den of the old farm house, huddled close to the potbellied stove with a cup of cocoa. Battle seemed so romantic then; exciting, even noble.

The first blast was deep and to port. It rattled the grates under his feet. Luke hunched over and squatted down, wrapping his arms around his knees. He absent-mindedly reached up and began to tug on his right ear. A second blast to starboard. His eyes went to the top of the compartment. The metal plates grew hazy; they looked almost wooden to him. Unfinished oak. His eyes were playing tricks on him. As the grates continued to tremor, he tightened his arms around his knees.

"Load the stern tubes!" the Kapitan shouted.

"We need to maneuver first, then we can load," Werner responded.

"We'll be fine. Don't question my decisions!" the Kapitan bellowed.

Why was the boat still shaking between the blasts? Luke tried to make sense of the blurred image around him. Then he understood – it wasn't the grates that were shaking; it was him.

Chapter Twenty Seven

"Solid echo, bearing three ten, range three hundred fifty yards!" Forky shouted.

Ken moved forward to the port-side porthole, scanning the gray water as if he could see the danger that ran below the surface. Waves, just a steady unbroken field of uniformly sized waves.

"Right in the middle of the search arc. Now to tighten the net." Hoffman smiled. "Tighten the swing. I want to get on them while we have a solid contact."

Ken thought about the big buck that got by him two falls ago. He'd grown excited and left his original course and tried to head it off sooner. It was faster than he'd guessed and kept ahead of him. He chewed on the inside of his cheek, thoughts festering his mind. Not too tight; you'll let them slip out.

"We lost them! The remote control tracking unit just went out!" Forky screamed from the CIC.

"Damn it! Not now." Hoffman smacked his hand against the bulkhead. "I'm blind up here! Get that damn thing back on line!"

Commander Swain cleared his throat. "Can't you track them manually from the lower sound room by using the JX sound-powered phone circuit?"

Hoffman's head snapped around. "How'd you think of that?"

He shrugged. "That's what we do at Security Command – electronic surveillance."

"Forky, get three men down there and patch in a dedicated line from the sound room to the CIC." He glanced at Ken. "Maybe you two will be more useful than I anticipated."

Forky stepped into the control room. "We had a good contact. Should we fire a second pattern?"

"Yes. But fire them from the K-guns."

Commander Swain moved toward the hatch. "With your permission, I'll go below and give them a hand in the sound room."

Hoffman waved him away. "Go. Get me some eyes in the water before they start shooting back." He paused, apparently realizing he'd been dismissive to a senior officer. "Ah, at your discretion, Sir."

Commander Swain raised a brow, gave Ken a wink, and exited. After he left, Hoffman turned to Ken. "We're blind. Any great insights now?"

Ken hesitated, thinking about chasing deer in dense brush when you couldn't see anything around, yet the deer sneaking through the brush could hear your every step and movement. The deer could pick what direction they wanted to go. Moving slow and in a straight line wouldn't work.

Hoffman exhaled forcibly. "That's what I thought. Farmers."

Ken's voice was soft at first, then grew louder. "She doesn't have bow tubes. She'll go to the right."

"What did you say?"

"Right. She'll go right."

Hoffman's head turned slowly toward the CIC. "Anything from the sound room?"

"They can't get a good fix. It could be a few minutes."

"We don't have a few minutes. A few seconds, if we're lucky."

"The sound room reports it's impossible to obtain cut-ons."

Hoffman looked to the steering mate, then at Ken. "Easy turn to one hundred and nine true and fire the pattern."

"Even on both sides?" Forky asked.

Hoffman paced around the room, then stared at Ken, narrowing his eyes. "No. She's going left to right relative to our attack, trying to get a shot at us. Double the charges on the starboard." Hoffman folded his arms over his chest. "You'd better be right, Lieutenant."

"Werner, get the spare torpedoes out from under the grates and move them to the stern." The Kapitain flicked his hand at Luke. "Take him with you. He may as well be of some use."

Luke remained huddled in a squat, staring at the bulkhead above him.

Werner stepped beside him, pointed toward the stern, then rested a hand on Luke's shoulder.

Luke looked up; the man's face seemed cloudy, distant, but his hand was comforting. He nodded. "I'll help you, Sebastian."

Werner grasped his wrist and pulled him to his feet. "It's Johann."

Luke shook his head. "Right. Sorry." He cleared his throat. "Lead the way."

Luke followed Werner's back, listening, as he hurried down the passageway. "We need to make sure the other fish are loaded and clear the racks before we can get the others out."

They hurried through the engine compartment, Franz reefed on a wrench at the base of the quiet diesel as they rushed past. The electric motor spun the shinny port shaft. The other remained still.

In the compartment aft of the engine room, three men worked to move a torpedo from the loading rails. It hung from a chain fall above the deck grates, swinging precariously. One man stood between the nose of the ordinance and the open tube, the others on each side attempting to guide it into the opening.

"Grab the fin and steady it," Werner said to Luke.

Luke grasped the fin just as a depth charge exploded near the stern.

The jolt knocked Luke to his knees, and the torpedo slipped from his grasp. Water burst out of a seal near the open torpedo tube cap. The man closest to the nose leaned on the ordinance to steady it. The other two scrambled for patching material and braces.

Luke stayed on his knees. Was the boat mortally wounded or just knocked about? The room seemed hazy.

Was that smoke or were his eyes playing tricks on him? He shook his head, trying to clear his vision.

Water shot across the room and began to flood the deck beneath the grates.

"Get a hold of the fin!" Werner shouted over the whoosh of water.

Luke remained on his knees. The boat groaned and snapped. Was she breaking up?

"I said, get up and grab that fin! Do it now!" Werner shouted.

Luke shook his head again, then dragged himself up and grabbed on with both hands. The room began to brighten as his eyes focused again. The stern settled downward as water continued to rush in, and the level rose. The man in front of the torpedo braced his feet against the front of the tube, leaning into the torpedo and attempting to keep it from striking the open tube cap.

The other two men shoved padding into the spray, bracing a metal pipe on the grates and into the wadding. Water continued to spray around the wadding, and the stern continued to sink.

Another charge rocked the starboard side. The torpedo swung into the rail with a deafening clank. At the same instant the metal pipe slipped from the grates, loosened from the wadding, and water shot across the compartment.

"Damn it! Get that patch in place!" Werner yelled.

"We're trying," one of the men shouted.

"Try harder. If we don't stop it, we'll go down!"

A charge exploded near the bow, raising the angle of the boat even higher. The torpedo rocketed back this time. The man holding the torpedo away from the cap disappeared into the tube as the nose stuffed him in like a ramming rod with a cannon ball.

The bow settled and the torpedo slipped back out; with it, came one of the man's legs. It landed on the grates still in the man's trousers, an empty pant leg on the other side. The bow continued to drop and the torpedo swung wildly, flinging Luke into the rail. The weapon continued on, shattering the metal rails, shoving them forward into one of the men working on the patch. The rail drove straight through the man's mid section and continued on into the pressure hull.

Spurting out from around the man's back, water mixed with blood sprayed in all directions. The flow of water had doubled.

"Get out! We need to seal off the compartment!" Werner yelled.

Werner grabbed Luke by the shoulder and dragged him toward the hatch. The third man was trapped in front of the torpedo and screamed for help.

Luke pulled at Werner. "We need to help him."

Werner looked at the man; the full weight of the torpedo rested on him. "He's a dead man. We need to secure this hatch before we all are."

Luke hesitated, then stumbled out as the water reached the bottom of the hatch and began to spill into the engine room.

Franz's strong hands grasped Luke's arms and dragged him through, flinging him to the grates. Luke lay on his back, staring into the eyes of the man in the far room as Franz slammed the hatch closed, and spun the lock tight.

"We could've saved him," Luke said.

Franz pointed to the batteries below the grates. "If sea water got to those batteries, it would make chlorine gas and we'd all be dead."

Werner staggered up the inclined deck. "We might be anyway if we don't stop our descent. The weight of the water is dragging us down."

Hoffman spoke into the microphone of the loud speaker. "All crew on the stern keep a sharp lookout for debris or oil. Report any sightings."

"Do you think we got them, Sir?" Forky asked.

"I don't know."Hoffman rubbed his temples. "Right rudder easy, 200. Bring us around slow so she can't get ahead of us."

Ken stepped out of the control room through the port hatch and moved to the solid steel chest high barrier that ran around the control room and CIC. The sea behind them was remarkably calm following the explosions. It seemed to Ken as if nature didn't recognize the power the ship had brought to bear. Was Luke dead? Was his body twisted up amongst the wreckage of the U-boat, sinking into the depths? He deserved it after what he'd done to Josh and Barbara. What he did to Maggie. Ken wanted to feel happy, but he wasn't.

Forky's loud voice drifted out of the control room. "Commander Swain reports a number of small pips resembling sea returns off our starboard at 1200 yards."

"Bring the boat to zero zero zero true. Arm the tubes, train all guns and torpedoes on 055 degrees true."

Ken moved around the back of the CIC and onto the starboard side, outside the open hatch to the control room.

"What?" Hoffman said. "Who's talking to me, the torpedo room or the K-gun crew?"

Ken listened closer. The K-gun crews and the torpedo firing room were on the same circuit and orders were getting confused.

"Damn it, no that's not what I said," Hoffman sputtered. "Forky, send the assistant gunnery officer to the torpedo room. Tell him to fire at his discretion when conditions are favorable."

"Aye, Sir."

Ken turned his attention back to the sea. His gaze followed the direction every gun on board was pointing to. Geez, didn't anything on this ship work right?

———

"Blow all the tanks! Get us some positive buoyancy!" the Kapitan shouted.

As Luke dragged his wet body into the control room, a tremor erupted from deep inside that reached up to his shoulders. The angle of the boat was steep and he could see the needle on the depth gauge inching deeper. Air hissed through the pipes and hoses, blowing water out of the ballast tanks. Yet the boat continued to slide deeper.

"One hundred and fifty meters," Werner called out.

"Continue blowing the tanks," the Kapitan replied.

"One hundred sixty."

The boat creaked and moaned. Luke felt like a chick inside an egg, with the egg being swallowed by a snake.

The hiss of the air began to trail off.

"The tanks are almost dry, Sir." Werner reported.

"Depth."

"One sixty-five and still sinking."

The Kapitan slowly rotated his head, looking around the control room, evidently searching for anything that might stop them from sinking, and certain death.

"Well, that's it then. A watery grave it is," the Kapitan said in a calm monotone.

Luke watched Werner close his eyes, slacken his body, and slump against the bulkhead. Luke's eyes moved to the depth gauge. "Ah...Kapitan. I think we've stopped."

Werner snapped straight and locked his eyes on the needle. "He's right. We've stabilized at one-seventy. And she's rising."

"Thank God." The Kapitan leaned on the chart table. "Control our ascent with water to the ballast tanks. Level us at one fifty and hold your course."

Werner reached for a red control valve. He tried to twist it, but it didn't budge. "The vent doors are jammed! I can't control the ascent."

"Get some leverage on it."

Werner picked up a short piece of pipe and stuck it between the spokes in the small red wheel. He pulled, but it didn't budge. Next he hung on it, adding his body weight. It creaked, then snapped off cleanly. Werner thudded onto the grates and the pipe bounced atop the grates with a clang.

"Shit!" The Kapitan said, looking at the top of the

compartment. "Looks like we've got an express ticket topside."

Werner looked up from the grates. "Do we prepare to abandon?"

"Sonar, what's the position and bearing of the destroyer?"

"Twelve hundred meters off our starboard bow at twelve knots, closing."

The Kapitan moved toward the periscope. "Swing the boat twenty degrees to starboard and give me full power on both electrics. If we can go fast enough, we might be able to pass under them and get a running start away on the surface."

Werner pulled himself to his feet. "We're going to try and outrun them on the surface?"

"Just until we can make repairs and get back below."

"We're going to put repair crews on deck with a destroyer on our stern?"

The Kapitan raised a brow. "Unless you have a better idea."

Chapter Twenty Eight

Forky rushed through the hatch from the CIC. "We've regained sonar contact! She's right where Commander Swain reported the pips."

Hoffman smiled. "How deep?"

"Three hundred feet and rising."

"She's coming up for a shot at us," Hoffman said.

Ken raised a brow. "Either that or she's hurt and doesn't have a choice but to surface."

"Either way we're not going to let her have a chance at us."

"What if they plan to surrender? Wouldn't the capture of the boat be valuable?" Ken asked.

Hoffman started to rock on his toes again. "Sure, but I don't think it's worth the risk to my ship and crew."

Ken watched Hoffman bob up and down. He'd known the officer for less than a day, yet his habits were already beginning to annoy him. "Can't you give them a chance?"

Hoffman stopped rocking, "No. I can't."

"You mean you won't."

"Yes, that's exactly what I mean." He locked eyes

with Ken. "Bring the boat right to zero nine zero and load all guns."

"You're giving up an opportunity here, Sir."

Hoffman kept his eyes on Ken, but turned his head toward the CIC. "Set the depth charges on shallow. She'll be on the surface or close to it."

"Contact Commander Swain. He'll tell you how important this could be."

Hoffman turned away. "Commander Swain made it very clear he didn't wish to take command. Now if you'll stop pestering me, I'll get on with sending these devils to the bottom."

Part of Ken wanted to see the U-boat sent straight to hell, but another part, something way down deep, told him there should be another way. A more productive way. "Permission to leave the control room."

Hoffman waved him off, his mind apparently elsewhere.

Ken spun around and leaned close to Forky. "How do I get to the sound room?"

Luke's eyes fixed on the depth gauge. The needle was sluggish at first, but the closer they got to the surface, the faster it moved. No one in the control room spoke. They, too, were staring at the little round indicator. He could feel the chill still in his body, mixing with his fear, to give him a steady, full-body tremor.

The sonar operator leaned into the passage and shouted to the Kapitan, "Sir, the destroyer has changed course. We are going to surface on her starboard side."

The Kapitan's head drooped. "That's it then. Our

deck guns would be useless against them and our torpedo room is flooded."

"Do we abandon ship?" Werner asked.

The Kapitan slouched against the chart table and glanced at Luke. "Take him and open the seacocks. Wait until we surface so the men can get out."

"Scuttle the boat. Aye Kapitan."

The Kapitan nodded. "Make sure to take care of your mother for me."

Werner rested his arm on the Kapitan's shoulder. "You be careful so you can come back and take care of her yourself."

The Kapitan rested his hand on top of Werner's, squeezed it, then moved to the speaking tube. "All hands. Prepare to abandon ship. Destroy all documents and code books." The Kapitan wiped a dribble of sweat from above his eye. "No one is to make any attempt to man the deck guns. I repeat, do not fire upon the destroyer. Get off the boat and away from her. The boat is going to go back down quickly, so don't waste any time abandoning her."

The depth gauge passed twenty meters. "You've been a brave and loyal crew. You've all done your duty. Now it is time to save yourselves."

Werner slipped beside Luke and paused in the hatch.

The Kapitan nodded at Werner. "Get going. We don't need to give the boat to the Americans."

Werner stared at the Kapitan for another instant, then turned his attention to Luke. "Follow me."

Men gathered personal items from beside their bunks, tied life belts around their bodies, and tugged knit caps tightly over their heads. The boat was still at a sharp angle upward and they steadied themselves by holding onto rails and bunks as they hurried to accomplish their tasks.

Werner spoke to them as he moved by, touching each one for an instant on the shoulder or cheek. "Make sure that vest is secure. Get on your warm sweater – the sea will be cold. Wrap your letters in an oil cloth."

When they reached the engine room. Franz was sitting in the center of the aisle, cross legged, a pint of liquor in his hand. "Can I offer you a drink, Oberleutnant?"

Werner scowled. "Didn't you hear the order? We're to abandon."

Franz wiped his soiled forehead with the back of his hands, nearly spilling the liquid as he did so. "I heard. What better time to fortify myself? I don't think they'll let me have this at the prison camp, and I've been hanging on to it too long to give it to the enemy."

Werner extended a hand. Franz grasped it and rose up from the grates. "We need to open the seacocks. Move yourself forward so the chlorine gas won't get to you."

Franz stuck a cork back into the bottle and stuffed it into his front pants pocket. "I'd better save a snort for when they pull me out of the water."

"He's a good man." Werner hesitated and watched Franz stagger up the passageway, then squatted down and tugged on a deck grate. "Give me a hand."

Luke spread his feet wide, placed them on either side of the grate, and lifted. The steel creaked and ground as they slid it on top of the decking, opening up a section of the floor. The batteries lay in rows under the grates, with pipes twisted and wound around them. Werner dropped waist-high into the opening, his head darting as quickly as his eyes to locate the valves.

"There!" Werner pointed. "That valve under your feet. Turn it counter clockwise when the boat levels. I'll get the one back here."

Luke knelt beside the opening, but couldn't reach the valve while facing aft. The boat was tilting too far upward for him to maintain his balance. He rose to turn around.

The boat apparently reached the surface. The bow lifted at a forty five degree angle. Luke grabbed hold of a rail that ran the length of the engine. His moist hands slipped on the smooth steel. He tightened his finger, his toes nearly lifting off the deck. The boat paused in mid flight. The deck grate began to slide back. Luke watched as it accelerated and dropped into the opening with a screech followed by a clank.

Werner screamed as the grate pinned his waist against the decking. The bow dropped with the pitch of Werner's voice. Luke landed on the deck, his feet on the grate pinning Werner in place.

"Get it off! Get it off!" Werner implored.

Luke scrambled to his knees and tugged on the grate. It ground on the other metal and moved away from Werner. He collapsed atop the batteries as Luke jerked the grate away. Luke released the grate and jumped down into the opening.

"Come on. Let's get you out of here."

Werner started to let Luke lift him, then pushed him away. "Neine. Get those valves open first."

"Let me get you out of here and I'll take care of the valves."

Werner slapped at Luke, missing him. "Valves, then me," he groaned.

Luke reached forward and twisted the front valve, rotating it counter clockwise until it stopped. Water spurted out of a pipe under the grates at the head of the engine room. He then leaned over Werner and turned the other valve. Water began to rush in from the stern.

Luke slung an arm under Werner's shoulder. "Now can we get out of here?"

The water began to rise around the batteries and crackle as the electricity met it. Fumes curled off the cells and wove through the grating.

Werner and Luke crawled out of the opening and onto their knees. Luke pulled at Werner's shoulder, the gas already stinging his throat and chest. "Can you make it?"

"I'm right with you."

Ken stepped out of the control room as one of the lookouts stationed around the platform yelled, "She's breaking the water!"

Ken squinted where the lookout was pointing the U-boat's dark silhouette rose from the water at a steep angle. It climbed upward, slowing as it rose, then paused as the base of the conning tower reached the surface. Ken could easily see the six oval mine doors on her forward deck. The bow dropped, coming down hard, and lifting white water into the air all around. The bow dropping lifted the stern of the boat. The tower replaced the bow as the highest point, and quickly, the whole profile of the boat was visible from the midline up.

"Fire all guns! Fire the starboard K-guns!" Hoffman

screamed. "Lay the charges in front of her so she'll sail into them."

His words had barely cleared Hoffman's throat before a burst from the 20mm deafened Ken. A trail of white plumes ripped across the surface of the water toward the boat and neatly pleated across the bow ahead of the tower. The rest of the starboard guns let loose. Ken clamped his hands over his ears.

The water exploded around the conning tower, the fire moving toward the stern of the U-boat as the Baker passed toward her stern.

The K-guns boomed and canisters flew into the air toward the bow of the boat. They splashed into the water around her bow and sank into the sea. The cannon pelted the boat as she continued to slip forward as if not feeling the insult. The first depth charge detonated, sending a geyser of water into the air behind the boat.

They hadn't led the boat enough. The charges were ending up at her stern before they could detonate.

A new sound. Hydraulics and high pitched screws.

Two furrows erupted in the water beside the ship as torpedoes were launched out of the Baker, and streaked toward the U-boat. Ken leaned on the armored rail and watched the trails get smaller.

The torpedoes disappeared into the side of the boat.

No explosions.

Hoffman screamed from the control room behind Ken. "Idiots! We're too close for them to arm. Do I have to do everyone's job?"

"We're slipping into the path of her stern, Sir." Forky's calmer voice followed.

There was a pause, then Hoffman again, his voice more restrained, "You're right. We can't pass by her stern and give her a shot at us. Full right rudder! Bring us around as fast as you can."

Thuds. Multiple thuds. Like a half-dozen men beating on the hull with sledge hammers. Slow at first, then increasing in intensity like a hail storm hitting a roof.

Luke hunched to his right as he half dragged Werner across the decking toward the control room. Werner attempted to stand, but his legs were unsteady and his feet seemed to have difficulty following their master's directions.

"Come on, one foot at a time," Luke urged.

"Leave me. Get out."

Luke looked at the dirty face of the man he barely knew. "I've left enough people behind. You're not going to die in here. Now help me, damn you!"

Werner pushed one foot forward, reaching for the side of the hatch to steady himself. Luke jumped through, then pulled Werner into the control room. Men scurried up the ladder to the conning tower hatch. The thuds were louder in the control room and seemed to be all around them.

Luke slammed the hatch closed and spun the lock, trapping the gas behind the door.

Werner coughed and reached up to Luke. "All right, I'm ready if you are."

The hatch to the tower opened, water rained down around them, and the thuds became sharper and tinny sounding.

A blur beside him, followed by a soft thump, that sounded like dropping a bag of grain on the bed of a truck. Luke looked down. A headless body lay front up, spurting blood from what remained of his neck. A corked liquor bottle peeked out of the dead man's front pocket.

"Franz!" Werner gasped.

Luke spun his head up toward the hatch. The sailors were getting spun around and knocked about by the bullets as fast as they could climb out of the opening.

Luke adjusted his grip on Werner. "Is there another way out?"

Werner continued to stare at Franz.

Luke shook him. "Pay attention. Is there another way out?"

Werner nodded toward the bow. "Forward escape trunk, ahead of the Petty Officers' quarters."

Luke churned his legs, pulling Werner with him, lifting and pulling him toward the bow. Werner tried to help, grabbing onto things as they passed, pushing forward, and sluggishly dragging his feet as he attempted to walk.

They pushed by the sonar room. It was empty, yet smoke streamed up from a pile of ashes on the deck from burned orders and instruction manuals. Others were stuffed into water pails, their dissolving ink leaving the pages and coloring the water.

Three men cowered in the Petty Officers quarters; two crouched down beside a bunk, the third sitting rigid between them.

"Get to the forward hatch," Werner's weak voice instructed.

They didn't respond. Luke felt Werner pull back against him. "Come on, follow us."

Luke continued to drag Werner past the men toward the base of the ladder in the next compartment. The men stayed in place, their eyes rotating around the room, searching for only God knew what.

"Come on. Get over here. That's an order!" Werner commanded.

The man on the bunk turned his head toward them, then slowly rose to his feet.

A shell tore into the quarters behind the bunk with a deafening explosion. The room instantly filled with smoke. Luke fell back against the ladder, his head striking a rung. Acrid smoke streamed through the hatch; Luke coughed as it attacked his throat, and his eyes burned. He pulled the top of his sweater up over his mouth, then laid his head back against the bulkhead. His hand left the sweater and found his right ear. He tugged on it.

The room appeared to shrink. Someone moved beside him. Jostling him. Nudging him. Luke closed his eyes.

The floorboards creaked next to Luke's ear as he lay on the Oriental carpet, under the dinning room table, in their house in Berlin. His twin brother wriggled behind him, Sebastian's arms clutched tightly to Luke's shoulders. Their father's shiny black boots paced the floor in front of him, the left boot sluggish and stiff. Two rigid, black boots rising up to the frill that lined the bottom of the table cloth, the boots continuing to move from one end of the table to the other. The cloth shrouded the rest of his father, yet the material wasn't dense enough to conceal the booming voice.

"Damn leg!"

Something whistled outside. Shrill, high up, and moving.

A second of silence, then an explosion.

The house shook, plaster rained down around the table, chunks flying apart as they struck the floor. The dust sifted down, coating the surface, turning it white. His mother's hand reached over Sebastian and tightened on his forearm. Luke pushed his head further into the musty carpet.

"It'll be all right, Ohren," she cooed. "Just listen to your father. He knows best."

The boots moved again – faster this time with less stiffness.

"Come on, you Doughboys. Just try and get me!"

Another explosion rocked the house, tearing out the front window and ripping the chandelier from the ceiling. It crashed down on the wooden table; splinters of glass pelted the floor. Luke turned his head and stared at the bottom of the table. Would something be coming through that next? Would the table be able to shield him if the ceiling collapsed? Was his mother right – could Father protect them?

Sebastian began to whine and squirm behind him. Maybe he should turn around and try to comfort him. Not being able to hear must be even more scary for him. Luke wanted to turn, rub Sebastian's neck, and sooth him like he'd done so many times in the past. But Luke didn't move. He lay still, eyes fixed on the bottom of the oak table.

"Shit, that was close!" Father said.

Another explosion followed. The floor felt as if it had been lifted and suddenly dropped. His father was *knocked to the floor, and the boots immediately had legs, the unevenly worn soles of black leather facing Luke. Smoke filled the room and curled under the table. Luke stared upward at the grain on the underside of the table. Even with all that was going on around him, he fixated on the wood.*

Darkness!

Luke reached out and pawed at the cloak. His hand ran across the familiar fabric. It was the quilt his mother had taken off a chair before they'd hidden under the table. He had difficulty breathing through the thick patchwork. The air under the heavy cotton was warm and stale. His lungs began to work harder and faster. Light streamed in through a thin place where the patches came together. He put his mouth to the tiny line of needle holes and sucked in a lung full of foul air.

His mother's voice sifted through the material. "Easy, child. Easy, Ohren. The blanket will help protect you from the smoke."

Luke wriggled in the quilt and brought his hands up over his ears. His mother's muffled voice spoke behind him; then his father's deeper one, followed by more explosions. He tightened his grip on his ears and felt himself shake. Sebastian twisted behind him, his warm body squishing them up against a table leg. The pressure hurt. The heat from his brother and the blanket made him wet with sweat. He pushed his lips harder against the cloth and sucked in the acrid air. He suddenly resented his brother. Sebastian was always making his father mad and often as not, Luke caught the brunt of the tirade that followed. It wasn't fair that they should both be punished for what Sebastian did. Luke wriggled, attempting to relieve the pain in his ribs from the table leg and push Sebastian away.

Then the pressure was gone.

Footsteps.

Luke removed one hand from his head and lifted the corner of the quilt just enough to peek out. Sebastian was sprinting through the smoke-filled room toward the front door, his mother chasing after.

"Nein! Nein, meine kinder!" she shouted.

The boots moved passed the table in the same direction.

"What the hell are you doing? Get back here!" his father's voice thundered.

Luke tightened the cloth around his face and watched as his father reached the shattered front door. His father paused and leaned on what remained of the front door. Then he turned into a dark silhouette as the doorway turned to mush and flying debris. His father bent at the middle and then was flung back, arms and legs trailing as he landed face-first onto the floor, skidding to the base of the stairs. His father lifted his head; it gave a tremor and bobbed, then fell forward onto the hard surface, still.

Luke cautiously squirmed out of the blanket. Keeping an eye on the doorway for his mother and brother, he crawled across the plaster-strewn floor toward his father. Reaching him, he moved close to his wide back, laid an arm over his midriff, and softly rested his head on his father's shoulder. He could feel his father's body lift and fall with shallow breaths.

Luke stared through the doorway into the street. All he could see was the hind end of a horse lying dead on the

*cobblestones and a heap of rubble on the far side, which
was a few feet away from his neighbor's house.*

*He nestled his chin deeper into his father's shoulder
and instantly longed for the pressure of his brother against
him, again.*

Someone shoved him from behind. Luke's head
scraped against the bulkhead, and spray from a punctured
pipe squirted into his face.

"We've got to get the hatch open." Werner coughed,
pointing upward.

Luke looked upward and continued to pull on his
ear. Smoke from the living quarters drifted across the
top of the compartment and settled around the wheel
to the hatch. He looked back where the three men had
been. Sunlight pushed through the smoke and lit up the
compartment. The man who'd been sitting on the bunk
lay face away on the far side of the aisle, crumpled against
the pressure hull as if he'd fallen asleep. His back was torn
open; his insides hung out and dangled on the grates.
The legs of the other two men lay sprawled, soles toward
him, in the passageway.

Luke stopped tugging on his ear. He stooped over
and wrapped his arms around Werner. "Climb up with
your arms. I'll steady your legs."

Werner reached for the rungs, grasping them and
pulling. "I don't know if I've got the strength."

Luke lifted him around his waist. "You've got the
strength. Now pull!"

Pushing with all his power, Luke felt Werner rise in

jerky steps. Soon Luke had to start climbing the ladder to keep pushing him from below. Werner stopped rising.

"What's the problem?" Luke's legs wobbled under the man's weight.

"Nothing. I have to open the hatch."

Luke's ears rang, but he could hear the latch turn and click. Sunlight streamed in around him as Werner pushed open the cover and crawled out on the deck. Luke rushed up the rungs... Water boiled around the conning tower and bullets glanced off the metal sides. Sparking and pinging off the metal sounded all around.

Several men huddled on the deck, behind the tower. The bullets were not going through.

"Crawl over to the tower! Get behind it!" Luke shoved at Werner's feet.

The deck was wet with seawater and blood. Bodies lay lifeless, strewn around the base of the tower. Luke could see the dark shadow of the destroyer on the horizon, her guns having gone suddenly quiet. The water around them calmed like a boiling pot being removed from a stove.

"Now's our chance. Move! Move!" Luke shouted.

Werner dragged himself over to the tower; Luke followed. He lay up against the cold steel structure, now twisted and perforated from the cannon fire. He leaned his head cautiously forward toward the destroyer. Its stern was beginning to swung toward them the bow away. She was coming around for another run.

The dark prow of another destroyer was steaming toward them from the other side.

The guns went silent. Ken stared at the U-boat

slipping into their wake. Men moved at the base of the conning tower. Many others lay still on her deck. Despite the hot afternoon sun, Ken shivered, then turned, and rushed into the control room.

Hoffman was talking into a radiotelephone to the Commander of the Card. "I'm coming around to put my port guns on her." There was a pause. "No, Sir. She won't be going back down with all the holes we've put in her. That is, she'll only be going back down once. For good."

Ken moved to the port side of the control room and looked out the hatch. The U-boat was reappearing on the far side and it would only be a minute before the bow swung enough to make another pass.

Lieutenant Commander Hoffman shouted behind him. "Forky, get Lieutenant Commander Kellog on the horn. The Thomas is going to foul our port side shot."

Ken squinted into the water behind the U-boat. The water reflected off the surface, obscuring much of the detail, but it appeared there were men in the water. The Thomas was bearing down on the boat, growing larger by the instant. Water boiled up around the U-boat again, but this time the guns aboard the Baker were silent. The Thomas had opened up on her.

"David, turn to starboard and let me get my guns on her," Hoffman said into the phone. "You're too close to put your big guns on her."

Ken watched as the Baker finished her turn and began to slip behind the U-boat. The Thomas continued to fire. Some of the bullets skipped over the surface of the water and ricochet off the deck of the submarine and splashed in the water around the bow of the Baker.

Zing!

An errant round buzzed passed Ken's head and thudded into the bulkhead of the control room.

"Check Fire!" Hoffman yelled into the phone. "U.S.S. Thomas, check your fire. We're taking strays!"

The water around the U-boat quieted.

"Jesus, David. What the hell are you doing? We're down range. Clear the area and let us in there."

There was a pause. The bow of the Thomas stayed on track, heading directly toward the U-boat.

"What do you mean you're going to ram her? Does Commander Young on the Card know your intentions?"

Ken spun around. "They're going to ram her? The Germans are abandoning ship already."

The Kapitan appeared at the top of the tower, his dress cap pulled snug over his scalp, and his heavy coat unbuttoned. He turned and began to climb down onto the forward gun platform as the second destroyer escort's guns opened up. The water ripped up in front of them, sending small plumes of water into the air.

Luke leapt to his feet, grabbed Werner by the collar, and dragged him toward the far side of the tower. The sailor beside them jumped to his feet and leaned over to help Luke with Werner. The 20mm rounds found him and flung him back against the tower. They pinned him there for an instant, tearing into him. His body jerked and lurched, new wounds appearing quickly, his insides painting the metal behind him.

Werner clawed at the deck as Luke pulled. They scrambled around the front of the conning tower and flopped back against it, facing the port side of the Baker. All her guns were facing toward them.

"We've got to get into the water," Luke said.

"You go. I can't swim with my hip damaged."

Luke searched the deck with his eyes. A dead sailor lay in front of the tower, ten feet away, a life vest around his bloody torso. The twenty millimeter projectiles continued to pelt the boat all around the dead and dying.

Luke didn't hesitate. He rose and rushed toward the man. Bullets tore into the decking behind him as he skidded to a stop at the man's side. He grabbed the front of the life vest and tugged, pulling the corpse into a sitting position. The fingers of his right hand struggled with the knots on the vest ties while his left held the man upright.

The top untied easily, but the lower part was too tight for Luke to separate with one hand. He released his grip on the man and his body flopped back on the deck. Luke put both fingers to use on the strap as machine gun fire tore holes into the deck on the far side of the body. Come on, you mother – come loose.

Luke's finger dug at the knot. I need a knife. I could cut it free. The strap moved and the top of the knot came loose. Yes! He tugged at the vest and dragged it off the man, twisting the dead man toward him, and dragging him as he retreated to the safety of the tower.

Luke slid on the deck and came to a stop beside Werner. "Here, this will keep you afloat."

He pulled the vest over one arm; Werner leaned forward and Luke slipped the second one in.

Werner's eyes watched Luke's face as he tied the vest in place. "You shouldn't be so eager to give away your life by taking such risks."

Luke cinched the top strap tight. "It's my life to risk. Besides..." Movement above him caught his attention.

The Kapitan had squeezed under the rail and swung his legs over the side of the gun platform. His toes rubbed against the metal of the tower, trying to grip the sides as he lowered himself down. Luke rose and reached out to steady the Kapitain's feet.

Before he could grab the Kapitan's feet, the man lost his grip on the rail and crashed down on top of Luke. A foot struck Luke in the forehead and another on his left shoulder. The two men's bodies intertwined and tumbled out onto the deck. The Kapitan tried to rise, but his heavy coat was caught under Luke's body. Luke rolled to the side, rose to his knees, and reached out to the Kapitan.

Luke's hands tightened on the heavy coat; then it felt as though he had been hit in the side with a baseball bat. Both men spun around and were tossed into the sea.

Cold water enveloped Luke. His breath had been knocked out of him and he wanted to inhale deeply. His face was still under water, and he knew he shouldn't breathe in; yet it wasn't that he shouldn't – he couldn't. The blow left his lungs flat. His mouth was open, undulating like a fish removed from the water, but he didn't feel the cold in his lungs. The water had no place to go. The Kapitan's coat slipped from his grasp. He swiped at the water, trying to find what was no longer there.

He felt a hand on his back. Pulling him. Lifting him. His face came out of the water and arms wrapped around him. Luke tried to cough, but nothing came out, just dry soundless convulsions. Without warning, as if someone released a valve, his lungs relaxed, and air rushed in. He gasped and greedily gulped at the air.

"Easy, Luke. You're going to be all right. Steady breaths now," Werner said.

Luke rested his head back against Werner's vest, letting the officer's arms support him from behind. Two other sailors swam nearby attempting to help the Kapitan. The U-boat lay stern low in the water, her bow beginning to clear the surface. A figure appeared on the top of the conning tower. Who was that? What was he still doing aboard?

Another shadow appeared behind him. Was that someone else? The figure grew. It was the bow of the destroyer escort ship. He turned and looked up as the ship struck the boat. The man's hands went up in the air and he dropped back down the tube of the tower, disappearing into the depths of the boat.

Loud crunching of metal on metal. Grinding and crashing. The boat was pushed on her side, turning the conning tower toward him. Water rushed over her decks and the tower plowed into the sea beside them, churning up the water around them. The momentum of the destroyer pushed the boat sideways. The coupled crafts slid toward them.

No. I'm not going to be run over by these boats. No, not after all this, he thought.

Luke kicked hard, trying to get away, but Werner's body held him firm.

"She's stopping," Werner said.

The bow of the ship sat high on the U-boat aft of the conning tower. The figures DE-102 were painted in white on her hull. The ship remained there for a few seconds, frozen together like a twisted, gothic sculpture. The grinding of metal returned and the prow of the ship eased back off the stricken vessel. The boat righted as the ship dropped away.

U-233 didn't rise up with the burden of the ship removed. Instead, she continued to sink by the stern. Slow at first, the water crept up her sides and wrapped around the conning tower; the bow rose out of the water and tilted toward the heavens. When she became vertical, U-233 paused, then dropped into the ocean. White foam and water billowed around her, yet she didn't cry out as she disappeared beneath the waves.

Luke lay weak in the water, bobbing in Werner's grasp, staring at the dented hull of the destroyer. He wondered if he could wriggle free from Werner and follow the boat down.

Chapter Twenty Nine

Ken hurried down the main deck of the Baker, pausing to examine each face of the German survivors. The officers, Petty Officers, and enlisted personnel had been separated into three groups. The wounded, in a fourth, were placed furthest back on the fantail. The American sailors made the enlisted men strip off their clothes, checking for weapons. Arranged in a makeshift line, the sailors were given hot showers on the deck, then issued a complete kit of survivor's clothes, and finally hot soup, and cigarettes.

A gunners mate sifted through a pile of discarded clothes, then leaned back on his haunches, and held up a couple of small, brass wheels. "Hey, Lieutenant, what do you make of these?"

Ken took the spoked, numbered wheels, and twisted them in his hands. "Who had these?"

The sailor pointed to a man cupping a bowl of soup in his hands, and staring wide-eyed at the wheels.

"In the confusion, it looks like someone forgot to toss these overboard. They look like some kind of code device. Get them to Commander Swain. He'll know what to do with them."

Ken continued down the deck toward the wounded. The boat's Kapitan lay on a stretcher. An officer, no older than himself, sat on the deck beside the suffering man.

Ken knelt down on the opposite side of the stretcher. "Have you served with your captain long?" The man looked into Ken's eyes, but didn't speak. His eyes held a detached sadness. "Do you speak English?"

The man nodded. "Yes, quite a bit, it was required at University."

"You were friends?" Ken asked.

"Yes, in a way," the man answered. "I thought he might be my stepfather one day."

"Its been a hard day on friendships," Ken said, looking down at the blood soaked bandages on the Captain's abdomen. "I'm looking for someone I thought was a friend. Did you have an American on board?"

The young officer glanced at his captain as if seeking direction, but the man was beyond being responsive. "Yes, he saved my Kapitan from drowning. He saved me, too."

"Did he make it off the U-boat?"

The man stared at Ken for a few seconds, then nodded, and motioned with his head, indicating for Ken to look behind him.

A figure lay against the bulkhead beside the stern K-gun, wrapped in a Navy issue blanket. He had the blanket pulled up around the back of his head and his face was turned away.

The man's head turned toward Ken and as it did, Ken felt the muscles in his stomach tighten and anger swell up inside him until he almost choked on it.

Luke!

Luke lay against the bulkhead, his face emotionless and calm.

"You son of a bitch!" Anger gripped Ken. His body began to shake. His eyes searched the deck for a weapon.

Anything.

A loose piece of pipe – a handle extension – lay on the deck near the K-gun. Ken grabbed it. His fingers clenched the steel pipe and he stepped toward Luke. Ken stopped at Luke's feet and put his other hand on the pipe. He raised the weapon, lifting it to shoulder height. He was going to bash that murderous traitor's head in. He deserved it.

Luke's gaze followed Ken. He didn't try to defend himself, nor even flinch at the sight of the raised pipe. His face was expressionless.

No fear.

No remorse.

The pipe wavered in Ken's hands. How could this monster be the father of Maggie's child?

Luke gave a prolonged blink and then almost imperceptibly nodded his head.What? Did he want Ken to kill him? It didn't make sense.

The pipe suddenly became heavy in Ken's hands. Luke's eyes flickered in the setting sun, becoming brighter blue.

The pipe wavered. He tried to draw it back to strike, but it didn't move. His rage frustrated him and he closed his eyes tight and screamed.

"Aarh!"

The clang of the pipe hitting the deck pried open his eyes. There on the deck was not his enemy, not the killer of his friends; it was just a defeated, familiar stranger.

Ken squatted down beside him. Luke slumped over limply against Ken's leg, his eyes vacant, looking southeast at the curved horizon of water as if trying to see over it and beyond. His right hand reached up toward his ear, hung still in midair, then dropped back to his side. "I really messed things up this time." His voice was weak and held a tremor.

Ken lifted the corner of the blanket. Luke's chest was mounded with red, moist gauze. Blood streaked down his shirt and disappeared behind his body."

"Corpsman!" Ken yelled.

"Don't bother. They've done what they can." Luke gasped, then coughed.

Ken tried to ignore the frailty in Luke's voice. "Corpsman!"

The young German officer knelt down beside Ken. "The doctor said there was nothing he could do."

"What?" Ken asked "What did you say?"

The officer rested a hand on Ken's shoulder.

Ken turned his attention back to Luke. "Why? Why did you do it?"

Luke tilted his head back and appeared to gaze up at the blue sky and wispy white clouds. "It would be a great day for a ball game."

"A ball game? What about Josh and Barbs?" Ken demanded.

"The weather's colder. I think I'd pitch a good game today."

Ken rested his hand on the warm steel bulkhead, then nodded as his voice softened. "I'd even play first if you wanted."

Luke's eyes didn't move, they continued to stare outward.

Ken put his fingers on Luke's neck.

Nothing.

He eased Luke's head away from the bulkhead, pulled the blanket over his face, and laid it back against the steel plates.

Two sailors moved in around the German captain, they checked him over, and then lifted the stretcher. The young German officer jumped to his feet. "Niene."

The flurry of activity broke Ken's trance and he rose. "Where are you taking him?"

"Orders to transfer him to the Card, Sir. They want to interrogate this guy, if he makes it," a sailor answered.

"May I go with him?" the German officer asked.

Ken looked at the weak, flaccid face of the Kapitan.

"I don't want him to die alone." The officer touched the side of the stretcher. "Please. I know I'm a prisoner, and don't have the right to ask, but he shouldn't die alone."

Ken looked into the man's eyes. Somewhere in the deep blue folds of the officer's irises Ken felt sincerity. "Sailor, have an armed Marine accompany you. This prisoner is going with you."

"But, Sir, we don't have orders for that!" he protested.

"I'm giving you the order, so get moving!" Ken commanded.

The young German officer stuck out his hand. "Thank you. I won't forget the kindness."

Ken hesitated, but shook the man's hand, then watched as they all moved forward.

"That was a smart move," Commander Swain's voice boomed behind him.

Ken spun around. "Sorry. What?"

"By doing him a favor, you've already begun to soften him up for the interrogation."

Ken stepped to the rail and turned his back to Luke's blanketed body. "I didn't do it for that reason. I did it because it was right."

The Commander moved in beside him. "We don't always have the luxury of doing the right thing. When it works out that way, it's a definite bonus, but in this business, the lines often get blurred."

Ken stared at the gentle waves lapping at the lighter horizon. "If you're trying to make me feel better, it isn't working."

"Things were a whole lot simpler a few days ago," the Commander said.

Ken rested his hands on the chain that ran around the edge of the ship. "No. They weren't simple. I was."

Chapter Thirty

Maggie sat on the blanket, arms wrapped around her shins. Rocking gently, she held her thighs tight against her chest and let her chin fall over her knees. Moonlight deepened the hollows beneath her eyes and shadowed the path of evaporated tears. Ken reached up, tucked a lock of hair behind her ear, and rested his hand on her shoulder for the briefest moment, then gently rubbed his fingers on her back, massaging the knotted muscles.

This was not the first time he'd sat beside Maggie in this very spot, quietly ruminating about what to say. But this was not the break-up they had two years ago. Ken was not thinking just now how to smooth over a broken heart – he needed to get at the deeper wounds they both shared and would always carry with them. But the words didn't come. Instead, his fingers continued to move along Maggie's back and the lock of hair fell forward on her face again.

Maggie shook the strands away with a twitch of her head, as if shaking off a pestering bug, then let her feet slide forward. She cupped her face in her hands, steadying both elbows on her thighs.

"It's just not real." She sighed. "They're gone. All of them"

Ken shifted and turned to sit facing her, then rested one hand on her lower leg. "I'm still here."

Maggie's voice hardened. "For now, sure, but you're going off to become some Spy Smasher like in the comic books. What am I supposed to do, stay home and mend your cape?"

The sudden burst of anger shook him, He hadn't expected it. He tightened his grip on her leg and pulled himself closer. ADon't blame this on me. I'm not the one who lied to everyone. I'm not the one who did this."

Her lower lip trembled. "But you're still going."

"I have to – it's my duty. Besides, after all this, what choice do I have?"

Maggie turned her face away to hide her tears. AHe offered to take me away. Did you know that? He wanted to go to California." She paused. "I should've gone. If I had just agreed to go, none of this would've happened."

Ken thought about her words. Suddenly more guilt rushed in; not the dread of abandonment – something else. He was thinking about the choice she made. If Maggie had gone with Luke, his friends would still be alive, but he wouldn't be with her. If he could go back and change things, what would he do? He shook his head. AThat's nonsense. Those kind of thoughts don't help. They mire you down and keep you from moving on." He moved his hand higher and touched a finger to her elbow. "And that's what we need to do."

"I want to move on, I really do. I know you said you'd love the baby and raise it as your own. But I can't help worry that you'll always see it as Luke's child. And even if you don't mean to, you might treat it differently."

Ken pulled her hands away from her face and replaced them with his hand. "I'll only see you in the baby's face. Luke is dead, and that's where he'll stay. I promise you this."

"Even if we have another baby later?"

Ken nodded. "Especially then."

"What about everyone else?"

Ken shrugged. "What about them? Luke's father is in prison and no on else knows anything. We simply need to get up every morning, put both feet on the floor, and make the best of every day we have together. As long we're upright, we can take those little steps in whatever direction we choose."

She put her hands on his arm. "I can do that." Maggie nodded her head as if trying to fully convince herself. "Let's start now. Take me for a walk around the lake and tell me how our life is going to be."

Author's Note

When I read another author's work, I find local dialect and accents, distracting and cumbersome unless they're lightly salted in. Because of this, I crafted with minimal dialect. The same applies to the German players in my story. I'm not fluent in German, nor did I wish to Anglicize the German language. I've added a few German phrases for effect, and that should suffice.

As for the main military actions, most are based on real events.

The incident involving shots fired at the coastal watch officer, at the dock, was taken from an interview with a patient from my practice who stated this happened to him. He further claimed to have contacted a Major Smith in Portland who arrived the following morning to discover U-boat parts in the shed. Although the U-boat engagement was fictional, the shots at his feet were not. A close friend told me he couldn't imagine the young officer would sit and toss stones at the wall to pass time after being shot at. But this indeed happened, and I felt compelled to include it.

A fishing boat did report a U-boat sighting that

prompted the dispatch of the K-14. The Blimp was lost off Mount Desert rock during its investigation of that sighting. The incident was officially recorded as pilot error, yet the minority opinion written in the incident report stated it was lost to enemy action. The report includes description of 30-caliber holes in the skin of the craft when it was recovered, and it was missing two of its depth charges. Further, the crew later captured from the sinking of U-233, revealed under interrogation, that they fought with a "Zeppelin." Several local boats and communities reported hearing gunfire at the time of the loss. However, the military didn't want the local residents to know how close the war was to home. Many incidents at the time were hidden or diluted, so as to not alarm U.S. Citizens.

A U-boat landed two spies on Hancock Point in November of 1944. The story was accented by their incredible luck getting to Bangor. When they reached Route One they were picked up by a taxi that had dropped off recalled Naval officers. The car seats were reported to have still been warm when the spies got in. Because of this luck, they did make the last train to Boston, by a mere ten minutes. Later, both were caught and sentenced to death. Neither man was executed and at least one of them is still alive at this writing.

A Canadian ship was sunk by a U-boat off the coast of Maine on December 3, 1944, with the loss of 42 lives. It is believed that the Germans sank the ship as a diversion to hide the delivery of spies to our shores.

U-233 was sunk in Casco bay by the U.S.S. Thomas and the U.S.S. Baker, much as the story appears in the book. The surviving crew was taken to Portland and imprisoned until the end of the war. They were on a mine laying mission at the time. The report states that the attacking vessels observed the U-boat reacting as though it was already damaged before the engagement.

The weather each day in the book was taken from my great grandfather's farm diary. He lived but a few miles from the scenes depicted here and kept track of the weather to develop trends for planting and harvest.

I've tried to include real people and their occupations throughout the book, including Sheriff Ray Foster, Emma Means, Dr. Hanson, Major Smith, Alton Bridgham, and good old Biscuit Gilman. It would be nice if these people didn't fade into total obscurity.